“First we will discuss
insisted, his curiosity piqued.

“Have you reason to fear him? Because if you have, you must just tell me and—”

“No! No, I have not,” interrupted Alice. “I have never so much as met Mr. Sayers before.”

“But you did know his sister?”

“We attended school together, Cecilia and I.” Alice twisted the reins in her hands and set Jacee’s head to shaking and his feet to shuffling uneasily.

“Miss Sayers spoke to you of her brother?” Spelling pressed. “Did she tell you something frightening about him?”

“It does not concern you, Mr. Spelling.”

But it does, Spelling wished to say. Only tell me what has happened to make you respond so to the mere sight of Sayers. Is it a Canterbury Tale that you never met the man before? *Have* you met him? *Are* you frightened of him? Or do you love him? Is that why you blushed to find him in the breakfast room? By gawd, Alice, please let it be fear. Please, do not be in love with him.

But Spelling said not one of those words aloud.

Zebra Regency Romance books by the author

Amelia's Intrigue
The Bedeviled Duke
Legion's Ladies
Camilla's Fate
A Devilish Dilemma
Balmorrow's Bride
A Season Of Virtues
Annabella's Diamond
Mutiny At Almack's
Lord Nightingale's Debut
Lord Nightingale's Love Song
Lord Nightingale's Triumph

Novellas

"The Valentine Victorious" (in A *Valentine Bouquet*)
"The Magnifikitten" (in *Christmas Kittens*)
"The Parson's Mousetrap" (in *My Darling Bride*)
"Rapunzel" (in *Once Upon A Time*)
"Rescuing Rosebud" (in *Winter Kittens*)
"The Emperor's Nightingale" (in *Once Upon A Kiss*)
"Fascination" (in *Notorious And Noble*)
"The Reprobate" (in *Mistletoe Kittens*)

LORD NIGHTINGALE'S CHRISTMAS

Judith A. Lansdowne

ZEBRA BOOKS
Kensington Publishing Corp.
http://www.zebrabooks.com

To my beloved grandchildren, Kelly and Joey.
No, my dears, this is not all that
Grandma's sending you for Christmas.

ZEBRA BOOKS are published by

Kensington Publishing Corp.
850 Third Avenue
New York, NY 10022

All Kensington titles, imprints, and distributed lines are available at special quantity discounts for bulk purchases for sales promotions, premiums, fund raising, educational or institutional use.

Special book excerpts or customized printings can also be created to fit specific needs. For details, write or phone the office of the Kensington Special Sales Manager: Kensington Publishing Corp., 850 Third Avenue, New York, NY 10022. Attn: Special Sales Department. Phone: 1-800-221-2647.

First Printing: November, 2000
10 9 8 7 6 5 4 3 2 1

Printed in the United States of America

Preface

Welcome once again to the world of Lord Nightingale. *Lord Nightingale's Christmas* is book four of the Nightingale Trilogy. It is preceded by *Lord Nightingale's Debut, Lord Nightingale's Love Song* and *Lord Nightingale's Triumph.* Yes, I do know that there are only three books in a trilogy—but I explained all that in the introduction to book one. Suffice it to say that this is an unusual trilogy—one that consists of four books.

If you have not read the previous three books in the trilogy, what's wrong with you, starting at the end? For shame! I should leave you to flail around on your own figuring out the various relationships, but I can't bring myself to do that.

All of the major characters in *Lord Nightingale's Christmas* were introduced in previous books. Since most of the characters are interrelated in one way or another, however, you may find the following helpful. Let me see now. The Chastains—Nicholas and Serendipity, the Earl and Countess of Wickenshire. Nicky's mama is the Dowager Countess of Wickenshire. Delight is Serendipity's younger sister and Nicky's sister-in-law. Eugenia, the Marchioness of Bradford is Nicky's cousin on his papa's side of the family and her husband Edward, the Marquess of Bradford and heir to the Duke of Sotherland, is Lord Peter Finlay's twin brother. Lord Peter Finlay's wife, Mary, is the daughter of the Reverend Mr. Butterberry. The nefarious Neil Spelling is

Nicky's cousin on his mama's side of the family, while Miss Alice Daily is either the legitimate or illegitimate daughter of the Duke of Sotherland (I'm not giving that particular tidbit away here) and therefore sister (or perhaps half-sister) to Edward and Peter. The villainous Henry Wiggins, Lord Upton, is Serendipity's second cousin—who inherited her papa's title and lands. Whew! I think I got the most important of the lot. Don't be intimidated by them. I promise they won't all sweep down upon you *en masse* in the opening chapters. Some of them, I assure you, will merely peek in from time to time.

Lord Nightingale's Christmas not only relates Nightingale's joyous celebration of the season with his extended family; it also wraps up the questions left dangling in the previous books and provides the opportunity for Lord Nightingale to once more play his own peculiar brand of Cupid, bringing together at last the most unlikely couple in the series.

One

It was nine days before Christmas, and in Lady Vermont's tangled mind, time was hastily running out. Her silver hair glistened in the candlelight as she raised her chin with considerable arrogance to study the gentleman before her. Her eyes, as gray as granite, darkened to the bruised color of rising storm clouds. Her hands, gnarled and palsied, clutched the cane she held before her as she sat upon the very edge of the puce horsehair sopha. "You must do it swiftly," she said in a tense, crackling voice. "Before Christmas, or Sotherland will carry her off to Northridge and she will be lost to me forever."

The gentleman nodded. "I understand. I will set out for Willowsweep with the dawn."

"How will you gain entrance? Have you thought of that? Willowsweep lies at the edge of a moor. Only the tiny village of Swiftinwhold is nearby. It will not be like London, where you may spend a day or two with a neighbor of the Wickenshires, make the Wickenshires' acquaintance at some entertainment or other and then simply stroll across the square to call on Alice. The Hadleys are close," she added abruptly. "Perhaps the Hadleys can be persuaded to—no, no, we never were more than vague acquaintances. Devil it, but I cannot so much as write to Alice at Willowsweep with Sotherland there. He will intercept any messages and destroy them. Beware, puppy," she hissed.

"Should Sotherland suspect you come from me, he will chop out your tongue before you have an opportunity to say yea or nay."

"Never fear," the gentleman assured her, studying the lady through eyes as tawny as a barn cat's back. "I will gain entrance to Willowsweep and Sotherland will not guess what I am about until it is much too late. You may depend upon it."

"I do depend upon it," snapped the ancient. "I depend upon that and more."

"And I depend upon you, madam. Do I succeed in restoring your granddaughter to you, my life is like to undergo a drastic alteration—especially if I must take her, as you suggested, over the Duke of Sotherland's dead body. If such should prove to be the case, words spoken between us by firelight and agreements made in shadows will be of little use to me."

"Phah! Do you think me some muling babe with pap for brains that I would forsake you if you are forced to take Alice over that devil's dead body?" grumbled the aged lady angrily.

"Not at all. However, it does pain me to point this out to you, madam, but you are not so young as you once were. What if I do the deed and return to find you in the grave? What then? Who will give me what I'm owed? Your Alice? I think not. I require there to be some reasonable security within my grasp before I set out for Devon."

"Monies," the lady scowled, reaching for the bell on the cricket table beside her and ringing it with frustrated authority. "Second sons! You are all alike. Your answer to every problem is to have your pockets lined with monies."

"If you object, then there is always Alan, m'dear," replied the gentleman, a most condescending smile on his lips. "I am quite certain that you may just as easily appeal to him to do this bit of a favor for you. He will not demand immediate payment of you. Of course, he will not do the deed either."

"Alan, bah! Staid, stuffy and self-righteous. A pattern card of propriety."

"But *not* a money-hungry second son."

"I have monies," muttered the old lady, ringing the bell again. "I have monies enough to make even you happy. Walters," she commanded as her butler appeared in the doorway. "Fetch my sewing box at once."

"Yes, my lady," the butler replied and hurried off.

"You keep your money in your sewing box?" asked the gentleman, cocking an eyebrow significantly. "It is pin money then and not nearly as much as I require."

"We shall see. There is brandy in that decanter on the sideboard. Pour a glass and bring it to me."

The gentleman smiled fully, the light of laughter softening his features and giving his tawny eyes a golden glow. "May I pour a glass for myself as well, or would that make me an audacious upstart in your eyes?"

"You have always been an audacious upstart. A moment ago, you were a guest here, Richard, and might pour yourself a glass. But no longer. When you require money of me, you make yourself my servant. You are no more deserving of my hospitality now than my fireboy or my kitchen maid."

"I see," the gentleman said with a chuckle. "Well, but this particular fireboy has developed a fierce thirst, my dear, and intends to help himself to your brandy do you approve or not. No, do not glare at me so. You are still a most formidable woman, Aunt Fiona, but I am no longer a child who shivers at the twitch of your eyebrow or shrinks when a dour expression rises to your face." With a grand flourish, he poured two glasses of the golden liquid and carried one to her. "There. Now, be very careful," he whispered wickedly, giving the glass into her hand. "Formidable old ladies have been known to choke to death on too large a sip of brandy, auntie."

In the Gold Saloon at Willowsweep on the evening of the seventh day before Christmas, Mr. Neil Spelling shuffled—rather like a crab—in the direction of the pianoforte. This had not been his original intent. He had originally intended to stroll with grace and nonchalance to the place where Lady Alice sat playing "The Winds of Winter Whisper Now," to sit down beside her and to suggest that they perform a duet upon the keys.

What the deuce is wrong with me? Spelling wondered as he watched himself shuffle awkwardly about. First I write Nicky a letter actually begging him to invite Sotherland, Alice and myself to Willowsweep, and now that he has done it, I act like a veritable looby.

"Cuckoo!" cried a voice from the far end of the saloon. "Avast villaincuckoo! Villaincuckoo!"

"Now who the deuce taught him to say that?" Spelling exclaimed as he ceased his awkward advance on Lady Alice and glared over his shoulder at the green-winged macaw which sat atop an enormous cage at the far end of the room. "By Jove, Nicky, cannot you keep that bird somewhere that people don't go? I do not know how you bear to have the featherbrain always about."

"There is a decided featherbrain in this room," whispered the Duke of Sotherland to the dowager Lady Wickenshire as they sat in matching chairs before the hearth, quietly watching and listening to the younger generation around them, "but it is not Lord Nightingale."

The dowager countess' eyes lit with playful laughter.

"Delight taught him cuckoo," offered the Earl of Wickenshire from the sopha, giving his wife's hand a delighted squeeze, "but that particular combination, I believe, is Nightingale's own invention, Neil."

"Ought to be stuffed and hung on a wall," muttered Spelling. "Wretched bird."

"You forget that Lord Nightingale was the one brought down Lord Upton at Wicken Hall and likely saved our lives, Neil."

"No, I do not forget that, or that he made you and Lord Peter rich. But that does not keep him from being a danged nuisance and annoying to boot."

"Will you never cry friends with him, Neil?" Sera, Lady Wickenshire inquired, suppressing a chuckle.

"No," stated Spelling succinctly.

"But he's so very beautiful," offered Lady Alice, who had ceased to play at the macaw's first utterance. "How can you despise such beauty, Mr. Spelling?"

"I do not despise his beauty, Lady Alice. It is his attitude that I despise."

"His attitude?"

"Indeed. He may look like an angel, but he bites people's fingers, steals things and throws objects at you when you are least expecting it. And he is forever calling me names."

"I could call that particular puppy some names," grumbled the duke for the dowager's ears alone. "What does he mean, to be looking at my Alice in such a way?"

"What way, your grace?" asked the dowager innocently.

"All calf-eyed and bumblebrained. He ain't falling in love with Alice, I hope, for he ain't about to have her. I have lost my heir to a mere miss and my Peter to a parson's daughter. I will not settle for your nephew as husband to my only daughter. No less than an earl will Alice have. I assure you of that."

"Come and sit, Mr. Spelling," Lady Alice said just then, patting the bench beside her. "Sera says that you play the pianoforte wonderfully well. Let us ignore Lord Nightingale and see if we cannot play a duet on the keys."

Spelling, about to expound further on Lord Nightingale's shortcomings, felt his lips go abruptly dry, his tongue swell to twice its size and the back of his neck begin to perspire. "I—I am—I do not play as well as you," he managed as he advanced, with a noticeable hesitancy, to the edge of the bench and gingerly seated himself. "I am a m-mere novice at it." Spelling placed his fingers upon the keys. Lady Alice placed her own fingers beside them. Spelling pulled his fingers away instantly and jumped up from the bench as though he had been burned.

"Cuckoo villaincuckoo!" Lord Nightingale observed.

The Earl of Wickenshire squirmed with glee on the sopha.

"Do not you dare laugh," ordered Sera, digging an elbow into Wickenshire's ribs. "Smile pleasantly, Nicholas, and be still."

Much later that same evening Spelling mumbled to himself as his valet helped him to slip out of the incredibly form-fitting coat he had ordered from Weston precisely for this particular excursion into the country.

"Pardon, Mr. Spelling?" asked the valet.

"What? Oh. Nothing, Carson. It has merely proved to be an arduous evening. I am exhausted."

"You did not—his lordship did not—"

"No," replied Spelling with some exasperation. "Really, Carson, you have got to get all that nonsense out of your head."

"I have made the attempt, sir, but we are actually at Willowsweep and—"

"And Willowsweep is not cursed, Carson. I am not cursed. Nicky is not cursed. I do admit there have been several—accidents—here in the past, but there is absolutely no cause for alarm. I would be much obliged, Carson, if you would simply dump that superstitious drivel out your ear."

"Yes, sir, Mr. Spelling," replied the valet, hanging Spelling's coat in the armoire and returning to untie the strings of his gentleman's breeches. "I shall attempt to do precisely that, sir. Oh, by Jove!" exclaimed Carson. Startled by an enormous crash of thunder, he jumped backward, forgot to let go the strings and cinched the waistband of Spelling's breeches tight around Spelling's waist.

"C-Carson! C-Carson, let go the strings," gasped Spelling, tugging desperately at his waistband. "L-let go the strings! I cannot c-catch my breath!"

"I am sorry, sir," Carson said, releasing the strings at once. "So very sorry. I have never before— It is this house."

"No, it's you," growled Spelling as he stepped out of his breeches. "I ought not to have brought you with me. You are far too excitable. It was thunder merely, Carson, nothing more."

"The entire house shook," protested Carson humbly. "I felt the entire house shake. I thought—I thought—"

"What?" asked Spelling as he slipped his nightshirt over his head. "What did you think? That the Witch of Willowsweep was just then crashing through our ceiling? I assure she was not and will not. She has been dead for two centuries and more."

"The Witch of Willowsweep?" asked Carson in a tiny voice.

"Blast and damn," muttered Spelling, noticing how his valet's hand shook as Carson handed him his nightcap. "I ought never to have said that, ought I? You do not know about Nicky's great-great-any-number-of-greats auntie."

Carson shook his head slowly from side to side.

"No, and I ought not to have mentioned her either. Forget I mentioned her, Carson. Wipe her from your mind."

"But a w-witch, Mr. Spelling."

"Yes, well, she was not truly a witch, Carson. An ordinary woman with an unfortunate face, merely."

"Did you know her, Mr. Spelling?"

"No, of course not. She died long before I was born."

"Just so," nodded Carson knowingly.

"Just so? Just so, what?"

"You did not know her, sir. You cannot possibly be certain that she was not a witch. Perhaps it was she laid the curse upon this place and upon you and his lordship."

"Bother it, Carson, you are impossible! Why would a woman who died before Nicky and I were thought of lay a curse on us?"

"Witches do those things," explained Carson nervously. "They do. Curse people who are generations down the line."

"Well, I am not even in the line. Just because Aunt Diana is Nicky's mother and her brother was my father, that does not put me anywhere in the line. Damnation, Carson, do cease quivering like a willow in a stiff breeze and take yourself off to bed. I cannot bear to look at you shaking in your shoes."

"Yes, sir," replied the valet, bowing and retreating at one and the same time. "I will, Mr. Spelling."

"And forget that I ever mentioned Elaina Maria Chastain."

"Who?" asked the valet, turning back with one hand lingering on the doorknob.

"Nicky's great-great-however-many-greats aunt. That was her name. Elaina Maria Chastain."

I have an enormous mouth, Spelling mused dolefully as he watched his valet shiver and shake his way, lamp in hand, into the corridor. An enormous mouth, and I never know when to clamp it shut. Cannot open it at the proper time either of late. What a perfect dolt Lady Alice must think me. I did not utter one coherent sentence all evening. And worse, I spilled my tea and crumbled my macaroon into bits without even noticing. And just when I wished to make a very good impression. Drat! Drat! Drat!

Spelling took lamp in hand and wandered into the adjoining bedchamber. He set the lamp on the night table and stepped up into the bed. Puzzling over his own behavior, he lay back and pulled the counterpane up to his chin. He stuck one arm out from under the covers to turn down the lamp wick, then pulled it back and closed his eyes. He was just entering into dreams when a horrendous screech followed by another and another set his teeth to rattling. "When the devil is that blasted bird going to stick his spoon in the wall," he shouted angrily to no one. "By Jove, I am going to strangle that creature and pluck his feathers to make a lady's hat. Why can he not have a night cover thrown over him without screeching like a madman in the midst of being murdered!"

"Goodness!" Lady Alice exclaimed as she jolted awake and sat straight up in her bed. "Someone is being murdered right here in this very house!" But then the screeches ceased and Alice recalled that she was not at home as her sleepy mind had assumed but visiting at Willowsweep. She sighed and smiled. "It was merely Lord Nightingale bidding us goodnight," she whispered to her wildly lurching heart. "Steady on. I ought to have expected it by now; we have been here an entire week and he has not failed to screech in that precise manner even one night."

With a stretch, a yawn and a weary blinking of her blue eyes, Lady Alice settled herself for sleep once again. Lord Wickenshire is a wonderful gentleman, she thought, but I am quite happy it is Sera who has married him and not myself. However did she grow accustomed to Lord Nightingale's screeching the first thing each morning and the last thing each night? He is quite a lovely bird, but I should not like to have the care of him. Certainly not for the rest of my days. And to think that Mr. Spelling was made to live with such a racket as that from his earliest childhood. No wonder he is not fond of the creature.

The very thought of Mr. Spelling made her smile. Really, she thought, he seems so different now than when we first met. I cannot think what has gotten into him to appear so shy and tongue-tied all of a sudden. He was so very outspoken and forthright when we met at Wicken Hall and at Grandmama's as well. And he was most polite and attentive at the Twilight Ball. He led me out twice, she mused, her eyes sparkling, just as he said he would do. But ever since he has arrived here, he has been most reserved. And odd. Oh, but he was so nonplussed to find his breeches wet through with tea and his macaroon all crumbled in his hand! How could he not have noticed what he had done until the dowager Lady Wickenshire pointed it out to him? It was all I could do to keep from laughing aloud.

It did not take overly long for Alice to find sleep again. Her breath came lightly, softly as Willowsweep settled around her for the night. The coals glowed red, unnoticed upon her hearth. The thunder faded from her hearing and the lightning flashed behind her curtains for eyes that did not take note of it at all. Even the creaking and cracking of the ancient house, the tiny dance steps of the shepherdesses on her mantel, the clink of the crystals from the chandeliers on the floor below, did not awaken her from her dreams.

It was only when sleet began to clatter against her windowpanes that Alice stirred. She mumbled incoherently and opened her eyes to a lightning flash so brilliant that it burned gold, red, orange behind her drawn curtains. This startling show of nature's brilliance was followed by the most tremendous crash. Alice fairly leaped from her bed and dashed to the window.

"Oh, my gracious," she whispered, tugging the curtains aside and staring out into the tempestuous night. Very near the house, one of the great oaks had been set ablaze. Flames danced frenziedly on the wind, illuminated the sleet, defined bits and pieces of the darkness and sent terrifying shadows and sparks spinning across the park. Lady Alice stared, her lips parted, her heart pounding.

What must I do? she wondered, engulfed by a mixture of awe and fear. Is it so close that the house is in danger? Ought I wake the entire household right this minute, or wait and watch and see if any sparks flare and float in this direction?

And then she caught sight of a movement among the shadows nearest the conflagration. She blinked, stared and blinked again. Were her eyes deceiving her or did she actually see the shadow of a man standing quite still a mere ten feet or so from the blaze?

Of course it is not a man, she told herself. The fire makes the shadows seem like a man, nothing more. And then the shadowman lifted his gaze and his eyes sparked in the firelight. Alice pressed the back of her hand to her lips. Beside him, she could now see a horse nervously pawing the ground. She let the curtains fall into place and backed away from the window. Who could it be standing out in the park on such a night as this and staring up at the windows of Willowsweep?

Two

"Will it not go out with the rain, Nicholas?" Sera asked, peering out at the burning tree.

"Quite likely it will," Wickenshire replied, hurriedly tugging on his old buckskin breeches. "Fetch my boots, Sera, eh?" he added, snatching a shirt from his chest of drawers and slipping it over his head. "I do not like to depend upon the storm to quell it, though. It is burning much too close to the house. Better to be safe than sorry. Thank you, m'dear." He took the boots she handed him and sat down to tug them on, then stood, stomping his feet into them more firmly. A moment more and he was exiting the chamber. "Stay at the window, Sera," he called over his shoulder. "If sparks should fly and catch on the roof I will wave up at you with both arms like this. Then you must raise the alarm and see that everyone gets out of the house quickly. I doubt it will be necessary, m'dear," he added. "Jenkins has heard the strike and seen the tree. I can hear him moving about above us. He will have the other men up and out in short order. And it will not take long to rouse the grooms and stable boys. We will extinguish the thing quickly enough." And then he was gone.

Sera hurried back to her post at the window. The tree burned heartily. A savage wind whipped flaming red branches against the sky, attempting, it seemed, to set fire to the storm itself. She watched, spellbound, as the lightning increased, the thunder roared ever more loudly, and a great chunk of the blazing oak burst from the rest of the tree and hurtled through the night sky to land, blazing, halfway between the lightning-struck oak and Willowsweep, setting the grass of the park afire. Sera fumbled with the window latch, shoved the casement outward. Already her husband's voice and the voices of other men swirled up to her. In another moment she spied them: Nicholas, the grooms, and most likely all of the capable male servants from the house rushed, armed with buckets, brooms and horse blankets, toward the now twin conflagrations that ignited the night sky.

"Hurry," she murmured. "Nicholas, please hurry. The wind gusts mightily in this direction." And then the younger Lady Wickenshire ceased to speak. Her eyes narrowed against the heightening brightness of the twin blazes and the increasing assault of the storm as a mixture of rain and sleet entered through her open casement. "What on earth?" she gasped as a shadow of a man on a wraith of a horse rose up before her. From the midst of the mounting holocaust that was Willowsweep's park, the shadowman appeared to rise like a veritable demon ascending from Hades.

Far down the east corridor, the Duke of Sotherland woke to the sound of a dog howling and the quick patter of tiny feet across the floor above him. "What the devil?" he muttered, frowning at the ceiling. Within a few minutes, there came a knocking at his chamber door. "What is it?" he called, rousting himself from beneath the counterpane and shrugging into his robe. "Just a moment. I'm coming. Now where the deuce are those slippers? Yes, yes, I'm coming!" One slipper on, one off, he hurried across the carpeting and swung the door inward.

"We are frighted," announced a little girl in a long flannel nightgown with a black-and-white cat cradled in her arms.

"Stanley Blithe is leaping all about an' howling. He is frighting us. Something is terrible wrong."

"Stanley Blithe," growled the duke at the enormous puppy dashing madly up and down the corridor. "Cease and desist, sir. Come and sit before me at once, you are frightening Delight."

"Oh, my goodness, he willn't listen to you either," observed the Earl of Wickenshire's little sister-in-law. "An' you are the bestest person we know in all the world at sounding angry."

"Mrrrrrow," agreed Sweetpea from the comfort of Delight's arms. "Rrrrrrrr."

A trace of a smile graced Sotherland's lips at the very solemn tone of Delight's voice and the appropriateness of her words. However, as he stood and watched the puppy, his smile faded. Something is wrong, he thought. Very wrong. He scooped the child—cat and all—up into his arms. "Lead on then, Stanley Blithe," he ordered, strolling rather lopsidedly along the corridor in his semi-slipperless state. "Show us what disturbs you, you demnable puppy, and I will put an end to it. You and Sweetpea are not frightened now, are you, Delight? Not now that I am with you, eh?"

"Uh-uh. You are the bravest duke in all of England."

"Just so," Sotherland agreed.

"Arrrroooooooh!" Stanley Blithe howled, skidding around a corner and into the adjoining corridor, coming near to knocking over one of the little cherrywood tables that stood in all the Willowsweep corridors with lighted lamps upon them to provide a semblance of light for anyone forced to wander through the house at night. "Arrrrroooooooh!"

"Dog makes enough racket to raise the dead," muttered Sotherland, trailing after him. "Takes after Lord Nightingale, that mongrel does. Surprised that old pirate of a bird am t up and squawking as well."

"Maybe it is robbers," offered Delight.

"Robbers?"

"Uh-huh. They are men who come in the night an' steal your things," she nodded solemnly, wisps of her fine blond hair escaping her nightcap and tickling Sotherland's cheek. "Robbers. Just like Lord Peter."

"Lord Peter is not a robber; Lord Peter is my son."

"But he came in the night and stole Lord Nightingale. It was on a stormy night, too, just like this one. An' ever'one was asleep, just like now. Even Stanley Blithe did not hear him."

"Arrrroooooh!" bellowed Stanley Blithe again, charging back to them and then dashing off once more around the corner.

"Well, if it *is* robbers, they will be running for the hills now that they hear the Hound from Hades on their heels," observed the duke. "No robber would be brave enough to face the animal who goes with that diabolical howling. Now why the deuce is he scratching at that door? I highly doubt a robber has hidden himself away in one of the guest bed-chambers."

"What is going on?" yelled a voice from behind the very door at which Stanley Blithe scratched. And then the latch jiggled, the door creaked open and Spelling, in nightshirt and cap, peered out into the corridor. "Devil of a racket going on out here. What are you about, Sotherland? Well, for gawd's sake!" he cried as Stanley Blithe charged straight past him and into the chamber. "What's got into that dog?"

"Something amiss," muttered Sotherland. "He is going to your window, Spelling. Draw back the curtains."

Spelling, stumbling over his own feet in the dim light from the corridor, rushed to the window, threw back the curtains and stared out into the night. "Oh, no," he hissed. "Not again. Not now. By Jove but this is all I need."

"What, Spelling? By Jupiter, will you look at that, De-light. Look way up there at the very front of the house. There's a fire in the park."

"Let go. Let go, duke. I got to ring the bell," Delight informed Sotherland as she dropped the cat and attempted to wiggle free of his arms. "I got to ring the bell. That is 'zactly what Nicky said to do when the Gold Saloon caught fire. So I did. An' because I ringed it so good, the squire and his men came an' helped us."

"Do not scramble away from me yet, m'dear," insisted Sotherland, holding tightly to her as he peered out the casement over Stanley Blithe's furry head.

"That will be Nicky there," observed Spelling, pointing at one of the figures backlit by the flames. "He has got every able-bodied man of his servants with him, too."

"I expect he will be appreciative of two more able bodies, Spelling. I will check on Alice and the dowager and take these imps down the corridor to stay with Lady Wickenshire, eh? If Wickenshire is out fighting the blaze, his Sera will not be asleep. Make haste, man. Don your breeches. It will take me but a moment to look in on the ladies and see they are all alerted. Then I will don my own breeches and join you in the park."

"Just so," Spelling agreed, moving hastily toward the armoire as Sotherland exited. He snatched a pair of breeches and a shirt from behind the double doors and slipped hurriedly into them. He found his boots, tugged them on, then grabbed the coat nearest to hand. A fire, he thought as he took one last hurried glance out the window. How does a fire keep burning in all that wet? And what the deuce is that horse doing out there?" he added, halting in amazement at a spectre-like beast rearing among the flames. "Why the devil would Nicky lead a horse *to* a fire?"

"You ought not to have invited the fellow to spend the night, Nick," Spelling grumbled over breakfast the next morning.

"Of course I ought," Wickenshire replied. "He helped us to quell the blaze, did he not?"

"Yes, indeed. Helped us to quell it after he started it."

"He did not start it, Neil. Lightning did."

"Yes, so he would like us all to believe. But what was the fellow doing out there in the middle of the night, in the middle of a storm, in the first place? I should ask him that if I were you." Spelling set his empty cup down with some vehemence upon the table, rose and made his way to the sideboard. "By Jove, if this don't look like gruel," he mumbled, peering into one of the serving dishes.

"It is gruel. Something to do with Sotherland. In memory of a grand jest, Sera informed me."

"Yes, well, Sotherland may have it. I am not about to touch the stuff. Kippers. Better. And a bit of bacon. Do not you so much as wonder how the fellow came to be in your park in the midst of the storm, Nicky?"

"Lost," Wickenshire replied succinctly.

"You are so incredibly innocent."

"No, am I? I thought I had outgrown innocence long ago."

"Well, you have not. Lost. A likely story. Knew no one would be out and about at such an hour on such a night, he did. Took advantage of it for his own fiendish purposes. You know nothing at all about the man, Nicky."

"He says he is Mr. Sayers from Overon; he has rented Dwyer Cottage from the Hadleys and he lost his way returning from Lydepool last night."

"Oh, certainly. And I am the Earl of Devon. I have rented Hadley's barn and I have lost my way while returning from London. Not at all likely. Intended to come snooping about, the fellow did. The fire surprised him and he could not get away unseen with all of us rushing out to extinguish the thing."

Wickenshire grinned around a bit of toasted bread. "All right, Neil," he said, once he had chewed and swallowed.

"Just why did this Sayers come snooping about on such a night, then? Whom do you suspect the fellow to be?"

"An exciseman."

"No. Why?"

"Who else would be roaming about in such a place at such a time? He was searching for Uncle Ezra's smugglers, most like."

"Well, he got himself near drowned and ended by fighting a fire all for nothing, then. Ought to have gone to Tivally Grange."

"Ssshhh. He may be listening even now."

"No, do you think so? Poor, unlucky gentleman," mused Wickenshire with a chuckle. "Searching about on such a night for smugglers when they are no longer anywhere near Willowsweep. To be out on such a worthless errand so near Christmas, too. Must apologize to him for his trouble, I expect."

"You make a jest of it, but I am telling you the truth, Nicky. You have invited a perfect stranger to shelter under your roof. And if he is not an exciseman, then he is most likely something equally as dangerous."

"You have proved dangerous any number of times, Neil, yet I have once again allowed *you* to shelter under my roof. Which brings to mind a question."

"What?"

"Have you truly developed a passion for Lady Alice or has her sudden rise in position sent you to counting your money again and made you determined to increase your income? You may as well tell me the truth of it, Neil, because I will learn the truth eventually. I always do."

"Lady Alice is a most extraordinary woman."

"Indeed. To spend all of her life as Miss Alice Daily and then in one brief moment ascend to become Lady Alice, the only daughter of the Duke of Sotherland, is most extraordinary."

"It has nothing at all to do with that," protested Spelling

at once. "I vow it has not. I began to love her before I ever knew she was anything but Sotherland's byblow. I know she is not what most people would consider beautiful, but I think her beautiful. And I—there is something about her, Nicky, that touches my heart and makes it want to fly. There is nothing I would not do to please Alice. That is love, is it not?"

"A beginning to love."

"I am beginning to love her, then. But I think it is a good deal more than a beginning. I would lay down my life for her."

"But will you lay aside your infernal, nefarious scheming?"

"I will!" exclaimed Spelling much too eagerly. "I will never involve myself in any sort of scheme ever again once Alice and I are married. I vow it!"

"Perhaps it is true love, then," nodded Wickenshire. "But you will not win her to wife easily. Sotherland is against you, Mama says. Wants no one less than an earl for the girl."

"I will convince him otherwise. I do not hold a title, but I am from a most acceptable family and I am rich as Croesus. That must count for something."

"Don't try too hard to convince Sotherland, Neil."

"But—"

"The person you need to convince of your desirability is Lady Alice. You must convince her of both your desirability and your love. If she comes to love you, she will convince the duke."

"Do you think?"

Wickenshire smiled. "Indeed. Lady Alice has no idea, as yet, of the power she wields over Sotherland, and so she does not make much use of it. But she is his daughter—a daughter he imagined lost to him forever. Why, the girl need merely wish for a thing within Sotherland's hearing and he will see it is hers. And if the thing she wishes for is you,

Neil, he will not stand against you. Not in the end. But you cannot go on as you always have, without a thought for anyone but yourself, and hope to win her. Ladies do not generally wish to marry gentlemen who are constantly involved in greedy, selfish plots and plans. They are more apt to prefer gentlemen who care first about them."

"I am not the one involved in plots and plans," Spelling protested, pushing a kipper about on his plate. "It is that fellow upstairs to whom you have given shelter. He is the one involved in plots and plans. I will lay you odds on it."

The fellow upstairs had just then tossed back the counterpane and set his feet upon the bright Abusson carpet. Bleary-eyed, Sayers stared about him for a moment, attempting to comprehend why his chamber had taken on such an interesting and unfamiliar aspect. And then he nodded silently to himself.

Willowsweep, he thought with considerable triumph. I am at Willowsweep. Not merely *at* Willowsweep, but actually inside the place. And by the simple project of helping to quell a fire, I have made myself welcome here so that I may come and pay calls without causing the slightest suspicion. What incredible luck it was that lightning should strike that oak just when I had determined to give up for the night!

With considerable satisfaction Sayers began to move about the room. He ran his fingers lightly over the finely carved mantelpiece above the hearth, lifted first one, then another of the china figurines that rested upon it. Then he studied the brass bound clock, taking it into both hands and turning it over. "Ancient old thing," he mumbled. He set it aside and moved his fingers carefully over the side bricks of the fireplace, then went down on his knees. He was, in fact, just preparing to peer up the chimney when the young footman, who had been scratching unheard at his door for an entire two minutes, opened that door and walked hesitantly into the chamber.

Hobbs stared at the visiting gentleman with some amazement. "Is there something wrong, sir?" he queried, stepping farther into the room. "Is the chimney puffing out smoke?"

"What? Oh, no, no. That is, yes, but merely a bit, and only one time. One time a few moments ago." Mr. Sayers rose hastily, the enormous nightshirt that Wickenshire had loaned him billowing around his slim form.

"How very odd," murmured Hobbs, setting the armload of clothes he carried carefully upon the bed and going to look at the fireplace himself. "Ought not to be puffing smoke, sir," he said, kneeling down before the hearth. "Especially it ought not when your fire is not so much as lighted."

"No, no, it ought not," replied Sayers. "Perhaps I was seeing things. Yes, most likely seeing things. Just awoke, you know. A fellow's brainbox does not always awake as quickly as his body. Dreams tend to linger."

"Yes, sir," nodded Hobbs. "Would you like me to start your fire for you? A bit of a chill in here to be sure. I cannot think why Jackie did not light it first thing this morning. Likely the lad forgot there was someone in this chamber, though he did lay it, so I cannot think why—"

"No need. No need," interrupted Sayers.

"But it is cold in here, sir.

"I am—fond—of the cold. Indeed, I am. Are these my clothes? And all cleaned and pressed? What an efficient household this is. I thank you for bringing them. You may go now."

Hobbs gained his feet at once and exited the chamber. "What a queer sort of gentleman," he murmured, shaking his head as he strolled toward the servants' staircase. "Queer as bodkins."

* * *

Lady Alice, having breakfasted in her chamber, went nowhere near the breakfast room. In a gown of soft brown velvet with bright gold trim, she strolled thoughtfully into the morning room instead. She was so deep in thought that she did not notice at first the vision of gentility strutting before the long row of morning-room windows.

"Take care, Alice," called Sera from her place on the silk-upholstered loveseat. "You will step on our fine gentleman else."

"St-step upon—gentleman?" Alice came to a standstill at once. "Sera? What on earth are you saying? Oh! Oh, Sera, only look at him!"

"Is he not splendid?" queried the younger Lady Wickenshire, her voice tinged with laughter. "And he is well aware of it, too, as you can plainly see."

"How on earth?" asked Alice, amazed, her blue eyes sparkling with amusement. "I have never seen such a thing in my life."

"They are his Christmas going-to-church clothes," announced Delight, peering up at Alice from beside her elder sister. "I have maked them special for him and he has tried them on and now he willn't allow me to take them off."

"Well, I can see why," Alice said with a grin, sinking down upon the edge of the closest chair. "He looks perfectly elegant."

"Uh-huh. He will be the verimost best-dressed gentleman at services on Christmas Day."

"The verimost best-dressed parrot, at any rate," Alice replied and gave one of Delight's ringlets a playful tug.

"Delight, Lord Nightingale is not attending services with us on Christmas Day," declared Sera.

"Uh-huh," responded the child, her light blond hair sweeping against her cheeks as she nodded emphatically. "Ever'one 'spects to see him there, Sera. And the Reverend Mr. Longfellow himself and even Mrs. Siely inquired particularly was Lord Nightingale going to attend."

"I am certain that they inquired in jest, Delight. Mrs. Siely would have the vapors to see a macaw at church, and the Reverend Mr. Longfellow does not actually expect—"

"Yes, he does. An' he 'spects that Lord Nightingale will sing for the congregation too. He does, Sera. That is why I am teaching him two new songs."

"Mornin' Genia!" exclaimed Lord Nightingale loudly from the floor, bobbing his head up and down, setting the high-topped little hat upon it to jiggling. "Mornin' Nicky! Avast me hearties!" And in a most peculiarly stylish manner, he began to shuffle his way across the carpeting toward Alice.

"Howdedo," he murmured in the most licentious tone as he reached the toe of her right slipper. "Howdedo, m'pretty. Howdo."

Alice stared down at the macaw in the tiny top hat and tails and giggled girlishly. "My, but you are a forward gentleman, are you not?" she queried.

Sera burst into laughter. "I cannot—" she gasped. "I do not—Nicholas did never teach him that!"

"Yes, he did," Delight offered. "Nicky taught him to say precisely that. It is the very first time Lord Nightingale has said it, too! We have got to tell Nicky at once. He will be verimost thrilled."

"Whyever would Nicholas teach him to say those precise words, and in such a tone?" asked Sera, attempting to suppress her laughter.

"For Lady Alice," Delight replied.

"For me?"

"Uh-huh. Nicky said, most serious, that if you was to spend Christmas with us and Cousin Neil was to spend Christmas with us, then you had best grow accustomed to—"

"Delight," interrupted Sera, her eyes beaming brightly at Lady Alice.

"What, Sera?"

* * *

There was little more he could do, really. Sayers studied himself in the looking glass and, though not quite satisfied with the manner in which his soft honey-blond hair insisted upon curling over his brow, he shrugged his shoulders, turned on his heel and exited the chamber.

He was not a tall gentleman, but his shoulders were broad, his hips narrow and his calves required not the least bit of padding. And though sparks from the fire the night before had left a mark here and there on his black velvet riding coat and his buckskin breeches, he was aware that nothing could be done about that and therefore ignored it, carrying himself as though he were dressed to the nines.

He might well have sought out one of the servants to direct him to the breakfast room. No one would have looked askance at him for doing so. Willowsweep, after all, was an enormous pile of stones. But he never thought to do it. Instead, Sayers wandered quietly along one corridor and into another, pausing now and again to peer up at this painting or that tapestry or a particularly fine cornice.

At the top of the staircase he ran his hand gently over the carved griffin on the newel post and his heart gave the tiniest little leap within his breast.

"I will thank Wickenshire most sincerely for the shelter he provided me, eat a bit of breakfast and take myself off," he whispered to the griffin. "I will not do one thing to arouse anyone's suspicions. Spelling did not so much as claim acquaintance with me last evening. He will not dare confront me now." Then Sayers descended the staircase, looking with interest at everything that came within his sight, and made his way down the first-floor corridor.

Three

"Nicky, Nicky, he has said it, an' just 'zactly right, too!" Delight exclaimed as she skidded around the corner into the breakfast room, Stanley Blithe bounding along beside her.

"No, has he?" Wickenshire grinned, gaining his feet as did the other gentlemen.

"Yes, and Lady Alice giggled and called him a forward gentleman. What is a forward gentleman, Nicky?"

"It is a gentleman who advances at much too great a pace," Alice said as she entered behind the child. "Good morning, gentlemen. I have come to see if we are still to go for our ride this afternoon, Mr. Spelling. You are not opposed to cantering over muddied ground?"

And then Alice's gaze fell upon Mr. Sayers. Her blue eyes widened considerably and one fine, long-fingered hand went to flutter at her breast.

"Lady Alice, may I present Mr. Sayers. Mr. Sayers, Lady Alice Finlay," Wickenshire said. "Helped us to extinguish our fire last night, Sayers did."

"How—how—k-kind of you," managed Alice.

"Why is your cheeks gettin' all redded up, Lady Alice?" asked Delight, leaning familiarly against Wickenshire's thigh. "Are you feelin' sickly?"

"Hush, Delight."

"But Nicky, her cheeks was not all red when we was in the morning room and that was just minutes ago."

"Perhaps she hurried very fast to keep up with you and is overheated," offered Mr. Spelling. "Come and sit down, Lady Alice. I will pour you a cup of tea, eh?"

"No. Y-yes. Thank you," nodded Alice, moving to take the chair Spelling pulled out for her. "I sh-should like a cup of tea. You are from Overon, Mr. Sayers?"

"Why, yes," nodded that gentleman.

"Well, by Jupiter! You are already acquainted with one another?" Spelling asked.

"No, no, we are not," Alice responded at once. "Mr. Sayers and I have never met."

"I should recall had we met," agreed Sayers, studying Lady Alice with a thoughtful frown.

"And yet you guessed he was from Overon, Lady Alice?" persisted Spelling carrying the teapot to the table. "Do gentlemen from Overon have a particular look about them, then?"

"N-not at all. I attended school with a young woman from Overon. Her name was Cecilia Sayers. We were close friends, Cecilia and I. Mr. Sayers quite resembles her and so I thought he might be a relation."

"There was a young woman at school about whom my sister, Cecilia, was accustomed to write," Sayers said quietly, his eyes fixed firmly on Lady Alice. "But she had no title."

"I was p-plain Miss Alice Daily then."

An expression of wonder quickly succeeded by a look of embarrassment swept over Sayers' features and he began at once to take a great interest in the rasher of bacon before him.

"Lady Alice is a plain miss no longer," Spelling said into the abrupt silence. "It is the most remarkable story. She is the daughter of the Duke of Sotherland."

"Cecilia," offered Sayers, glancing up and then hastily down again, "is engaged to be married."

"How very nice for her," Alice replied, fastening her attention desperately on Spelling as he added sugar and cream to her cup, then poured the tea. She had to keep herself from staring open-mouthed at Mr. Sayers somehow. Perhaps concentrating upon Mr. Spelling and the tea would prove the answer. With a noticeably shaking hand, Alice picked up a teaspoon and began to stir the steaming liquid.

Early that same afternoon, the Duke of Sotherland stood in the foyer of Willowsweep, tugged on his gloves, adjusted his hat firmly on his head and turned toward the door, his spurs jangling.

"You are in a precious hurry to ride off and get yourself a chill," observed the dowager Lady Wickenshire from the second step of the staircase.

"Chill does not concern me," replied Sotherland.

"No. That much is quite obvious. What is it concerns you to send you riding out on such a damp, cold day?"

"You know very well," the duke grumbled, turning to face her. "And you need not cock your eyebrow at me in such a manner. I will not have my daughter prancing about the countryside with Spelling and no one else."

"They will take Bobby Tripp with them."

"A groom. Bah!"

"Bobby Tripp has been with us since he was six years old and is to be trusted implicitly. He will keep a sharp eye on my nephew and your daughter."

"Indeed. Good for him that he does. And I will keep a sharp eye on them all."

The dowager Lady Wickenshire could not but laugh. It was a pleasant laugh and Sotherland's frowning countenance brightened considerably at the sound of it. His frosty blue eyes warmed a bit and the corners of his mouth turned upward. "You think me an old fool, madam."

"Indeed, but a loving old fool."

"I am not loving."

"Yes, you are. There is a fine heart hidden away beneath your crustiness, your grace. Sera and I, among others, have caught a glimpse of it, you know."

"Perhaps. Perhaps so. But I am not accustomed to the use of it—this heart. It is more trouble than aid. Witness how I stumble about like a blind man where Alice is concerned."

"Only because having a daughter is so very new to you," the dowager said, descending the last of the steps and crossing the foyer to lay a hand on one of Sotherland's coat sleeves. "Show Alice that you trust her, your grace. Bobby Tripp is the only escort she requires for propriety's sake."

"Is you goin' out, Duke?" interrupted a small voice from the top of the staircase. Sotherland and the dowager looked up to see an extraordinary pile of greenery adorned by red ribands and balanced on tiny feet clad in red slippers peering down at them over the landing rail. "You did not say you were going out. You are not going very far, are you? You have not decided not to help me dec'rate the staircase?"

"Decorate the staircase?" queried the duke.

"You forgot," sighed Delight. "An' I was dependin' on you."

"No, no, I did not forget," protested Sotherland. "I just did not think that we need decorate it this very afternoon."

"Oh."

"To tell the truth, my Alice is about to go for a ride with Mr. Spelling and I thought to go along to keep her safe."

"She is verimost old," asserted Delight. "Cannot she keep her own self safe?"

"In general I expect she can, but—"

"She will have Mr. Tripp and Mr. Spelling, too. Mr. Tripp

and me fetched in the dec'rations this verimost morning just because he had to ride with Lady Alice this af'ernoon. How many gentlemen does it take to keep Lady Alice safe? Thousands and thousands? A 'tire regimend?"

"Delight," commanded the dowager, a dimple flashing in one cheek as she called up to the little pile of greenery, "do not plague his grace. If he feels he must accompany Lady Alice, then he must accompany her."

"But Nicky is giving her Jacee to ride. An' Jacee is a perfeck angel, so Lady Alice willn't fall off or anything. Why does she require every gen'leman in the house to keep her safe if she is to ride Jacee?"

"Delight, enough," declared the dowager.

"But I will be forced to dec'rate the staircase all alone and I might trip an' fall right down the steps an' die. I should think at least one gen'leman would want to keep *me* safe."

"Delight," chuckled the dowager somewhere between exasperation and hilarity.

The Duke of Sotherland stared up at the talking greenery, then gazed for a moment at the front door with a footman poised in anticipation beside it. "Open that door, fellow," he said gruffly, replacing his hat on the foyer table, "and tell those who await that I will not be joining them this day. Say that they must go on without me."

"You are going to help Delight rather than guard Alice?" the dowager asked, her eyes sparkling merrily.

"Indeed, madam. What else am I to do? The child might fall down the steps and die. We cannot have that, can we?"

"You are most silent, Mr. Spelling," Lady Alice offered, drawing her mount to a halt at the edge of a small wood. "Is it—is it something I have said or done keeps you from speaking?"

"No, of course it is not. What an extraordinary thought!"

"Not so very extraordinary," sighed Lady Alice, gazing with a visible melancholy into the woods. "You have not behaved at all like yourself since first you arrived here to find me present."

"N-no, I expect I h-have not."

"There, you are stuttering again, just as you have done for days. Either you stutter at me, Mr. Spelling, or you do not speak to me at all. And you seem forever in some brown study when I am near to you. Why, last evening you did not so much as notice that you spilled—"

"Yes, I know what I did not notice," interrupted Spelling, the back of his neck abruptly burning with embarrassment. "I am sorry, Lady Alice, that I have been—distracted. I will attempt to do better."

"You are certain I have not said or done anything to give you a distaste of me?"

"You could never do that."

"I fear I could, and without so much as realizing. I have—I have done so to—to—people—before, I think."

"I find that impossible to believe," Spelling replied, so moved by the sadness of her tone that he reached over without the least bit of self-consciousness and placed his gloved hand on one of hers. "You must not blame yourself, Lady Alice, for my foolishness. I realize I have been acting rather odd, but it is merely because I have come to—like you very much and—"

"I have come to like you, too," Alice interrupted, looking up at him with eyes that smiled through unshed tears.

"You have?"

Alice nodded. The sleek white feather on her red riding cap nodded as well. "You were so very kind to me, you know, when you learned of my supposed parentage. You did never let on, Mr. Spelling. Not a word to anyone. You came to the Twilight Ball and called me Lord Bradford's cousin as cool as you please, and then you danced with me. Twice. I am so grateful to you for that."

"There is no need to be grateful for that," Spelling replied. "I promised to call you Bradford's cousin and I kept my promise. I wished to meet you at the ball and dance with you, so I did. Twice."

"Still you *are* kind, Mr. Spelling, and courageous as well. Only consider: the world believes his grace to be the Devil Incarnate, and yet you were willing to ride out with me today despite the threat of his riding between us."

"Well, perhaps that took a bit of courage, but I am not kind," murmured Spelling.

"You are not?" Lady Alice's lips curved deliciously upward. "Oh, Mr. Spelling, what a clanker! I suppose that next you will say that you are not truly courageous either."

Spelling's dark, brooding eyes sparked at the upward turn of her lips. His heart shuddered the merest bit. He wished, beyond anything, to take her into his arms and hold her there forever. But he had no right to do so. Not yet. And then he remembered her red cheeks and shaking hands of the morning. "Why did Sayers upset you so?" he asked. "He came near to making you swoon."

"He never did!"

"Yes, indeed he did. I will go so far as to think that even Nicky noticed, though there is no telling with Nicky. If there is something about Sayers frightens you, you must tell me at once."

Lady Alice brushed a straying curl from her cheek with one gloved finger and pinned her gaze on the small track that followed the boundary of the woods. "Shall we race the length of the tree line, Mr. Spelling?" she asked hastily. "I should enjoy to ride at a spanking pace for a bit."

"Not quite yet," Spelling replied, his curiosity piqued. "First we will discuss Sayers, I think. *Have* you reason to fear him? Because if you have, you must just tell me and—"

"No! No, I have not," interrupted Alice. "I have never so much as met Mr. Sayers before."

"But you did know his sister?"

"We attended school together, Cecilia and I." Alice twisted the reins in her hands and set Jacee's head to shaking and his feet to shuffling uneasily.

"Miss Sayers spoke to you of her brother?" Spelling pressed. "Did she tell you something frightening about him?"

"It does not concern you, Mr. Spelling."

But it does, Spelling wished to say. Only tell me what has happened to make you respond so to the mere sight of Sayers. Is it a Canterbury Tale that you never met the man before? *Have* you met him? *Are* you frightened of him? Or do you love him? Is that why you blushed to find him in the breakfast room? By gawd, Alice, please let it be fear. Please, do not be in love with him.

But Spelling said not one of those words aloud. "You are correct, of course," he said instead, noting the splendid way in which Alice had tilted her nose upward and the soul-stirring manner in which her eyes accused him of overstepping the bounds. "I merely thought that— No, I did not *merely* think anything," he corrected himself, his need to know leaping to the fore as her gaze drifted from him. "I intend to know, Lady Alice, what caused you to color up in Sayers' presence. He made your cheeks burn and your hands shake. Why is that?"

"It is none of it your concern, Mr. Spelling."

"It is," Spelling protested. "It is my concern because—" *because I love you,* he would have said, but he could not quite get his mouth around those words. "It is my concern because Sayers had no business to be lingering about Willowsweep's park last night," he said instead. "Whatever you know of him, I wish to know as well."

"I know nothing of him but what Cecilia has told me and what I have gleaned from the letters he sent to—her," Alice replied, her lower lip trembling. "Nothing more."

* * *

"I tell you, Sera, her cheeks grew just as red as yesterday's roses and her hands began to shake as though she had the palsy. She would not look at the man. It was the oddest thing," Wickenshire said, clasping his hands behind his back and staring out at the glowering afternoon sky through one of the casements in the small drawing room.

"Perhaps there is something scandalous in Mr. Sayers' past, Nicholas, and Lady Alice is aware of it." Sera was concentrating on the sketching pad in her lap, moving her pencil carefully and cleverly over it.

"I cannot think that to be the case."

"No," smiled Sera, studying his broad shoulders, "you never can think the worst of anyone, not even Neil, though you do attempt it with him."

"I have learned to attempt it with Neil," replied Wickenshire, turning to face his wife. "So, will you ask her about it?"

"Do not turn just yet, Nicholas. I have almost finished."

"Finished what?"

"My sketch. I am making a sketch of you staring out that window for Bedazzler. Turn back around, do. Yes, and clasp your hands behind your back again. Good. It is not my place to be inquiring into Alice's private life, my dearest. However, perhaps I may persuade her to volunteer the information. If she does, I will share it with you."

"They both declared they had never met before."

"Yes, well, perhaps they have not. Perhaps Alice merely knows of some gossip involving the gentleman. Do you not think it the least bit suspicious, Nicholas, that Mr. Sayers should be in our park in the middle of the night?"

"No. He is new to the area and lost his way in the dark. He found our drive and rode up it. I would do as much myself. I would, in fact, come up and pound on the door hoping to raise one of the servants on such a night as last night. Dwyer Cottage is ten miles to the northeast of us, m'dear. Closer, of course, if you do not go by the road. The gentleman was in the vicinity, eh, but not quite in the right place? Nothing at all suspicious in that. May I move now, Sera?"

"Yes, you may move in this direction and very quickly too. Your son is kicking me again, Nicholas. My, what an insistent little heir he is. He cannot wait to make his appearance."

In the time it took for the cat to wiggle a whisker, Wickenshire was sitting beside her on the sopha. He placed his hand upon Sera's stomach and then he smiled the most whimsical smile. "No matter how hard Bedazzler kicks, I think she's a girl," he said. "Oh! That was a mighty one! I will like to have an heir, Sera, but I will like to have a daughter just as well. Only think what a joy to have a girl to grow as sweet and stubborn as her mama."

"Sweet and stubborn! For shame, Nicholas! And what fun to have a boy as innocent and whimsical as his papa. But no matter which we do have, we must think of a better name for the babe than Bedazzler, dearest. I warn you, Delight will think it a prime name, but your mama will faint dead away do we christen the child such a thing as that."

Built of fieldstone and timber long before the erection of Willowsweep itself, the ancient barn brooded, sullen and somber, at the northernmost edge of the treeline along which Spelling and Lady Alice raced. Behind it, amidst the woods, a stream, swollen by the night's storm, rushed with angry mutterings along its rock-filled bed, west, toward the sea.

"Ugly old place, is it not?" Spelling observed, bringing his horse to a standstill.

"It gives me duckbumps," Alice replied with a shiver.

"No, does it?" asked Spelling, dismounting. "Duckbumps?" he asked with a puzzled frown.

"They are not quite as large as goosebumps."

"Oh. It is an old barn, merely. Nicky was accustomed to keep some of his sheep here until he built the new barns."

Spelling, having failed to pry any information from Alice concerning Sayers, and quite certain that he had set up her hackles because of his persistence on the subject, hoped that showing her this particular place would make her feel more kindly toward him again.

"Wretched place for sheep," he continued. "Floods every spring. If you do not anticipate correctly, you end by having to scurry about and carry the animals to safety. Smelly, daft old things, sheep. Do not appreciate being carried. Kick at you. Make an inordinate amount of noise."

Why the devil am I rambling on about sheep? Spelling wondered. She does not care a fig about sheep. I do not care a fig about sheep. But how do I actually invite her to accompany me into a barn? Do I just say it? Lady Alice, would you like to stroll into the barn with me for a bit? No, she will slap my face for me, and rightly so. Sounds absolutely lecherous. And why the deuce am I standing here like a simpleton, holding to my horse's reins, instead of strolling over there and lifting her down from the saddle? Have I lost my mind completely?

With a distracted shake of his head, Spelling nudged himself into action. "Allow me to help you down, eh?" he managed as blandly as he could, though the mere thought of placing his hands upon that slender waist sent rivulets of perspiration down into his collar. "We will stretch our legs a bit. Take a—a closer look at the barn—if you like. You have been asking to see where we discovered the feathered serpent."

"And this is the place?" Alice's eyes grew large with wonder as she leaned to put her hands on Spelling's shoulders and felt his hands close about her waist as he lifted her to the ground. "Oh, Mr. Spelling, how kind of you to remember that I wished to see it. But I did never expect you to bring me here."

I am kind again, thought Neil, absurdly angry at the word. Why must she persist in thinking me kind? I have never been kind in all my life and I am not kind now. I am not.

"I cannot think what possessed Mr. Quinn to hide such a treasure in a place like this," Alice's excited voice interrupted his thoughts. "I would fear to trust anything of value inside such a barn. Why, a strong wind might send the building crashing to the ground at any time."

"No, it would not," offered Spelling, releasing his hold around her waist and then tugging in vague aggravation at his neckcloth. "I know it looks frail. Nicky is forever saying that it will fall down if you puff on it. But it has stood where it is for near four centuries."

"Four centuries, Mr. Spelling?" Alice's disbelieving gaze stopped him fidgeting with his neckcloth and set him to fidgeting with his hat instead. "Surely Willowsweep is not as old as that?"

"No, but this building is. It was not always a barn."

"It was not?"

"There are myriad legends concerning it, though no one knows for certain what it was to begin with or who actually erected the thing. Would you care to s-step inside for a moment? M-merely to see where the statue was concealed?"

"I would like that of all things," Alice replied, tucking her arm companionably through Spelling's. She knew that she ought not to have done that. His grace would have frowned gravely. But she did not care. At the moment she cared only about Mr. Spelling, who had lurched directly into discomfort and stuttering again ever since she had refused to speak of Mr. Sayers.

Mr. Spelling fears I am angry with him, she thought. It would be cruel of me to allow him to continue to think that he has offended me. It is not his fault, after all, that I cannot confide in him about Mr. Sayers. "What a strong arm you possess, Mr. Spelling," she said softly. "I may depend on you to support me, may I not?"

"Yes. Certainly. Not to worry." Spelling felt his cheeks burn and the back of his knees grow weak. This is not me, he thought in amazement. The mere presence of a woman's arm in mine is nothing to me. I am a gentleman of the world. By Jupiter, that the mere touch of her hand on my sleeve should affect me so!

"Are we not going inside?" asked Alice quietly.

No, I am going to stand here frozen in the glow of your incomparable eyes, blinking like a madman, for the entire afternoon, Spelling thought. "Of course," he said. "You cannot see where we discovered the statue else. Tripp, are you coming?"

They entered through a door made of split logs bound with wide metal bands. It swung noiselessly inward to reveal a hard-packed earthen floor, a moldering pile of hay, pens that had once held Wickenshire's sheep, and high above, ancient wooden planks that formed the floor of a loft. Bits of gray daylight trailed in through the door behind them and dappled down through spaces in the planking from a hole in the thatched roof.

"Not a very appealing place," Spelling said.

"No. There is something frightening about it."

"Would you rather not continue? We need not."

"Oh, I am not such a poltroon as all that, Mr. Spelling. Frightening it may be, but that will not keep me from investigating this hidden niche my brothers spoke of."

"Quite right," nodded Spelling. "Ugly old place, but there is nothing here to harm anyone. In the loft we found the thing."

"Then to the loft we go," Alice replied. "Lead on, Mr. Spelling. I am not so delicate that I cannot climb a ladder."

They ascended to the loft, Spelling first, Lady Alice in his wake and Bobby Tripp bringing up the rear.

"There have always been rumors about a priest's hole in

this barn," Spelling said, taking his handkerchief from his pocket as he crossed the loft and spreading it on the floor to kneel upon. "Why anyone would put a priest's hole in a barn, I cannot imagine." As Alice moved to peer over his shoulder, Spelling took a ten-penny blade from his waistcoat pocket, pried at a stone and tugged it out. He set it aside and pried at another. In a matter of moments a space appeared between the stones of the inner wall and those of the outer wall.

"My, but they must have had an exceptionally tiny priest," observed Alice with a giggle that made the inside of Spelling's ears quiver with delight.

"This is not all of it," he replied. "We had no need to uncover it all. Stuffed right in here, it was," Spelling added, sticking his gloved hand into the niche behind the inner wall. "Well, I'll be jiggled!"

"What? What is it?" asked Alice.

"There is something else in here. There was nothing else in here when we fished the feathered serpent out. We made certain of it." Spelling withdrew his hand and stared. "By Jove, will you look at this!"

Four

They were within sight of the house at the far end of the lower pasture, allowing their horses to proceed at a leisurely pace, when Lady Alice reined in her mount and exclaimed excitedly, "Mr. Spelling! Look!"

Spelling, his mind occupied with explaining to himself where the prize they had discovered in the barn could have come from, assumed that Lady Alice had taken note of the sunken well house and the stone rows and circle that had stood forever in the pasture. "Ancient old things," he muttered. "No one knows what they are, except the well house, of course, but legend has it that you will be cursed should you destroy them. Rubbish, of course, the legends."

"What? Whatever are you speaking of, Mr. Spelling?"

"The stone rows and the circle and the well house."

"The what?"

"The stone rows and the circle and the well house. You do not wish to go and peer at the stones today, do you? Moldering old things, really."

"It is not a group of stones I see, Mr. Spelling. It is a gentleman."

"What the deuce!" Spelling exclaimed as he halted his horse beside hers and stared in the direction in which she pointed.

"M'gawd!" exclaimed Bobby Tripp, urging his horse around the two riders and making his way to the gentleman who stretched his length upon the ground. "He bean't dead," Tripp called, dismounting and kneeling beside the inert figure. "He be breathin', Mr. Spellin'."

Spelling dismounted and strolled hastily forward. "Do you know the man, Tripp?"

"Never seed him afore in m'life. There be his hack. Over there," replied Tripp, pointing. "Lost his seat some'ow, the feller did."

"Likely the horse stepped in a hole and threw him off," agreed Spelling, all thought of the trinket he had discovered fleeing his mind. "Fetch the animal, Tripp. I will see what can be done for this fellow. You may need to ride for a hay wagon to take him to the house."

"It is not Mr. Sayers?" asked Alice, studying the gentleman from the safety of her saddle. "His hair is much the color and length of Mr. Sayers'."

"No, not Sayers," Spelling replied, rolling the man over. "One of the neighbors, most like. Ride everywhere in the winter, they do. Make themselves free of each others' fields until the farrowing begins."

"Uhhhh," groaned the gentleman, and blinked open his eyes. "What? Where?"

"Taken a spill," offered Spelling.

"A spill?"

"You and your horse parted company over something."

"Do you not remember what happened, sir?" asked Alice, urging Jacee a bit closer to the gentleman.

"N-no. T-took a spill, you say?" he asked, attempting to lever himself upward into a sitting position.

"Do not move about too much just yet," commanded Spelling. "Best to see if you have broken anything first."

"Just so," nodded the gentleman, gingerly flexing one arm and then another. "Ouch! Sprained a wrist, I gather, though m'fingers work, so it cannot be broken. Is that my horse?" he asked as Bobby Tripp led the animal up.

"What do you mean, is that your horse?" asked Spelling,

shaking out his handkerchief and proceeding to tie it around the gentleman's brow to cover a cut there. "It is the only animal out here besides our own. It must be yours."

"Yes, it must, must it not? How odd that it does not look the least bit familiar. You do not look familiar, either. Do I know you?" the gentleman queried, gazing blearily at Spelling.

"I am Wickenshire's cousin. Do not generally come to the country. Not to Willowsweep at any rate."

"Willowsweep," mumbled the gentleman, accepting Spelling's help in attempting to gain his feet. "Ouch! Twisted an ankle, too, I think. Where the deuce is Willowsweep?" And then the gentleman groaned the tiniest groan, and if Bobby Tripp had not lunged forward to support Mr. Spelling in his efforts, the man would have tumbled, senseless, back to the ground.

"It is veritubly raining strangers, Nicky says." Delight, her pale ringlets swinging, bounced down the gayly decorated staircase and into the foyer to stare up at the Wickenshires' butler. "Last night it rained Mr. Sayers and this afternoon, Mr. Duncan. We are going to call him Mr. Duncan, because he thinks p'rhaps that is his name. But I didn't see it rain this afternoon, did you, Mr. Jenkins?"

The butler gave a shake of his head. "I do not think that his lordship intended those particular words to be taken quite so literally, Miss Delight."

"Oh. Do you know who Mr. Duncan is?"

"No, miss, I regret to say that I have never seen the gentleman before in my life."

"That is verimost sad, because I have asked everyone else, even Jackie, and you are the very last person who might have knowed him. Poor Mr. Duncan. Our duke says that it is very frighting not to know who you are. I expect

Mr. Duncan is 'ceptional frighted. Are we going to do it now, Mr. Jenkins?"

"It is very near dinner time, miss."

"Yes, I know. And you an' Jackie and Becky an' Jem will be 'ceptional busy soon. That is why I hurried," Delight replied, reaching up to take one of Jenkins' hands into her own. "All the gentlemen are busy tending to Mr. Duncan, and all the ladies are busy talking about him. That is why now is so excellent a time. No one will even notice we're gone. This is going to be the verimost best Christmas surprise, Mr. Jenkins. Everyone will be amazed at it."

"Indeed," nodded Jenkins, allowing himself to be tugged along by this little sister of the younger Lady Wickenshire. It did occur to the elderly butler that perhaps he ought not to aid the child in the preparation of her Christmas surprise. It might prove, after all, to be far too amazing for the present company. But then he recalled, as he often did, the very sad and serious lad Lord Wickenshire had been and the difficulties with which his lordship had been forced to contend as a child, and he smiled softly to himself. "There can be not the least harm in it," he murmured. "And it will make his lordship laugh."

"It will?" asked Delight.

"Pardon? Oh, yes, it will. His lordship will think it a marvelous thing."

"Just what I thought," nodded Delight.

"You cannot remember anything else?" asked Wickenshire, seating himself beside the canopied bed.

"Nothing," replied the gentleman. "Nothing beyond Duncan, and I am not certain, actually, whether that is my name or belongs to someone I once knew. It just rose up into my mind and lodged there—rather comfortably—which is why I think it may be—my name, I mean."

"Just so," sighed Wickenshire. "And you cannot recall how you came to be lying on the ground in the lower pasture?"

"He took a spill, Nicky," Spelling offered. "Easy enough to see that."

"Yes, but it is odd that his horse shows not the least damage. Not so much as a strained tendon. I don't recognize you at all," Wickenshire said. "Forgive me, Duncan, but you do not so much as resemble any one of my neighbors. Well, perhaps you are someone's in-law come for the holidays, eh? I will send Bobby Tripp and one of the stable hands out to ask if any of the neighbors are missing a guest."

"Think whoever lost the fellow would be out seeking him by this time," declared Sotherland, pacing the chamber. "Devil of a thing, to lose a guest and not so much as send your servants out to find him. Unless, of course, whomever the fellow belongs to is *pleased* to have lost him."

Spelling would have laughed at that, but a particular uneasiness crept upward between his shoulder blades and kept him silent. This gruff, unpredictable duke was, after all, the father of the woman he loved—the first woman he had *ever* loved. He dared not misstep and he had no idea whether Sotherland's words had been intended seriously or not.

"Well, we must call you something," Wickenshire said. "Duncan seems most familiar, but perhaps it is your surname, and if you cannot remember your title . . ."

"I may not have a title," offered the gentleman in the bed.

"No. True. But you are a gentleman. Your speech and clothing prove that much."

"Devil of a puzzle, is it not?" grinned Duncan abashedly. "For a grown man not to remember who he is—embarrassing."

"Well, but it ain't your fault," Wickenshire replied. "I have heard of such things happening. Perhaps once you have rested, eaten a decent dinner and slept the night away, your memory will be restored to you."

"I hate to be such a bother," murmured Duncan. "Surely someone hereabout misses me?"

"I have no doubt of it," Wickenshire assured him. "Likely there will come a knock on our door within the hour. And if not—well—you are no bother to have about. I shall give you the loan of a footman, eh? Hobbs will look to your comfort, bring your dinner to you on a tray and spend the night on a cot in your dressing room should you require assistance."

"I thought someone was coming to knock on the door in search of him within the hour," observed Spelling.

"Yes, well, if they do not," Wickenshire responded. "If they do not, he shall have Hobbs."

"Avast me hearties!" squawked Lord Nightingale in welcome as the family and guests gathered in the Gold Saloon before dinner. "Mornin' Nicky. Mornin' Genia. Howdedo, m'pretty. Knollsmarmer!"

"Rackety old bird," Spelling said, strolling up to the cage and eyeing the macaw cautiously.

"Villain!" shrieked Nightingale right back at him.

"I am not a villain, you old pirate. At least, I will not be much longer. Here, I brought you something," Spelling added, taking a pine nut from his pocket and offering it, on the palm of his hand, to Lord Nightingale.

Nightingale glared at him through one amber eye, bobbed his head up and down, sidled forward to the edge of the roof of his cage, sidled back again and studied Spelling most seriously.

"You will not take it?" asked Spelling. "It is nothing but an ordinary pine nut, Nightingale. I vow it."

"Villain," muttered Lord Nightingale quietly, beginning to edge his way sideways toward the pine nut once again.

"Maggotyscoundrel," he mumbled, stretching to reach the offering and turning it carefully about with his beak. "Seascum."

"That is going too far," protested Spelling with a scowl. "Of all the things to say. Who is it taught you that particular phrase? I have a good mind to—"

"Oh, Mr. Spelling, you are going to give Lord Nightingale another chance to be your friend!" Lady Alice exclaimed, coming up beside him to watch as the macaw took the pine nut and retreated back across the top of his cage. "What a fine thing for you to do. You will not regret it, I think. Everyone here seems most fond of the creature."

"Yes," agreed Spelling, his exquisitely tied neckcloth becoming significantly tighter than it had been a moment before. "I realize that everyone here has succumbed to the old pirate's charm. I thought that, perhaps, I have been mistaken in him all these years."

Lady Alice smiled the grandest smile and placed her hand on Spelling's sleeve. "You are not so stern and implacable as you pretend to be, I think."

Stern and implacable? The very words caused Spelling's toes to curl inside his shoes. Never, in all his years, had anyone ever referred to him by such terms. Handsome, yes. Cool, yes. Rich as Croesus, indeed. Even—if one included Nicky—cowardly, untrustworthy and scheming. But stern and implacable? What on earth had given Lady Alice such an impression as that?

"I am not—that is—I mean to say—I have never *been* stern or implacable in all my life," Spelling sputtered. "I cannot think why you should—"

"Oh! I do apologize, Mr. Spelling. Truly, I do. I was referring only to your apparent relationship with Lord Nightingale. Only that."

"Yo-ho-ho Harry Chismer!" Lord Nightingale squawked loudly, flapping his wings enthusiastically and shuffling again toward Spelling in search of another pine nut.

Spelling directed his gaze away from the incredible blue of Lady Alice's eyes and back to the green-winged macaw. "Wait just a moment, Nightingale. I have brought another. Let me just remember where I have put the thing."

Spelling knew precisely where he had put the thing. In his right coat pocket. But Lady Alice's hand rested on his right coat sleeve and he was loath to move his arm and lose the slight, but intoxicating, touch of her. So, to prolong that touch for a moment more, he began to fiddle with his left coat pocket as if searching for the pine nut there.

Nightingale bobbed his bright red head impatiently, then reached out and caught the seam of Spelling's coat with his beak and hoisted himself over onto Spelling's shoulder. "Hungry," he mumbled, nudging at Spelling's cheek with the top of his head. "Nightingalehungry."

"Yes, well, remember that I am not dinner, you old pirate," Spelling warned. "What the deuce?" He removed his hand from his pocket and held up a silver trinket on a silver chain. "By Jupiter, I had forgot all about this. Carson must have transferred it from my riding coat into this one. Now, why did he not think to ask me a thing about it?"

The trinket sparkled in the lamplight as it twisted and turned on the end of its chain. It winked, wobbled and glistened enticingly. All thoughts of pine nuts flew from Lord Nightingale's brain. He stared at the trinket. He lifted one foot, set it back down, lifted the other, set it back down, as he stood on Spelling's shoulder. Then he spread his wings partway, gave them a hurried flutter and lunged for the prize. He seized it in his beak, ripped it from Spelling's grasp and soared off with it to the very top of the nearest drapery.

"Nightingale!" cried Spelling. "No! Bring that back at once, do you hear?"

"Oh! Oh, my!" Lady Alice exclaimed, her fingers closing on Spelling's arm most intimately as her gaze followed the macaw's flight. "Mr. Spelling, he must not eat that. He will die!"

"Eat it?" Spelling, who had thought to go after the bird at once, stood stock still, relishing the increased pressure of her fingers through his sleeve and hoping for it to last a moment longer. "He knows very well that falderol is not to eat. He will more likely drop it and break the thing."

"Break what?" asked Wickenshire, approaching them from across the room. "What is it Lord Nightingale has done to offend you now, Neil?"

"Nothing. I am not offended, only parted from my prize. And if I am not reunited with it swiftly, there will be parrot pie for tomorrow's dinner, Nicky."

"Mr. Spelling, you would not," Lady Alice protested.

"Of course he would not," Wickenshire replied, noting with some interest Lady Alice's possession of Spelling's arm and Spelling's decided inclination to remain motionless. "If Neil has not made a pie of Nightingale in all these years, he is certain not to do so tonight. He has had any number of opportunities. Must get him to tell you about some of them, Lady Alice. Stay right where you are, Neil," he added, grinning widely. "No need to actually move. I will get the trinket back for you."

Wickenshire crossed determinedly to the draped window. "Come, Nightingale," he ordered.

Lord Nightingale glared down at him, gave the dangling trinket a shake and then dragged it farther along the curtain rod. "Knollsmarmer," he muttered as he dragged it. "Yo ho hoho Murry Curstmurgle."

"Come, Nightingale," Wickenshire tried again.

"Mornin' Nicky," the macaw replied and flapped his green wings enthusiastically.

"I don't understand it," mused Wickenshire. "He knows to come when he is called. He has done it any number of times. What is it he stole, Neil?"

"It is a necklace or a charm of some sort," offered Lady

Alice, having taken one of Spelling's hands into both of her own and now patting it consolingly. "We discovered it in your barn by the stream this very afternoon. Our discovery of Mr. Duncan wiped all thought of it from our minds, I'm afraid, or we would have brought it to your attention earlier."

"In the barn? A trinket?"

"Wanted to see where we discovered the feathered serpent, Lady Alice did," explained Spelling. "Discovered this falderol in the same place, Nick."

"You could not have done," Wickenshire replied. "We made certain that niche was empty."

"So I thought. Perhaps it fell down from higher up somewhere. It is not much tarnished. Either been wrapped in something or has not been in the barn for very long. What the deuce is Nightingale doing now?"

"Godres ye wassail," sang Lord Nightingale merrily as he gave a flap of his wings and sailed from the curtain rod to the chandelier in the center of the Gold Saloon, the trinket swinging from his beak. "Merrygen'lemen among theleavesso greeeeen."

"Nightingale," commanded Wickenshire, while across the way Sera, the dowager Lady Wickenshire and Sotherland watched, laughing. "Come down here at once, sir. That particular trinket is not a toy for parrots."

Tenderly, Lord Nightingale balanced the silver chain with its pretty silver trinket over the bronze circle of the chandelier. Carefully, he ambled to the unlighted candle nearest himself. His red head bobbed. His chest feathers ruffled. The crowning feathers on the top of his head rippled upward. His wings of glorious green fluttered.

"Nicky, watch out," warned Spelling. "Do not go any closer."

"He would not dare," Wickenshire replied. "We reached an understanding about such behavior long ago, Nightingale and I. I am going to lower the chandelier, Neil. Grab the trinket as soon as it is within your reach, eh?"

So saying, Wickenshire took himself off to the far corner of the room, undid the rope that held the chandelier aloft and began to lower it. "Go, Neil," he urged. "I am doing it as slowly as I can, but Nightingale will notice what is happening in a moment and fly off again."

"Oh, no," Spelling replied with a shake of his head. "I am not going over there."

"Mr. Spelling, whyever not?" asked Lady Alice. "You cannot be afraid of a bird, sir?"

Yes, I can, thought Spelling as he slowly shook his head in the negative. I can be afraid of that particular fowl. Devious feather duster. But I am damned if I will look the coward in front of Alice.

Lifting his chin the slightest bit, Spelling gave Lady Alice's hand a pat, then stepped bravely, though somewhat reluctantly, toward the chandelier. The chandelier came lower; Nightingale turned his back on Spelling. The chandelier came lower still. Spelling raised his arm as high as he could above his head, jumped upward and snagged the trinket. At which precise moment, Nightingale turned back around and tossed a candlestick down on Spelling's head. "Villain!" Nightingale cried and scurried to the next candle, plucked it from its base and tossed it in the direction of the backtreading Spelling. "Bitevillain!"

Five

"Sixteenth-century Spanish," declared Sotherland, studying the trinket as the gentlemen enjoyed their after-dinner port. "Perhaps we ought to go out and take a closer look at this particular barn of yours, Wickenshire. First the feathered serpent and now this. What else might it disgorge?"

"Wander about in it too much, it will fall down around our ears, and then one day it will disgorge *us,*" Wickenshire replied with a grin. "You have not seen it, Sotherland."

"No. I might have done. Prepared to accompany the beetlebrain here and m'daughter on their little expedition this afternoon, but little Delight talked me out of it."

"God bless you, Delight," mumbled Spelling under his breath as he poured himself another glass of wine.

"Eh? What, Spelling?" growled the duke.

"Nothing. Merely observing what a fine child Delight is."

"Indeed she is. This is a silver starfish fastened about the coin to keep it on the chain," continued Sotherland. "I have seen such before. A bit of polishing and it will be a splendid ornament to grace your lady's throat, Wickenshire."

"I found the thing," muttered Spelling into his wine.

Wickenshire noted and nodded. "So you did, Neil," he said, taking the trinket from Sotherland and tossing it to

Spelling. "Still be there, had you not discovered it. It is yours to keep."

"Truly?"

"Truly. Someday there will be a particular lady whose throat you will wish to grace with it, no?"

"Y-yes. Yes, there will. Some day soon, I should think."

"Just so. A magnificent trinket worthy of even a duke's daughter," teased Wickenshire, the remark freezing Sotherland's eyes to blue crystal and causing Spelling to shift his gaze away from both gentlemen. "Time to join the ladies, no?" Wickenshire continued, thoroughly amused by both Sotherland's and Spelling's reaction to his statement. "Must not abandon the ladies to their own resources for too very long. They will be plotting mischief else, without us there to protest against it."

Together the gentlemen rose, abandoned their port and tramped off down the corridor into the Gold Saloon. "Yo-ho-ho, Merrgle Misfit!" Lord Nightingale greeted, rocking from side to side on the back of the sopha while the ladies turned from where they stood in a group before the largest of the two hearths and smiled benignly.

"Jenkins, what the deuce are you doing up there?" asked Wickenshire, staring at the elderly butler balanced precariously on a short ladder leaned against the mantel.

"He is helping us to make a change, Nicky," replied Sera blithely. "I have decided that that horrid painting of dead fowl and gasping fish must go. It is the most depressing thing, and your mama and Lady Alice agree with me entirely."

"Now?" asked Wickenshire. "You are changing paintings now?"

"Yes, dear," smiled Sera. "Right this moment, before we get to placing ivy about the frames for Christmas. You do not mind, do you, Nicholas? We have sent James and Mackelry upstairs to fetch a painting to replace it."

"Oh," murmured Wickenshire, rubbing at the back of his

neck with one hand and turning aside in order to whisper to Sotherland. "Is this something that ladies do because of—because of—the vagaries of increasing?" he queried, bewildered. "I ask because we put that particular painting above the mantel the day before you arrived, Sotherland. Counting this one, five different paintings have occupied that particular space."

"Ladies in the family way are most unpredictable," Sotherland replied in a hushed voice. "You do not mind to have the paintings switched about, eh?"

"No, but a week ago Sera declared that painting to be just the thing. Whoa, Jenkins. Steady on!" Wickenshire called and moved quickly across the room to take the painting from the awkwardly wobbling butler. "Not a job for a man alone. Heavy old thing. Climb down, Jenkins," Wickenshire ordered, leaning the painting against the side of the armchair beside the hearth.

"But I am to replace the painting with—"

"Climb down, Jenkins," interrupted Wickenshire. "I have kept you with me for all of my life. Once I went so far as to board up the fourth-floor windows on this very house so that I might save on the tax and pay your salary. I am not about to lose you now. Climb down at once. I will hang the painting that Lady Wickenshire has chosen. James and Mackelry will assist. You must stand back near the doorway, eh, and observe whether I have got it straight or not."

"Yes, my lord," agreed Jenkins with a most stoic expression, though he breathed a sigh of relief.

Just as Jenkins' feet stood once more upon the carpeting, James and Mackelry appeared in the doorway, carrying between them a large painting in a gilded frame.

"What the deuce?" murmured Spelling, as the footmen brought the painting to the bottom of the ladder which Wickenshire was in the process of climbing.

The earl looked down at Spelling's low-key exclamation

and then echoed it. "Sera, are you certain that you wish to hang this particular painting here?"

"Oh, yes, Nicky," Serendipity replied. "It will be just the thing. We ought to have a picture of one of your ancestors gazing out over the room in which we spend most of our time."

"Yes, but this particular ancestor, my dear?"

"Indeed. You have invented so many stories about her for Delight, that we have all grown exceedingly fond of her."

"This cannot be Glorianna, Queen of the Faeries," observed Sotherland, stepping forward to view the portrait more fully.

"No," smiled Sera. "But she has been kissed by Glorianna just as Delight has, and so Nicky has made up innumerable stories about Elaina Maria for my little sister."

"Hand it up then," ordered Wickenshire. "As long as you are certain, my dear. Neil, hold this ladder steady, will you? Yes, I have got it now, James. A bit farther and—"

Lady Alice gasped.

"I cannot believe it!" Serendipity exclaimed. "Why did we not take note of it at once?"

"By Jupiter!" observed the Duke of Sotherland, stepping forward, his eyes raised to the portrait Wickenshire was hanging above the mantel. Placing his arm subtly about the dowager Lady Wickenshire's waist, Sotherland pointed toward the portrait. "Madam, will you look at that."

"What?" asked Spelling, busily supporting Wickenshire's ladder and so unable to see the portrait around the earl's broad back. "What is it that you are all staring at?"

Wickenshire, above him, leaned back away from the portrait to see for himself what had caused such a reaction in those below and whistled a low, long whistle. "I cannot think why I never noticed it before," he said softly.

"What?" asked Spelling again. "Noticed what? It cannot

be the wine stain on her cheek. We have all of us noticed that over and over."

"No, I never did," offered Lady Alice softly. "It is quite like little Delight's unfortunate birthmark."

"Exactly like Delight's," Sotherland agreed.

"Well, if that is all . . ." said Spelling. "Nothing extraordinary in that."

"It is not all, Neil," interrupted Wickenshire. "My great-great-however-many-greats aunt appears to be sporting the exact same trinket around her neck that you discovered in the barn."

It occurred to Duncan, as his dinner tray departed with Hobbs, that Wickenshire was a rather fine fellow. For, although every gentleman might be expected to offer aid to an injured stranger and to provide him shelter in such circumstances as now existed for Duncan, not many would send up their finest brandy for him to sip after such a prime dinner as he had just eaten.

But what will he do tomorrow when no one has come to claim me? Duncan wondered. Will he send me off in his carnage to some country inn and place me in the care of the innkeeper? "Well, cannot be faulted in the least if he does," he sighed. "Christmas is near upon us and a complete stranger cannot expect to be taken into the bosom of someone else's family. Yes, come in," he called at the sound of scratching on his chamber door.

"Are you feeling more the thing, Mr. Duncan?" asked a little voice, as a head topped by a ruffled nightcap from beneath which pale gold ringlets sprouted peered around the doorframe at him.

"I am feeling quite the thing," Duncan replied.

"Oh, good! Then you willn't mind if I come an' visit."

"No, not at all. I should like to have a visitor."

Being very careful to close the door softly behind her,

Delight stepped across the carpeting on tippy-toes until she reached Duncan's bed. "May I?" she asked most politely.

"I expect so," Duncan responded. "Must I take your hand?"

"Oh, no. I am verimost good at steps."

"Are you? In such a long robe and bedroom slippers?"

"Uh-huh," Delight assured him, climbing up the three steps and bouncing down beside him on the bed. "I am called Delight and you are called Mr. Duncan."

"Exactly so. I am most pleased to make your acquaintance, Miss Delight."

"I thought you would be."

"You did?"

"Uh-huh. It gets lonely when ever'one else is downstairs an' a person is up here without nobody, expected to go to sleep. I did not want you to be lonely."

"I see. What is it that you have in your hand, my dear?"

"One of your stockings."

"It is?"

"Uh-huh. It has got a hole in it."

"It has?"

"Uh-huh. Right here. See?" With rather much of a flourish, Delight held the stocking up under his nose, one tiny finger wiggling through the hole in its toe. "It is your stocking I have comed to talk to you about," she said gravely.

Duncan stared at the wiggling little finger and then at the child, thoroughly entranced. "I am certain I did not intend to put a hole in my stocking, Miss Delight."

"I know you did not. But now that it has one, will you be wanting it back?"

Duncan would have chuckled, but the expression on the child's face was so very serious that he thought better of it. "I expect I shall need it, hole or not, when I leave. Unless you know of someone willing to lend me another."

"Jackie says that he will give you the loan of two of his

that match. They do not have any holes at all in them either."

"And Jackie is?"

"Jackie is the fireboy. He makes all the fires in all the rooms in the whole house. Well, perhaps he does not make quite so many as that, but he makes a frightful number of them."

"I see. And do you think that Jackie's stockings will fit me, Miss Delight?"

Delight studied the gentleman in the bed, worrying her lower lip with her teeth as she estimated the length of him. She held his stocking as high in the air as she could and studied that. "Well," she said with a sigh, "if Jackie took the toes of his stockings and me the tops and we stretcheded them with all our mights, they would be bound to fit you. And they do not have one hole in them either, did I tell you that?"

"I believe you did. Perhaps you will tell me as well what you intend to do with my stocking if I give it to you?"

"Well, that is just the thing," said Delight, scooting up to the head of the bed and plumping herself against Duncan's pillows, so close to him that he must place his arm around her shoulders or have it sat upon. "We are making a surprise for Christmas, you see, and this is the most elegant stocking we have got yet. It has got little clocks on it, did you know? We do not have any stockings at all with little clocks on them. It is perfeckly 'squisite. And we need a most 'squisite stocking to be our angel."

It was near ten o'clock as Spelling peered down from the window of the Gold Saloon at the two shadows in the garden. "They will freeze to death out there. What can they be doing?"

"Hush, Neil," answered Sera as she directed Jenkins to place the tea things on the low fruitwood table before her.

"Lady Alice merely wished for a breath of fresh air and his grace went to keep an eye on her. She sat too near the hearth during our game of whist and grew sluggish from the heat."

"Well, I am the one ought to be strolling through the garden with her, not Sotherland. Whoever heard of strolling about a garden with your daughter?"

"I shall stroll through the garden with my daughter," Wickenshire announced, "if I have a daughter."

"Yes, but not when she is of an age to be courted, you will not," Spelling protested.

"Perhaps not then, but Sotherland did never know his daughter until a few months ago. Do not pout, Neil. Give the man an opportunity to know his girl before you take her from him."

Spelling turned from the window and noted the teasing light in Wickenshire's eyes. "You are quizzing me. You do not believe that I will ever have the girl."

"Perhaps you will and perhaps not, Neil," the dowager Lady Wickenshire observed. "But if you are ever to have the opportunity, you must make some determined effort to gain the girl's attention. You cannot be forever shuffling about like a man fresh risen from the grave when she is in the room."

"I am not doing that, am I, Aunt Diana?"

"Perhaps not quite. But you do tend to look terrified whenever she speaks to you."

"That is only because Sotherland glowers at me as if he will have my head on a platter should I answer her in the wrong tone."

"A demon, Sotherland," Wickenshire said with a grin. "What is it Lady Vermont is wont to call him?"

"The Devil Incarnate," Spelling answered. "And she is not mistaken in it, I think."

"Balderdash!" protested the dowager. "The duke is nothing of the sort. He is a man made hard by fate. He can be softened. We have all of us seen proof of that. Is Eugenia not married to his heir and Mary to his younger son? If you truly love this girl, Neil, we will all do our best to be of help to you, but you must learn to deal decisively and forthrightly with her father. You do love Lady Alice, do you not? You do wish to have her hand in marriage? Your letter to Nicky was not filled with lies merely to gain admittance to this house for some nefarious reason?"

"You read my letter?" Spelling asked in a squawk that sounded so like Lord Nightingale that the macaw turned hurriedly to stare at him. "Obmigawd! You read the letter I sent to Nicky? Did you read it as well, Sera?"

Serendipity nodded. "It is not a letter of which to be ashamed, Neil. It is a very—sensitive—letter."

"Ohmigawd," choked Spelling, his cheeks flaming. "Nicky, how could you have allowed them both to—"

"We have not only read it, Neil," interrupted Sera, rising and crossing the room to take his arm and steer him to a seat upon the sopha. "Nicky's mama and I have sprinkled it with lavender and pressed it in the Bible to give to Lady Alice once you are married. She will treasure it forever."

"Are you mad?" sputtered Spelling. "Treasure it forever? That ill-worded, ink-splotched mess of a letter? I crumpled it up and threw it on the floor three times at the very least before I got up the nerve to send it. I still cannot believe that I actually posted the thing. And you have sprinkled it with lavender and pressed it in a Bible?"

"Your grace, Lady Alice, just in time for tea," chirped Sera in warning to Spelling. "Come in. Sit. I am just now about to pour out. Alice, do sit upon the sopha beside Neil. Just scoot Nightingale out of your way if he bothers you."

"Yes, and you shall have this chair beside me, your grace," the dowager added. "That way we will be able to have a bit of a coze, you and I, and leave the children to their own devices."

"I have not the least intention of leaving them to their

own devices," muttered Sotherland, taking the seat beside the dowager and crossing one long leg over the other. "I intend to pay close attention to all that goes forward."

"Incorrigible scoundrel. You ought to be flogged for what you are putting that poor boy through."

"I, madam, am doing nothing to your nephew. I have not laid a hand upon him," whispered the duke back.

"No, but he fears you may."

"Right to fear it, too. I have said it before and I will say it again. I will not have less than an earl for a son-in-law and you would do well to believe me."

"You do not mind to share the sopha with me, Lady Alice?" Spelling queried, standing and waiting for her to take a seat.

"No, Mr. Spelling. Of course I do not," she replied as she sat. "I expect I have missed a great deal of conversation while strolling through the garden."

"N-no, not—not—anything of significance."

"Tarra mistlemay," inserted Lord Nightingale, sidling along the back of the sopha in Spelling's direction as that gentleman took a cherry tart from the plate before him. "Godresye merrrrrrry gen'lemen," and he came to a halt just behind Spelling. He stretched forward and nibbled at Spelling's collar.

"Lord Nightingale is so very precious," Lady Alice observed. "I do believe he is interested in your tart, Mr. Spelling."

"He would be," Spelling responded as the macaw's beak moved upward. "Nightingale, cease and desist. Nibbling on my collar is one thing, nibbling on my hair is entirely another. Here," Spelling offered, taking his cherry tart in hand and breaking off a tiny bit. "You may try this if you wish." Cautiously Spelling held the piece of tart toward the macaw.

Lord Nightingale studied the offering thoughtfully.

"You are kind, Mr. Spelling," Alice observed with a smile.

"I am attempting to be."

"I can see. Oh, he is stepping down onto your shoulder. How prettily he does it. He has every confidence in you, Mr. Spelling. I do think it reveals something of a gentleman's character, the manner in which animals relate to him, do not you? The creatures of nature are never misled with flowery phrases or charming manners, as are we."

"Just so," agreed Spelling, hoping with all his heart that Lord Nightingale had decided to forget their altercations of the last twenty years or so in favor of the cherry tart. Take it, you old pirate, he thought as Lady Alice smiled at them both. I will bring you pine nuts every day for the rest of your life, you peabrain, if you take it.

Lord Nightingale stretched forward, inspected the offering, stood upright, ruffled his chest feathers and bobbed his head excitedly. "Heytheremister Isaw Hiram kiss yersister," sang the macaw rowdily, and stretched toward the tart again.

"Will Nightingale take it or not?" asked Wickenshire quietly of his wife.

"Of course he will," Sera replied.

"Like to make a wager on it?"

"Yes, I would. I will wager five pounds, Nicholas."

"So much?"

"Indeed. On behalf of Bedazzler. If I lose, I will put five pounds of my pin money into the little treasure box and if you lose, you must do the same."

"Well, if it is for Bedazzler," grinned the earl.

Spelling held the piece of tart in fingers that had begun to shake the slightest bit. Take the tart you danged feather duster, he thought. Take it now, before it crumbles to nothing and the cherries smear all over my fingers. Take it and show Alice that you have deciphered my character and approve of me.

"Howdedo," mumbled Lord Nightingale. Then, he inched forward on Spelling's shoulder, opened his beak and clamped down forcefully on Spelling's thumb.

"Ouch! Danged, demented piece of fox bait!" Spelling exclaimed, jumping up and sending Lord Nightingale into a jubilant flight around the room.

"Oh, Mr. Spelling!" Alice cried, standing up beside him. "He bit you! What a naughty bird you are," she called out to the soaring macaw. "Look what you have done to poor Mr. Spelling. Not only have you hurt him, but you have made him get cherry tart all over himself! You must allow me to care for your wound, Mr. Spelling. It is my fault that he has bitten you."

"Your fault? No, never."

"Yes, indeed. It was I encouraged you to offer him the bit of tart. We shall just go down to the kitchen, you and I, and wash the wound. Certainly Cook will find something in the still room to apply to it and something with which to make a bandage."

Across from them, the dowager Lady Wickenshire smiled the most pleasant smile at the Duke of Sotherland.

"You delude yourself, madam, if you believe that I will allow her to take him to the kitchen alone," stated Sotherland. "It ain't going to happen."

"Should you care to place a wager?" queried the dowager.

"Tuppence."

"A guinea."

"Very well. A guinea."

"Done," nodded the dowager, who then rose to her feet and crossed to Mr. Spelling. "Is it bad, Neil?" she asked, placing one hand on his shoulder. "Let me see."

Mr. Spelling, discomposed by the bite, the unexpectedness of Alice's response and now his aunt's interest, stuck his poor thumb directly under the dowager's nose.

"Neil," she exclaimed, "it is bleeding!" Placing one hand on her heart and the other on her brow, she sank to the floor.

Wickenshire, Sera and Sotherland were on their feet and

rushing to her in an instant. Spelling knelt down beside her at once, as did Alice.

"She has fainted," Sera said in the most bewildered voice. "I cannot believe— Nicholas, fetch my hartshorn at once, darling. Will you help me, your grace, to get her on the sopha?"

The Duke of Sotherland nodded, bent down and lifted the dowager up into his arms.

"Alice, will you see to Neil while I see to my mama-in-law?" continued Sera. "I cannot think why— She is generally not so delicate as to allow a little blood—"

Alice took Spelling by the arm and urged him from the room just as Sotherland placed the dowager Lady Wickenshire gently down upon the sopha. Lacking anything else to hand, the duke tugged his handkerchief from his pocket and began to wave it with exceeding energy before her face. The younger Lady Wickenshire praised him for it and urged him to continue while she looked about for something more appropriate to promote a breeze.

"I do not think it could have been that little bit of blood on Neil's thumb," Sera mused aloud. "She has never been one to faint at the sight of blood. Perhaps she rose too quickly. Oh, I cannot think what could have happened. Is she not awakening yet? Here, here is the fan Nicholas bought for me in Edinburgh."

Wickenshire arrived moments later, hartshorn in hand. "Mama," he whispered, waving the hartshorn beneath her nose. "Mama, wake up."

The dowager groaned and pushed the hartshorn away. One lovely blue eye opened, and then the second. "What happened?" she asked breathlessly.

"You fainted, Mama."

"Did I? What a gudgeon."

"Not a gudgeon," protested Sotherland, peering down at her from behind the sopha. "Any woman might—"

"Has Alice taken Neil to the kitchen to tend to his wound?" she interrupted.

"Yes, Mama," replied Wickenshire. "Do not worry about Neil."

"No, no, I do not," she said, and gazed up at Sotherland, a smile quivering on her lips. "Neil is in excellent hands, and I am soon to be a guinea to the good."

"Oh, Nicky, her mind is wandering," gasped Sera. "A guinea to the good? What can she mean?"

Sotherland's worried expression changed to a scowl as he stared down at the dowager and then he smiled and then he burst out in the loudest guffaw. "You minx! To send us all into a panic for a guinea!"

"Not merely for a guinea." Lady Wickenshire smiled up at him. "For hope, your grace. For my nephew. For an opportunity."

Six

"Nightingale will never like me," sighed Spelling, watching as Lady Alice wrapped a strip of linen around and around his thumb. "I have failed your test completely."

"My test?"

"Yes. You know, the one about creatures knowing what is in a person's heart."

"I did not say that precisely."

"No, but it is what you implied. I have never thought of it before, but you are likely correct. From the moment I was old enough to toddle around my father's study, Nightingale clearly detested me. He knew me for a villain even then."

Lady Alice ceased in her ministrations and gazed into Mr. Spelling's sad, dark eyes. "A villain? As a babe in leading strings? Oh, I think not. No one is born a villain. You must not take my ill-conceived words so seriously," Alice said, longing at that precise moment to brush a splendidly shining curl from his furrowed brow. "I do believe that animals see things in people that we do not, but I form my own opinions of my acquaintances and what is in their hearts. All by myself."

"You do?"

"Certainly. Please do not allow this little mishap to spoil the holiday for you, Mr. Spelling. We are going to have such a splendid time."

"We are?"

"Oh, yes. We must bring in the Yule log and fashion the kissing bough. There is more of the house to decorate, baskets to fill, gifts to wrap, surprises to plan. And his grace tells me that there are Christmas traditions in Devon that I will find most surprising and enjoy immensely. All this and more await us in the company of Lord and Lady Wickenshire, who are the most gracious host and hostess I have ever met. And of course, we have your aunt and little Delight, Stanley Blithe and Sweetpea, all eager to keep us entertained. Are you not having a splendid time already, Mr. Spelling?"

"Ah, yes!" answered Spelling as he rose and pulled back Alice's chair so that she might rise as well. Ghosts of Christmases past hovered about Spelling at that precise moment. Visions of Lord Nightingale danced in his head. "I used to enjoy Christmas enormously," he said with a wistful sigh. "Aunt Diana and Nicky would come to spend the entire twelve days of Christmas with us in London. There would be roast goose, plum pudding, minced pies. My mother would make gingerbread men—one for Nick and one for me. He was a sad, quiet boy, Nicky. As young as I was, I noticed that. But then Uncle Ezra would come and pound upon our door, all dressed up as Father Christmas. He could make Nicky laugh. Always. And he made me laugh as well. How odd," he added quietly as Alice placed her hand on his sleeve and allowed him to escort her from the kitchen.

"What is odd, Mr. Spelling?"

"That I should remember Uncle Ezra in such a pleasant way," he replied as they traversed the corridor. "I have not thought of him as Father Christmas for years and years."

Alice gazed up at him as they turned toward the staircase and she studied his proud profile. He was a handsome gentleman with hair that seemed brown but was actually a vibrant mix of colors when the light caught it.

His perfectly straight nose was neither too long nor too short; his teeth were white and even.

And he has the eyes of a poet, she thought as he glanced down at her, his memories surging up around him. His eyes betray his every emotion. Joyous or sad, they touch a person's soul.

If only I had never heard of Mr. Sayers, Alice thought as her slippers whispered along the corridor carpeting beside the soft clomp of Spelling's shoes. Why must that man appear here? And why now? Mr. Sayers cannot have known that I would come to spend Christmas at Willowsweep. What ought I to do about him? she wondered. Ought I just go on pretending that I know him not? I wonder what his grace would do? And then Alice smiled the most tender of smiles.

"What is it?" asked Spelling quietly. "I have never seen you smile quite like that before."

"I happened to think about his grace," Alice replied softly. "He is truly the finest, sweetest gentleman."

"Do you think?"

"Oh, yes. He has been splendid to me since first we met. I cannot possibly imagine the frightful grief he has suffered because of my mother and my grandmother, and yet he is determined to be the best of fathers to me."

"He is?"

"Do you not see it in him, Mr. Spelling?"

"He is always so—so—gruff with everyone."

"A mere facade. He hides behind his peevishness to protect his heart from further damage. You should hear the tales my brother Edward can tell. Edward was the only one, you know, who grew up with him at Northridge."

"I have heard some of those tales. I do not envy Bradford his childhood in the least."

"But had his grace raised all of us—had mother and grandmother not tortured him so ceaselessly for so very long—all would have been different with him, I think. Even in so brief a time as that from my brothers' marriages until now, he has altered greatly."

Spelling gazed down at her in something approaching wonder. He had not noticed much alteration in the Duke of Sotherland, but then, he did not know the gentleman well at all. "Perhaps I ought to make more of an effort," he murmured, mostly to himself.

"An effort, Mr. Spelling?"

"To—to become better acquainted with your father."

They stepped together into the Gold Saloon.

"Villain!" shrieked Lord Nightingale at the sight of them and soared in a great circle around the room. "Bite! Villain! Bitevillain!" And with a gracefulness beyond that of the most exquisite of hawks, he landed on Spelling's shoulder.

"You, my Lord Nightingale, have been a naughty bird," Alice declared, removing her hand from Spelling's sleeve and tucking it through the crook of his arm instead.

"Howdedo m'pretty," responded Nightingale in his best come-hither voice while rocking seductively back and forth on Spelling's shoulder.

"Do not 'howdedo m'pretty' me," Alice said. "That particular phrase will get you nowhere. You have hurt Mr. Spelling and you have made him sad as well. Such dreadful behavior, my lord! And from a gentleman! Only look at the damage you have done." With great show, Alice removed her hand from the crook of Spelling's arm, stepped in front of him and with both hands lifted his bandaged thumb up within Nightingale's sight.

The macaw glared at the large, white linen bandage. Tentatively he made his way down Spelling's arm, stretched forward and nibbled at the thing.

His hand caught between both of Alice's, Spelling could not pull away from the macaw's beak, though he truly wished to do so.

"Villain," muttered Nightingale, pecking gently at the bandage. "Bitevillain."

"Yes, you did, and you had best never do so again, do you hear? No bite villain. Never again," Alice scolded.

"At least both my Alice and that old pirate recognize a villain when they see one," observed Sotherland in a whisper.

"Neil is not a villain," the dowager replied ardently.

"Villain," mumbled Lord Nightingale again as he eyed the bandage, then Alice, then the bandage. "Nobitevillain."

"Precisely," agreed Alice. "No bite villain."

"No," murmured Nightingale. "Nobite. Nobitevillain. No, bite villain," and he clamped down with great enthusiasm on Spelling's bandaged thumb.

The bandage was so thick, however, that Spelling felt merely a bit of pressure. His fear of being bitten dispensed with on the instant, and his hopes of befriending the bird for Alice's sake firmly in mind, Spelling smiled broadly. "What a scoundrel," he said, wiggling the thumb about with the macaw's beak still clamped to it. "Did you attend to the manner in which he switched the order of your words about to serve himself, Lady Alice? Nightingale, you are a scoundrel. A pirate and a scoundrel." Then Spelling reached into his pocket with his free hand and produced the pine nut that had lingered there since before dinner. "Would you not rather have a taste of this?" he asked the parrot. "I should think it tastes better than a bandage."

Lord Nightingale released the linen at once, seized the offering and shuffled sideways back up Spelling's arm to his shoulder where he settled himself nicely and inspected the treat with enormous delight.

"And how is our mysterious Mr. Duncan?" queried Serendipity as she stepped into her husband's dressing room later that same evening. "I assume you have received word as to the gentleman's condition. Have you?"

The Earl of Wickenshire nodded and opened his arms

for his wife to walk directly into them. "Ate his dinner with great enthusiasm and has since gone off to sleep. Hobbs will sleep on a cot in the gentleman's dressing room to-night."

"So, you do not trust this Mr. Duncan, Nicholas?"

"It is not just that, m'dear. He has been injured. Someone ought to be nearby in case he should wake and require help in the night. And Hobbs is the best choice. Jenkins can manage without him as long as James and Mackelry are available."

"I ought not have sent Jenkins up that ladder," mused Sera, her head resting comfortably against her husband's chest.

"No, that you should not have done. He is not as agile as he once was, and I do not wish to lose him, Sera. He was more father to me than my own father."

"I know. It was foolish of me. I merely expressed a wish to exchange one painting for another and Jenkins immediately fetched the little ladder from his pantry and set about doing the thing."

"Because he adores you, my dear."

"No."

"Yes. You and Delight both have won his heart completely."

"There is some conspiracy afoot with Delight and Jenkins," Sera observed.

"Is there?" With one graceful movement, Wickenshire swept his wife up into his arms and carried her into his bedchamber. "I do not doubt it. Christmas fast approaches." He set Sera gently on the bed and bestowed a lingering kiss upon her lips. "I have noticed a peculiar smile flitting about Jenkins' lips of late."

"Yes, and a particular sparkle in his eyes."

"Just so," nodded Wickenshire, climbing in on his side of the great oaken bedstead and tugging the covers warmly over them both. Leaning back against the pillows, he placed his arm protectively around his wife's shoulders and the two gazed comfortably into the fire as it flickered on the hearth just beyond the foot of the bed.

"I spoke with Alice about Mr. Sayers, Nicholas."

"You did?"

"Um-hmm. After dinner. Before you brought the gentlemen to the saloon."

"And did she tell you what it was that made her color up?"

"I think so," mused Sera. "She said that she had developed a tendre for the gentleman as a school girl."

"I thought they had never met."

"They had not. It was his sister kept speaking of him and how remarkable he was. Alice said she made the greatest hero of him in her imagination. And then, to discover him sitting at table, well, she was embarrassed."

"Embarrassed? No cause for embarrassment that I can see. Women are odd creatures."

"We are?"

"Yes, but it is a perfectly lovely sort of odd," Wickenshire replied, kissing Sera's nose and then placing a hand softly against her stomach. "Tell me, what did Bedazzler do when Nightingale bit Neil the second time?"

"He laughed."

"How do you know?"

"Well, he was laughing so very hard that he was rolling all about and kicking like a little creature gone wild."

"She is a sharp one, our Bedazzler."

"Indeed he is."

Wickenshire chuckled. "We shall never settle it between us, you know. Bedazzler must settle which pronoun is applicable. You are not overwhelmed, Sera? With all these guests, I mean."

"Oh, Nicholas, for goodness sake! I am pleased to have company for Christmas. It is not as though I am required to clean the rooms and make the beds and cook the dinners.

They are a pleasure to me, our guests. I only feared that you might be opposed to it at first because I am—I am—"

"What?"

"Well, because it is so obvious that Bedazzler is—"

"A jolly little elf of great goodwill?"

"No," giggled Sera.

"What then?"

"Because Bedazzler is so—so—obviously present."

"Does it bother you to have others see that our Bedazzler is obviously present, Sera?"

"No, it does not. I cannot imagine hiding away as though our pending child were something to cause me shame."

"Our pending child?" Wickenshire tickled his wife's ear with his tongue. "Our pending child, Sera? Great heavens, what a phrase! Does it trouble our pending child to be seen by our guests? Eh?"

"I think Bedazzler likes all the company. He certainly enjoys Neil. Each time Neil is in the room, he seems to pay the strictest attention. And then he laughs and laughs."

"My child a Neil fancier? I hope Lady Alice *will* have my cousin then. I will not fear to send Bedazzler to visit Neil if Lady Alice is there to keep them both out of the briars."

"Nicholas, you still did not say."

"Say what?"

"If you are—if it—if you gave over and invited everyone just to keep me happy, but are actually—"

"What a peagoose!" interrupted Wickenshire. "If you are not bothered and Bedazzler is not bothered, then most certainly, madam, I am not. You are the two most important people in all the world to me, and there is nothing I will not happily do including the setting aside of generally held traditions. I will set aside Christmas if you wish."

"Oh, no, do not you dare, you tease! Bedazzler and I are so looking forward to Christmas!"

* * *

Jenkins closed the door of Lord Nightingale's cage and covered the cage with the ancient shawl that the earl had inherited along with the bird. Nightingale shrieked and squawked.

"Yes, goodnight to you too, my lord," murmured Jenkins. It was odd how one grew accustomed to the ear-piercing sounds of Lord Nightingale's move toward slumber. Equally disconcerting were the sounds of his rise into morning, to which one also grew accustomed. Jenkins crossed to the main mantel to extinguish the last of the lamps in the Gold Saloon and stared upward at the portrait of Elaina Maria Chastain. "It is about time," he whispered up to her. "You have been tucked away for too long. It is about time you shared a bit of happiness with the family."

It was queer, indeed, that for all the years he had been in the service of the Wickenshires, Jenkins had never once considered this great-great-innumerable-greats aunt of the present earl as any but a malignant blot upon the family name. Not until Miss Serendipity Bedford had arrived with little Delight had he given the least consideration to how the poor Spanish lady must have suffered for that wine red blemish on her cheek. To be sent away and her husband with her to this wild place so that her existence would not embarrass the remainder of the family; to be scorned by barbaric English peasants for that mere accident of birth; to be labelled for all time the Witch of Willowsweep.

And I am just as guilty of maligning her as those who knew her at first hand, he told himself as he made his way along the corridor from one room to the other, checking the window locks and the hearths, lowering the lamps as he went. I used that poor lady shamelessly when first we came to restore this house. "I ought not to have done that," he said quietly as he turned and made his way up the staircase to the second floor. "But Christmas is a time for forgiving. Perhaps, wherever she is, she will forgive me for my part in that little escapade."

"ARRRRRRRohhhhhhhhhEEEEEE!"

The shriek came so unexpectedly that Jenkins jumped straight up into the air. "What the devil was that?" he asked himself as his feet once again touched the floor. "Not Nightingale."

"ARRRRRRRohhbhhhhhhEEEEEE!" came the shriek again and somewhere above Jenkins' head something struck solidly against something else. Then came the sound of feet meeting the floor above him, a pause, and then footsteps hurrying across carpet, doors opening and slamming shut. Feet met floor audibly on the second story as well. Doors opened and heads poked out around door frames into the corridor.

"By Jupiter, that was not Nightingale!" exclaimed Spelling, limping out into the hallway with one shoe off and one shoe on. "I have listened to Nightingale for almost my whole life, and that was not him. Jenkins, did you hear?"

"Yes, sir," nodded Jenkins.

"It was the w-witch," mumbled Carson, trembling, barely visible behind Spelling's shoulder. "It was the W-Witch of W-Willowsweep screeching."

"Yes? And what was that enormous whop-bang at the end of it, Carson?" asked Spelling. "She slipped and fell flat on her—"

"I thought this witch died a century or more ago," muttered Sotherland as he trundled up to them in robe and slippers. "Explain to your man, Spelling, that dead witches seldom wander about shrieking at the top of their lungs, and rarely if ever fall upon their—"

"It sounded a good deal to me as though someone had stepped on Stanley Blithe's tail," interrupted Jenkins. "Though what could have fallen with such a bang afterwards, I cannot think."

"Stanley Blithe sleeps in the nursery with Delight, does he not?" asked Sotherland. "Well, by Jove, Jenkins, why are we all standing about here then. The child—"

"Did not come from the nursery," interrupted Spelling. "Came from the fourth floor. Nursery ain't on the fourth floor; nursery is on the third."

"Even so, Delight is most likely frightened near to death, Spelling. One of us ought to go up to the child at once."

"Likely on her way down to us at this very moment," observed Jenkins as the door to the servants' staircase burst open and the household staff, in various states of disarray, flowed excitedly out into the second floor corridor. "Just so," Jenkins added as Stanley Blithe rushed out from behind the mumbling group of humanity with Sweetpea close behind while Delight appeared at the very end of the line, Cook holding to the child's hand.

"Jenkins, what the deuce could have made such a racket as that?" called Wickenshire, approaching from the master's chambers, tying his robe as he came. "Delight, come here to me at once. You are not frightened, are you, m'girl?" he asked, as she ran to him and he swept her up into his arms.

"Did you hear it?" Delight asked. "It were 'ceptional loud."

"Indeed. You are not the least frightened, are you?"

"Uh-uh. But it was the dreadfulest noise."

"She were goin' to see what made it, lordship, when I catched ahold of her," offered the cook. "All the way to the top of the stairs she and them little creatures were."

"Does any one of you actually know what happened?" Wickenshire asked, gazing at his staff.

"The W-Witch of W-Willowsweep," Spelling's valet replied, his voice atremble.

"The what?" asked James, the first footman.

"The W-w-w-witch of W-w-w-willowsweep."

"Of all the dashed nonsense," James replied. "Surely, Mr. Carson, such a civilized person as yourself does not believe in witches. I expect something has broke in one of the empty rooms, my lord," he added. "Sounded quite like something large rubbing together and then falling. Perhaps one of the beams—"

"A beam?" asked Spelling, appalled. "Great glory, Nick, do not tell me that the entire house is going to fall down on our heads. I thought you had repaired everything."

"Well, everything that I could see required repairing."

"Where is my Alice?" asked Sotherland abruptly. "She must have heard that noise. She cannot have slept through such an unearthly shrieking and bang as that."

"Unearthly," whined Carson softly, shrinking even farther back behind Spelling.

"Lady Alice was thinking to go to you, Sotherland," explained Wickenshire, "when I met her just outside her door. I requested her to fetch my mama and the both of them to stay with Sera until I ascertained what was going forward. You do not mind that I—"

"No, no, excellent idea, Wickenshire. Keep the ladies stowed safely out of the way."

"Jenkins, I expect you and I had best go up and see what we can see. If it was a beam, we shall be forced to move everyone to the east wing. Pray, Jenkins, that it was not a beam."

"Wait just a moment, Nicky. I will don my other shoe and accompany you," offered Spelling. "Three pairs of eyes will be better than two."

"Rrrrrmphh," offered Stanley Blithe, sitting patiently on his haunches in the crowded hall.

"Mrrrrrr," Sweetpea observed, and she arched her back, set her tail high and began to rub against Sotherland's leg.

"Wretched animal," grumbled Sotherland, gazing down at her. "Lindsey, pick the danged cat up," he ordered his valet. "Here, Wickenshire, give me the child."

"Will you take her to the ladies until I return?"

"I may. It depends upon whether she is inclined to be a rascally scoundrel or not. Are you inclined to be a rascally scoundrel this evening, m'gel?" he asked, taking Delight's hand firmly into his own once Wickenshire had set her slippered feet firmly back upon the carpet.

"Uh-uh. An' Stanley Blithe is not 'dined to be a rascally scoundrel either. And neither is not Sweetpea," Delight added, gazing hopefully up at the duke.

"So. You would have me entertain the lot of you, eh? Well, we will see," replied Sotherland, leading Delight back toward his chambers, the enormous puppy bouncing ahead while Lindsey, with Sweetpea in his arms, stepped smartly along at the rear. "We will see how well all of you behave. I warn you, Missy, one misstep on the part of Stanley Blithe or that cat and they are out in the corridor on the instant."

"They willn't misstep. Not once," Delight assured him. "I will sit in your lap to keep you warm and Stanley Blithe will lay right down on your feet to keep them warm and Sweetpea will curl up on your bed to keep the sheets warm and—and—I will tell you the most amazing story!"

Seven

"Since there is nothing to be seen in any of these chambers, perhaps it was something inside the walls, my lord," Jenkins offered quietly as the three stood gazing about them at the last of the attic rooms.

"Inside the walls?" asked Spelling.

"Of course! Inside the walls!" exclaimed Wickenshire. "Clever of you, Jenkins, to have thought of that. Do they lead all the way up here, the passages?"

"Oh, right, the passages," Spelling muttered, the oddest look on his face.

"They lead into every room in the house on all of the floors," Jenkins said. "A regular rabbit warren of passages, they are, my lord. Now, let me think. The entrance into them from this particular room ought to be . . . Indeed! It will be right behind that little chest of drawers."

The chest of drawers proved to be stuffed full with linen and took all three of the men to move it away from the wall. Then, as Wickenshire held a lamp aloft and Spelling a brace of candles, Jenkins studied the wall paneling. He ran his hand slowly across it and then nodded. He pushed lightly against the dark wood and a door swung inward.

"Only think, Nicky," Spelling observed, as he followed Wickenshire through the opening. "A man may travel from here into any room in the house," and then he sneezed. "Dusty," he observed and then sneezed again. The brace of candles wobbled unsteadily in his hand, the flames flickered wildly. "Oh, damnation," he muttered, "the candles have gone out."

"Jenkins, fetch us another lamp, will you," Wickenshire requested, handing the useless brace of candles to his butler. "It is not worth the time to relight these. Neil will simply sneeze them out again. Fetch the lamp from the corridor."

Jenkins nodded, turned and left the passage, and then he popped his head back in. "Do not go wandering off, will you, my lord, not you or Mr. Spelling? The floor is worn and treacherous in spots and there are steps in the most unlikely places."

"No, no, we shall stay put until you return, Jenkins." Wickenshire raised his lamp high above his head and stared up at the ceiling of the ancient servants' passageway. "Looks all right here, Neil. No beams hanging loose."

"Only thing hanging down at all are spiderwebs," Spelling replied. "Empty ones. Apparently the spiders abandoned this place long ago. Cannot say I blame them."

"Now what the deuce?" Wickenshire asked, lowering his gaze to a stack of wooden boxes. "Jenkins? Jenkins, what are these?"

"Wh-what are what, my lord?" asked the butler, stepping back into the passageway with a lamp in hand.

"These boxes. They are not some of Uncle Ezra's goods? He has not decided to reestablish himself at Willowsweep?"

"Never! Those boxes have been there for years, my lord."

"Most likely thirty or forty years," Spelling commented and then silenced himself by biting at his lower lip.

"How many years, Jenkins?" asked Wickenshire. "Do you know?"

"That I cannot say. A number of them her ladyship brought when first she married your father, my lord. But his lordship and she did never remain in this house for more than a se'enight at a time, so a good many of them did never get so much as opened up, much less unpacked. And the others—"

"Yes? And the others?"

"Well, I cannot guess, my lord, what the others may be. Those nearest the bottom—the barrel-like ones and that great chest—there is no telling to whom they belonged."

"Likely belonged to the W-w-witch of W-w-willowsweep," said Spelling in imitation of his valet, even going so far as to set his hand to trembling. "Most likely c-c-cursed."

"Enough, Neil," admonished Wickenshire, though his eyes glowed with laughter. "You ought to be ashamed to have set Carson to fretting over poor, dead Aunt Elaina."

"I did not set him to fretting," Spelling protested righteously. "He set himself to fretting. A master at it, Carson is. Best fretter in all of England."

"What do you imagine is in that great trunk, if it is not some of Uncle Ezra's goods?" asked Wickenshire.

"Most likely old clothes turning to powder as we speak," Spelling replied at once. "There is nothing here that could have made that dreadful noise, Nick."

"No. Let us proceed in this direction, shall we? We will not need to descend any steps, I think. The sound did come from this floor, you say, Jenkins?"

"Indeed, my lord. James was positive it came from the fourth floor and I believe so as well. You will wish to shuffle sideways a bit, Mr. Spelling, and you as well, my lord. Narrow, this. Not made for gentlemen with broad shoulders. Not made for gentlemen at all."

"Yes, I remember how tight some of the places proved to be in the passage that leads to the stable. Though parts were fairly wide. Do you truly think these passages made for the servants, Jenkins?" asked Wickenshire. "Why should the household servants find it necessary to travel under the stable, for instance?"

"To carry in the luggage, my lord."

"Or to carry out the dead," said Spelling in an eerie voice.

"Neil!"

"Well, if Aunt Elaina was actually a witch, she might—"

"She is not your aunt, Spelling. She is mine. And I will be obliged if you will cease defaming her."

"I was merely jesting, Nick."

"Yes, but if you continue to do so, you may slip and say something most inappropriate when Delight is in the room. It will not do at all, Neil, to have my little sister-in-law begin to think that that wretched birthmark on her face labels her as anything except a precious child kissed by a good faery."

"I am not so dullwitted as to say anything of the sort in Delight's presence," responded Spelling, peering about him. "Have come to like that little rapscallion. Would not hurt her feelings for all the world. Now why have I suddenly gained so much room about my shoulders? It feels as though I have stepped into—what the devil is this?"

"What? Neil? Where have you gone?"

"Here, Nick. Behind you and to your left. Bring the lamps."

"Well, I'll be deviled," breathed Wickenshire, holding his lamp aloft. "Jenkins, come here. What is this?"

"It is a room, my lord," replied Jenkins.

"Yes, and one that you led us right past. Am I to believe that you did not know this chamber existed, Jenkins?"

"There are so many passages, my lord."

"With rooms attached right to them?"

"There are s-several, I expect, my lord, but—"

Spelling's ear caught a particular tone in Jenkins' voice and it set him immediately to wondering. It also set him to interrupting the butler's response at once. "That old sea chest appears to have fallen from that table, Nick," he said, redirecting Wickenshire's attention. "That will be what made the whop-bang. I will lay you odds on it."

"A safe wager on your part," Wickenshire agreed. "Neil, look at this place," he added, walking deeper into the chamber and turning about in a circle. "It looks as though—as though—some lady resides in it and has just now stepped out for a moment."

Spelling glanced once at the silent Jenkins, then gazed about him, his suspicions rising. A looking glass in a gilded frame with a dressing table and bench set tidily before it stood in one corner. To the right of it, a most ornate chair and beside that a petite little sopha. Directly across from the sopha, a bed with a lace coverlet and silken draperies. And in the center of the room, on a faded carpet, lay an old trunk on its side with its lock broken open, spilling its contents out onto the floor.

"And there is not a bit of dust or a spiderweb anywhere about," Wickenshire whispered. "B'gawd, Jenkins, what is this place? How does it come to be here? And who the devil has taken up residence in it?"

"And what made that horrendous shrieking sound?" added Spelling, his eyes narrowing as he captured Jenkins' nervous gaze. "Who or what made that gawdawful sound?"

"Are you for certain sure Mr. Duncan is fine?" asked Delight as Sotherland settled her on his lap before the hearth in his bedchamber sitting room.

"So said Hobbs when we rapped upon the door, m'gel. You heard him say so yourself. Mr. Duncan did not so much as cease to snore through all that commotion."

"He must be very tired then," Delight observed, wiggling about to find the most comfortable position.

"It does make a man tired to be thrown from his horse and turn his ankle and have his head bitten by a rock."

Delight giggled.

"What? Why do you laugh?"

"Because rocks do not bite, Duke."

"No? Well, one bit our Mr. Duncan. Perhaps it was a magic rock, eh? Here now. Here comes Lindsey to make us cozy," added the duke as his valet appeared with a coverlet and lay it over the laps of Delight and the duke both. "That will be all, Lindsey. Off with you."

"Yes, your grace. The cat, your grace, is lying upon the bed. You do not mind, your grace?"

"No, no. At this moment it may lie wherever it likes. Now, off to bed with you. Evidently the house is not falling down around our ears."

"Just so, your grace," Lindsey replied, bowing curtly and exiting the chamber.

"I believe I shall keep Mr. Lindsey," mused the duke. "He has lasted far longer than any other valet I have ever had in my life. Yes, I do believe I shall keep him."

"And you b'lieve you will keep us, too," declared Delight confidently, snuggling against Sotherland's chest while her fingers played idly with the lap robe.

"What makes you think so, urchin?"

"Urrrph!" offered Stanley Blithe, who had made himself comfortable by lying on Sotherland's feet.

"Not you, you audacious puppy. I was speaking to your mistress here. What makes you think I will, Delight?"

"You are goin' to keep us because Stanley Blithe is the verimost handsomest and bravest dog in all of the world and Sweetpea is the verimost smartest of cats and because I tell the best of stories to you when you cannot sleep. You will not like to lose any one of us, ever."

"Well, you had best be about telling me a story then, or I am like to forget that you can."

"I am going to. An' you must pay attention. This is the story of Glorianna and the little handmaiden girl."

"And what is a handmaiden girl?" asked Sotherland, just to prove that he could be annoying if he wished.

"Do not you know what a handmaiden girl is?"

"No. I have never had a handmaiden girl."

"Well, she is a little servant girl whose job it is to wash everyone's hands in the whole household."

"And you know this because you have one of these girls here at Willowsweep?"

"Uh-uh. I readed the word in a book and I figured out what she did all by myself."

"Well done," nodded Sotherland, attempting to keep a straight face. "So, Glorianna and the little handmaiden girl. Get on with it. I am prepared to be thoroughly enthralled."

"I do hope that nothing serious has happened," said Sera, placing a shawl about her mama-in-law's shoulders. "Such a noise! I thought at first Stanley Blithe had been attacked by goblins."

"More likely he was frightened by a giant mouse and screamed for Sweetpea," smiled the dowager.

"You are not dreadfully concerned?" asked Alice as she settled cozily at one end of the flowered fainting couch in the sitting room attached to the master bedchamber.

"No," replied Sera and the dowager simultaneously.

"But the gentlemen—"

"Gentlemen must always investigate everything," the dowager offered. "They cannot bear for the least little mystery to go unsolved. They will discover what it was and return to tell us and that will be that. You will see, my dear. It will turn out to be something dreadfully pedestrian."

"Such a noise as that?"

"Indeed. Something scraping against something else as it fell and nothing more," Sera replied, settling down beside Alice. "And having solved it, tomorrow Nicky and Neil will return to the mystery of Mr. Duncan. No one has claimed that gentleman, you know. Evidently he is a stranger in these parts, for Bobby Tripp could not get any of the neighbors to own him."

"Almost as mysterious as Mr. Sayers," the dowager observed.

"Mr. Sayers is not mysterious," Alice replied on a tiny breath, her cheeks glowing a sudden pink.

"You do not think so?" asked Sera most seriously. "An unmarried gentleman come to spend Christmas alone in a rented cottage? A gentleman who is known to have at least one sister? You did say that you knew his sister?"

"Yes, but—"

"Alice, my dear, can you think of the least reason why he should not wish to spend the holiday at home with his sister and family?" the dowager queried. "I should think he would wish to do precisely that. Or, if he does not get on with his family, I would think him more likely to be in town, or celebrating Christmas at the home of some friend."

"Just so," nodded Sera. "That is where the mystery lies. Why should Mr. Sayers come into the wilds of Devon all alone and at this time of year?"

"And was he truly lost the night of our fire, or was he lingering outside Willowsweep for some other reason?" added the dowager Lady Wickenshire.

Both the dowager and Sera gazed at Alice with such intensity that she colored up even more and put her hands to her flaming cheeks. "Good heavens, you cannot think that I know the reason for Mr. Sayers' presence?"

"We are quite prepared to learn that you truly do not," said Sera as she took the girl's hands from her cheeks and held them tenderly in her own. "We have, however, discussed it, Nicky's mama and I, and it has occurred to us, Alice, that though you may not know the reason for Mr. Sayers' presence, you may yet *be* the reason for Mr. Sayers' presence."

"And then, very late at night when everyone was asleep, the little handmaiden girl an' her bosom friends sneakeded up the magical staircase which the elderly old elf had taked them up before, but that no one else even knowed about, and they peeked into Glorianna's special room where the fine old elf had let them play. There was no one there. So they walked on tippy-toe right into the room and right up to the most 'squisite trunk."

"A trunk?" asked Sotherland. "What sort of trunk?"

"A 'squisite trunk made of wood with a curvy top an' iron bands around it," Delight explained, wiggling around to sit up straight in the duke's lap so she might turn and look him in the eye. "I will bet you have never seen any trunk like it, not even as old as you are, because it was a 'cessively ancient trunk."

"It must have been excessively ancient if I have never seen one like it," agreed Sotherland.

"Ancienter than ancient. And the little handmaiden girl an' her friends was thoroughly impressed by it when they had been up in the room before, and they thought to open it up and see what was inside even though the elf had forbade them to do it."

"No!"

"Yes! But it was way high up on a spindly old table, an' so they could not reach it very good or see inside it either. So the little handmaiden girl thought to lift it down."

"Quite right."

"But it was very heavy, so she had to tug and tug."

"Did not her friends help her?"

"They tried. Lady Pea stood on the table and walked all around the trunk thinking how to go about it, and Sir Stanley sat down on the floor an' thought an' thought what would be best to do. But the little handmaiden girl could not be patient for too very long or someone might go to her little bedchamber and fine that she was not no longer there, and that would be terrible. So she tugged and tugged and wiggled and tugged, and the most dreadful thing happened."

"What?" asked Sotherland, his cold eyes grown warm.

"The little handmaiden girl stepped on Sir Stanley!"

"Oh, no, not that! Poor Sir Stanley."

"Well, he was so surprised that he cried out afore he

even thought about how quiet they was s'posed to be. And the little handmaiden girl was so startled that she spunned around an' stepped on Sir Stanley again. And he cried out twice as loud."

"Great heavens!"

"Uh-huh. An' just then, the trunk toppled right off the end of the spindly table and fell—whop! crash! bang!—right onto the floor!"

"The little handmaiden girl must have been thoroughly discomposed."

"Uh-huh. She was thoroughly disposed an' could not think at all what to do."

"No, well, I should think not. What a dreadful thing! Only think if Glorianna should discover them there!"

"Or the elderly old elf who had told them not to look in the trunk in the very first place! So they all ran right out of the room and dashed down the magical staircase as fast as they could and they did not even ever see what was in the ancient trunk. They did not get one peep inside of it. The end."

"The end?" queried Sotherland, wiggling his eyebrows at her and setting her to giggling. "It cannot be the end."

"Yes, it is. That is the end."

"Well, did not the little handmaiden girl and her friends learn a great lesson from that adventure?" prodded the duke.

"Oh! Uh-huh. They learned a very great lesson from their 'venture an' that is the moral of the story."

"What is?"

"The lesson."

"Yes, m'gel, but what was the lesson that the little handmaiden girl and her friends learned?"

Delight paused and twisted her hands together in her lap in great consideration. "Not to go about tugging trunks off of tables in the verimost middle of the night," she declared at last. "And they will never do it again."

The Duke of Sotherland, though he had never known his

own daughter at such a tender age, found Delight's story equal to a number of stories his son, Edward, had chosen to tell as a lad. He had scolded Edward severely for telling such clankers and sometimes had sent the lad straight up to his room without his supper as well. But Sotherland had grown a deal less severe since Delight and others of the Wickenshire household had entered his life, and besides, Delight was not a lad but a sweet and tender little girl. He could not bring himself to treat Delight in anything near the same manner in which he had treated his son. He could not, in fact, even grumble at the shining, innocent little face that peered up at him so pensively. Deep inside himself he felt the oddest sensation—something turning slowly about—somewhere in the region of his heart.

"I am pleased to hear that they will never do it again," he said, hoping to make a definite point. "They ought not."

"No. But what ought they to do? Because they do want to see what is in the trunk, Duke. Really, truly, they do."

"They ought to take a grown-up person with them the very next time they sneak up the stairs."

"Do you think so?"

"Um-hmmm. A very ancient grown-up person. And they ought not to do it in the middle of the night."

Sotherland studied the little girl thoughtfully. He imagined that her magical staircase must be the servants' staircase. He guessed that Glorianna's special room must be a storage room on the fourth floor. And he knew without a doubt that Wickenshire, Spelling and the butler had gone off on a fools' errand. Nothing untoward had happened at all. A little girl had simply stepped on a dog and knocked over an old trunk. But he was damned if he was going to let the cat out of the bag and pitch the child into deep briars. He would simply accompany her next time and see that she did not upset the entire household again.

Eight

Mr. Duncan, cleaned and scrubbed, dressed in a puce riding coat donated by Spelling, as well as a pair of Spelling's breeches, one of Spelling's best shirts, Spelling's stockings and a pristine neckcloth—also Mr. Spelling's—and with a piece of sticking plaster on his brow, proved to be a most impressive gentleman. His honey-blond hair curled alluringly about his ears and at the nape of his neck. A dimple flashed temptingly in his left cheek when he smiled and he had the most delightful way of tilting his head, just so, when he spoke. Alice, who stood at the entrance to the morning room, studied him thoroughly as he engaged in conversation with Sera and the dowager.

"No, please, do not disturb yourself, Mr. Duncan," she protested as he took note of her and made to stand at her entrance. "You are looking a good deal better this morning."

"Feeling better as well," offered Duncan. "You are Lady Alice, I think? The young lady to whom I owe my life?"

"I am Lady Alice," replied Alice, "but you hardly owe me your life, sir. I simply spied you stretched your length upon the ground. It is Mr. Spelling who rescued you and brought you here. He and Lord Wickenshire's groom."

"Ah, but if you had not spied me, I should have lain there the entire afternoon and night and like as not frozen to death."

"I highly doubt that," the dowager said, resting her knitting in her lap and studying the gentleman. "You would find it most difficult to freeze to death, Mr. Duncan, in such temperatures as we have had this winter."

"Is that so?" asked Duncan. "I find I do not remember much about the weather. Well, even so, Lady Alice, I am most grateful for your sharp eyes and tender heart."

"You are quite welcome," Alice replied. "I was pleased to be of service," she added as she settled upon the edge of a carved oak chair very near to where Sera sat comfortably upon the sopha.

"Mr. Duncan does not yet remember who he is, from where he comes or where he was bound," offered Sera, setting a final stitch into the monogram on one of the handkerchiefs she was making her husband for Christmas. "He proves to be a mystery even to himself, Alice."

"Which I do regret," sighed Duncan. "It is the most perplexing thing, really. Apparently, I was not bound for anywhere near this particular estate. Not one of the neighbors seems to be missing me." He grinned. Alice noted that his grin was just a bit lopsided, which somehow made it most endearing.

"Mr. Duncan," she said softly, "I doubt not that some young lady somewhere is even now m tears over your disappearance. She must be thoroughly discomposed by your unexplained absence and ready to go out searching for you herself. I certainly would be. Perhaps, if you think back, you will discover another name in your mind that seems familiar. A particular young lady's name."

"We have already suggested that," Sera said before Duncan could answer, "but Mr. Duncan claims there is not a one comes to mind, though I, too, cannot believe that there is not a young lady somewhere thoroughly distressed by his absence.

So, Alice thought, Sera finds him attractive as well. But how could she not? Only look at the man.

"You do not, perchance, find the name Sayers familiar to you?" asked the dowager softly.

"No, I cannot say that I do, my lady."

"I ask merely because your hair is quite like his and there is a vague resemblance about the lips. Well, but there is nothing in that, eh? Your nose is quite the picture of my nephew's, and yet I am positive there is no relationship there. Are you quite certain, Mr. Duncan, that you do not prefer to be in the billiards room with the other gentlemen?"

"Yes, madam," nodded Duncan. "Not feeling up to it. My wrist, I think, will not yet support a game of billiards. And besides, this is a most pleasant room and the company incomparable." His glance swept the room, coming to rest, in the most admiring fashion, on Alice. He did not remove his gaze from her until Jenkins arrived at the threshold.

"Mr. Sayers," announced Jenkins, ushering that gentleman into the morning room.

"Ladies," Sayers greeted with an all-encompassing bow. "I hope you will not think me forward for paying a morning call?"

"Not at all, Mr. Sayers," responded Sera. "Come in and be seated, do. We have been wondering how you go on at Dwyer Cottage. Oh, and may I introduce Mr. Duncan," she added, as that gentleman rose.

"Duncan," nodded Sayers, spreading the tails of his coat and lowering himself into a wingbacked chair. "You are a relative of Wickenshire's as well?"

"A guest, merely. A most unexpected guest."

"Jenkins, perhaps you should tell his lordship that Mr. Sayers has come to call," suggested Sera, amused by Jenkins' propensity to communicate his mind to her without so much as putting a crease in his face or a furrow in his brow.

"Indeed, my lady," Jenkins replied, turning about on his heel and setting off down the corridor. Will tell all the gentlemen, not just Lord Wickenshire, he thought. Especially

I will be certain Mr. Spelling understands me. Fine thing it is, Mr. Spelling for once attempting to behave like a decent gentleman and doing a fine job of it, too, all to impress Lady Alice, and she in there with two gentlemen making calf eyes at her while he is nowhere about. Let him know plainly that Mr. Sayers has arrived and that Mr. Duncan remains. Once Mr. Spelling divines that there are *two* very odd wolves sniffing around the duke's little lamb, he will be up the corridor in the twitch of a cat's whisker.

"Mr. Duncan has joined the ladies in the morning room, my lord," Jenkins announced as he paused upon the threshold to the billiards room. "And Mr. Sayers has arrived to pay a morning call as well."

"Just so, Jenkins. Thank you," Wickenshire responded, lining up his shot. "I have only to make this and Spelling his next and the game will be over. I expect we have lost already, but—"

"Losted to me!" interrupted Delight joyously as she peered up at Jenkins from the far end of the billiards table.

"Lost to *us,*" corrected Sotherland, laying a hand on one of Delight's shoulders. "You, m'gel, are a very apt apprentice, but not the only member of this team. It is better than ice-skating, billiards, is it not?"

"No," Delight replied thoughtfully, "but it is verimost more fun than ice-skating without ice like we did this morning 'cause that was terrible."

"Yes, I agree. We will never attempt skating on brown grass slick with frost again," agreed the duke. "Definitely not a good substitute for ice, that. Sayers, you said, Jenkins?"

"Yes, your grace," replied the butler, a most speaking gaze firmly fastened upon Mr. Spelling.

"Give it up, Nicky," Spelling urged, stepping toward the wall and racking his cue. "Our team surrenders outright."

"Are you certain, Neil?"

"Positive. Join the ladies for a bit. Likely Sera is wishing to have us there to help entertain." For a brief moment Spelling's gaze and Sotherland's met. Just so, you old demon, Spelling thought. Neither you nor I nor Jenkins is pleased to think of Alice in the presence of those gentlemen, regardless of who is present to chaperone her.

Mr. Spelling, however, was not destined to linger long in the morning room. Bundled in his greatcoat against a wind that grew more chill moment by moment, he soon discovered himself strolling beside Sayers toward the paddock while the others of the household remained in conversation before a pleasant fire. "I cannot think why you brought it up, Sayers, or why you wish to actually see it," Spelling muttered. "And right this moment, too. Ugly old thing."

"I did not bring it up. You did when you mentioned finding Duncan. It is ancient, Wickenshire says."

"I expect it is, but that does not make it any more pleasant to look upon. A well house is a well house. The new one is next to the stable. You would not rather—"

"No, no, I should like to see this ancient one. It is beyond the paddock?"

"In the lower pasture. A ten-minute stroll, no more."

"Good," nodded Sayers, rubbing his gloved hands together. "Very good. I ought not have pulled you away from Lady Alice's company, eh? Unfeeling of me. Delightful young woman."

"How do you know that?"

"What?"

"That Lady Alice is delightful. You have only met her once before and she said nothing worth saying."

"Well, but one knows these things, Spelling. A fellow simply knows. Any young woman whose father happens to be a duke must be delightful, must she not?"

"No."

"You do not find Lady Alice delightful?"

"That is not what I meant. I meant that just because her father is a duke, she is not necessarily delightful."

"Oh, yes, she is, at least to any man who aspires to power and fortune. A magnificent prize Lady Alice will be for the gentleman who can win her heart. That Duncan fellow, now. With such a face and form as he possesses, he is already three steps ahead of you in the race for Lady Alice's heart, old man."

"I was not aware that I was engaged in a race."

"Well, you are. I should wrap that muffler tighter around my neck if I were you, Spelling. You cannot afford to take a chill. Not with that Duncan fellow right in the house. Do you spend one day in a sickbed and he will steal the march on you. Or perhaps I will steal the march on you myself."

Spelling stuffed his hands into the pockets of his greatcoat, where they balled into fists of their own accord. "I cannot believe that you are here, Sayers. I cannot believe that you came all the way to Devon, rented Dwyer Cottage and had the audacity to come snooping around Willowsweep in the middle of the night. And now you think to set yourself up as my adversary in the battle for Lady Alice's heart? What the devil has got into you? And while I am thinking about it, why did the very sight of you discompose her so?"

"Perhaps because she formed a tendre for me when she was young? M'sister Cecilia did, ah, mention as much to me at one time. That her friend Alice had conceived a passion for me."

"Without so much as meeting you?"

"Young girls are like that," said Sayers, his cheeks whipped red by the wind. One hand clung to his beaver as he turned to see whether or not Spelling was likely to accept this explanation.

"But there is nothing between you?"

"I was merely jesting, Spelling, about winning Lady

Alice's heart. Though had I known that Miss Alice Daily was to become Lady Alice one day, I might have done things differently back then. I might have—well, never mind. How goes it, Spelling, your search? Have you found anything yet?"

"This," sighed Spelling, extricating the Spanish coin on the silver chain from his pocket.

"It was hers?" asked Sayers, halting in his tracks and taking the trinket into his hand.

"I expect so. She is wearing it in the portrait Wickenshire has of her."

"Hers," Sayers repeated worshipfully, staring at the coin.

"But not yours," Spelling said, snatching it back and striding forward again. "What the devil *are* you doing here?" he asked. "You nearly made a muck of everything, Sayers. I had to pretend to Wickenshire that I imagined you to be an exciseman to keep him from at all suspecting that we might know each other."

"An exciseman?" Sayers laughed and his eyes sparkled in the sunlight. "An exciseman, Spelling?"

"It was the best I could do. I had to pretend to be suspicious of you myself to make him less suspicious."

"He was not suspicious of me in the least."

"Not of you, no. But he would have been of me after he thought about it. If I had not had my wits about me and protested against you, he might have begun to suspect that we are known to each other. And then he would have begun to take more notice of where I went and what I did in the house."

"Perhaps so. Perhaps you are correct, Spelling. But the opportunity did present itself—the opportunity to rent Dwyer Cottage—and I could not but think what a delicious opportunity it was. A chance to explore on my own while you go about the search. Who knows what I might—see."

"Oh for gawd sakes, do you mean to tell me that you

were lingering around outside the house in the midst of that storm because you actually thought you might see—"

"Yes."

"You are mad, Sayers," Spelling sighed. "If you did not possess that ring and I have a tremendous need for it, I would have nothing at all to do with you."

"But I do possess the ring," smiled Sayers, looking Spelling triumphantly in the eye and not taking note at all of where his feet were going. "And you know what you must do to obtain it, yes? What the devil!" he cried out suddenly as he stumbled and fell to the ground and then bounced three steps farther down.

"Ought to watch where you walk," Spelling said very quietly. "You have just discovered the wretched well house. No telling what else you may stumble into, Sayers, if you do not pay attention to where you tread."

Lord Nightingale cocked his head to the left and then to the right. He raised his left foot, stretched his toes, replaced his foot and raised the other.

"So," Duncan observed, "this is the gentleman who woke me with such a start this morning."

"Indeed," Alice replied. "Lord Wickenshire has gone so far as to order Lord Nightingale's cage kept covered until a decent hour because there is nothing else can be done to keep him from greeting the morning so raucously."

"Nothing else but to delay the morning, eh? And he is just as noisy at night, you say?"

"Equally as nerve-racking."

"But he is not nerve-racking in between," offered Delight, standing between Duncan and Lady Alice, holding to Alice's hand. "He is a perfeck gentleman in between."

"So I see," Duncan replied. "He is your pet?"

"Uh-uh. He is not nobody's pet. He is Lord Nightingale."

"Just so," agreed Alice. "He is Lord Nightingale and

subject only to the King. Well, to the Prince Regent, I expect I must say, at this moment."

"Oh, an independent lord, is he? Well, I ought to have known from the manner in which he glares at me. Do not stare so, my lord. I shall keep to my place, I promise you that."

"How can you?" asked Delight, glancing upward in surprise.

"How can I what, m'dear?"

"Keep to your place when you cannot remember what place you come from?"

"Ah, yes. Now that is a bit of a problem, but I will remember sometime soon. I must."

Alice's heart went out to the gentleman the instant he said the words. The look of bewilderment on his face touched the softest and most sentimental part of her and she felt herself compelled to offer him some consolation. "Certainly you will remember, Mr. Duncan. And you will turn out to be someone of noble birth, I should think."

"Me? Of noble birth?" He smiled at that and his smile affected Alice even more than his look of bewilderment had. She thought at once how handsome he was and how courageous to face the unknown with a smile as he did. And though his hair reminded her of Mr. Sayers, still, it was clear to her that other than that, the two men were not alike at all.

"Wrenwrenwrenwren," muttered Nightingale, just as Alice had lost herself in Mr. Duncan's smile and forgotten all about the bird. "Wrenwren wrenwren."

"Oh, you ought not to ever even say that," Delight warned, stepping forward and inviting the macaw to come down from the top of his cage and step onto her shoulder. "I have told you over and over that you ought not. It is a terrible thing."

"It is? Wren?" asked Duncan, freeing Alice from his

gaze and focusing on the child. "And why is that, may I ask?"

"Because of the Wren Hunt," offered Lord Wickenshire from the doorway to the Gold Saloon. "Sera has sent me to fetch the lot of you."

"Lord Nightingale hunts wrens?"

"Not at all. You are not from the west country, I think, Mr. Duncan, or you would know about the Hunting of the Wren. It's somewhat of a tradition here. I should think not even as nasty a bump as you took would cause you to forget it."

"They kill a wren an' hang it by its feets from a pole," offered Delight in a most excited whisper. "An' the wren boys procession it off to its funeral and everyone follows them. An' if you give money for the funeral, the wren boys will give you one of the wren's feathers for good luck."

Alice stared at the child, horrified. "Who does this?" she asked, her hand going to her heart.

"The men and boys hereabout," Wickenshire replied, stepping into the room and crossing to Delight. "You, my girl, are not supposed to know about that. Your sister will comb my hair with a milking stool does she discover you have even heard of it. Who was it told you about *that* little Christmas tradition?"

"Jackie."

"Barbaric," breathed Alice, taking hold of Mr. Duncan's arm.

"Merely a custom," Wickenshire replied with the shrug of a gentleman accustomed to the violence of country life. "The Hunting of the Wren has taken place here on St. Stephen's Day for a century or more," he added, taking note of the manner in which Mr. Duncan's hand moved to cover Lady Alice's most gently.

"And who taught Lord Nightingale to call himself wren?" Alice asked. "Delight, dear, you did not?"

"Uh-uh. I think Cousin Neil taughted him."

"Oh!" exclaimed Lady Alice. "Oh!"

* * *

Spelling could not understand what it was that disturbed Alice throughout dinner that evening. He looked up from his soup and smiled at her. She glared back at him as if she would drown him in his soup bowl. He chewed and swallowed a portion of his salmon and bestowed upon her what he thought to be a most speaking glance. She raised her nose into the air as if she smelled the foulest odor. He accepted a bit of braised beef from James, cut a piece and, lifting it to his lips, gazed wistfully across at Alice. He found himself pierced clear to the soul by her icy glare. And to make matters worse, she was seated beside Duncan and turned to that gentleman quite often with a most companionable smile on her lips. All this set Spelling's stomach to lurching about with confusion and dread, and when the syllabub arrived at table, Mr. Spelling's inside was quaking just as much as the dessert's outside. By the time the ladies withdrew, a most enormous lump had risen in his throat and demanded to be drowned in port. And, by the time the gentlemen joined the ladies in the Gold Saloon, Spelling was listing decidedly to the right.

"I would have a private word with you, Lady Alice," he blurted out right in the midst of a lively game of crambo.

"That does not rhyme at all, Neil," the dowager Lady Wickenshire pointed out helpfully. "The verse is: From out the crimson sky did Cupid soar."

"And raised his bow and fired at the boor!" Spelling supplied in frustration. "I would have a private word with you," he added, bestowing the most pleading look on Alice, who sat upon the very edge of the sopha beside the dowager.

"Said stricken boor whose face had turned bright blue,"

offered Wickenshire from where he stood leaning against the back of Sera's chair. " 'Oh, no, sir, I dare not,' replied the girl."

"The crimson of the sky began to swirl," provided Duncan handily. "See clouds of gray arise; hear thunder roar."

"I shall say not one word to you, you boor," Lady Alice spat. "I find you, sir, a wretched, hateful thing."

"And then she doffed her cap and tossed it in the ring," finished the duke with a most interested tilt of an eyebrow. " 'Begone, you fool,' quoth she, 'or stand and fight.' "

"What have I done? I do not have the faintest idea what I have done," cried Spelling in frustration.

"My goodness, Neil, that not only does not rhyme, it is not even your turn," protested Sera quietly, studying first Alice and then Spelling.

"Damn the rhyme!" Spelling bellowed, rising from his chair and placing his hands on his hips. "Damn the game! Why will she not speak to me? What have I done?"

"You know perfectly well what you have done, Mr. Spelling," Lady Alice replied icily, tilting her chin upward.

"No, I don't. I have not the least idea."

"You are a brute, and a rudesby as well. Your speech betrays you as such."

"I did not mean to say damn. I apologize for that. But you glared and scowled at me all through dinner and you are doing the same right this moment. Why?"

"Because you are a beast," said Alice primly.

"Why am I a beast?" asked Spelling, totally ignoring the interested gazes of all present.

"Mr. Duncan, though he cannot so much as remember who he is, has more sensitivity in his fingernails than you do in your entire being," Alice replied testily. "*He* knows what you have done. *He* was as appalled as I. How dare you teach Lord Nightingale to name himself the wren in time for the hunt on St. Stephen's Day? Did you think it a jest, Mr. Spelling?" she asked, all thought of the onlookers disappearing from her mind as she rose and stood toe to toe with Spelling, planting her own hands on her own hips. "Let me tell you, sir, there is nothing at all humorous about it. To think of that lovely bird, dead and dangling from a pole, his feathers given away for coins."

"I—but I—" stuttered Spelling, staring directly down into the blue crystal of Alice's eyes.

"How unfeeling! How despicable!"

"B-but you do not understand."

"I *do* understand. You have always detested Lord Nightingale. The kindness you attempted to show him last evening was but a bit of drama for my sake alone. A lie, Mr. Spelling, to convince me that you are possessed of a good nature."

"I am possessed of a good nature. I am. I have not always made the best use of it, but—"

"Enough. I do not wish to hear another word."

"Wren!" Lord Nightingale cried raucously from atop his cage at the other end of the room. And then the brilliantly colored macaw took flight, circled the room once and came to land on Spelling's shoulder. "Wren," he said again, more quietly.

"You see, sir. You are condemned by your own word!" Alice exclaimed. "Straight from Lord Nightingale's mouth!"

"Not," muttered Nightingale then, stroking his beak along Spelling's shoulder and tugging at that gentleman's collar. "Not. Nightingale. Notnot. Nightingalenot. Nightingalenotwren."

"That is what I was attempting to teach him," sputtered Spelling, his mind fluctuating between frustration and relief. "That is precisely what I was attempting to teach him to say. I should like to know what is so very despicable and insensitive about attempting to get him to say that he is not a wren."

"Nightingalenot wren," mumbled the macaw, climbing slowly down toward Spelling's coat pocket by the simple means of grasping Spelling's coat sleeve in his beak, setting his nails into the weave, then grasping with his beak again. "Hungry," he mumbled. "Mornin' Nicky. Yohohoho. Murky Listerliss."

Nine

"I am amazed that the duke is not here," Sera observed, watching with sparkling eyes as Spelling and Lady Alice busily twisted greenery around the hoops to form the kissing bough the following morning. "I expected him to be sitting right between those two, keeping a keen eye on things."

"Tossing obstacles into Neil's way, you mean," Wickenshire said, peering over his shoulder to observe the two for himself. "We have Delight to thank for Sotherland's absence. She came down early to the breakfast room. I discovered her whispering most excitedly into Sotherland's ear. No sooner had he finished the food on his plate, than off they went together with Stanley Blithe and Sweetpea trailing along behind. Hand up the ribands, Sera. I am ready for them. Though why we are decorating the library shelves, I cannot think."

"Because I wish the entire house to look festive."

"Well, hand up the ribands then."

"Sera is determined to turn this house into a forest," Spelling said. "I have never heard of ivy and red ribands draped along library shelves before."

"His lordship is so very considerate of her," Alice responded quietly. "Whatever she wishes, he provides. I do believe he is the kindest, most generous person I have ever met."

"I expect he is," Spelling replied.

"Why do you say so in such a tone, Mr. Spelling?"

"Because I have never thought of it before."

"Never thought his lordship kind or generous?"

"Never considered those particular qualities of my cousin to be something admirable. But they are, are they not?"

"Exceptionally admirable. Why should you think them not?"

"B-because—because they always seemed to me to make him vulnerable to—people inclined to take advantage of him."

"Allow me to hold that in place while you tie it, Mr. Spelling. There. I expect it does make him quite vulnerable. Most good men are good precisely because they have the courage to *be* vulnerable. Only see how he allows Mr. Duncan to remain here when he knows nothing at all about the gentleman. And yet, what would poor Mr. Duncan do if he were sent out into the cold, not knowing who he is or from whence he came?"

"I do not trust Duncan."

"And yet, you have given him the loan of your clothes and of your valet as well, I think."

"He must wear something, and Carson has a deal of time to waste at the moment."

"Even so, you are being generous to a stranger, just as Lord Wickenshire is.

"Well, we cannot have Duncan strolling about naked."

"No," grinned Alice, beginning to twist another bit of ivy into the bough. "We certainly cannot have that. Mr. Spelling, I must—I am—I know I did apologize to you last evening, but—"

"All is forgotten," Spelling interrupted before she could go further. "I can understand, you know, how it must have disturbed you to hear Nightingale mutter 'wrenwrenwren' like that. I understood the moment you said as much. There is no need to apologize again."

"But I thought the very worst of you, Mr. Spelling, on the instant, without so much as waiting for an explanation."

"As to that, you ought not let that bother you. Everyone thinks the worst of me. And it is all my fault, too."

"Oh, Mr. Spelling!"

"Yes, it is. I have had a most villainous inclination my whole life long. Ask anyone. They will tell you how it is with me. I am always involved in some nefarious nonsense. I did never think anything of it, actually, until . . ."

"Until when, Mr. Spelling?"

"Until I stood with you in your grandmother's gazebo and Bradford came raging up to you and I heard how your grandmother had lied. And then, of course, at Wicken Hall, when you first met your father and learned how terribly her lies had harmed your family. I had grown most accustomed to lying, myself, by then," Spelling mumbled ashamedly, lowering his gaze to the slowly forming kissing bough. "I had never stopped to think before how my lies might harm someone else—how dreadfully they might harm someone else, I mean. I have always been accustomed to think only of myself. But I will not think only of myself again," he added, raising his gaze to see if Lady Alice was actually listening to him. "Never again."

Alice's gaze met his on the instant. Her hands stilled on the ivy and her heart leaped within her breast. Mr. Neil Spelling was not so gloriously handsome as Mr. Duncan. He would never be. His hair, the color of autumn leaves, his eyes as dark and clear as boiled coffee, the generally straight, narrow line of his lips, combined too often to give him a most brooding aspect that kept any description of him as gloriously handsome at bay. And yet—and yet—

"You have—you intend to imply, Mr. Spelling—that just as you have attempted to befriend Lord Nightingale, you have also begun to mend your ways because of me?"

"Just so. At least, I *wish* to mend my ways because of you, but I am not certain it is possible."

"All is possible, Mr. Spelling. All we need do is to try our very best and there is nothing cannot be accomplished."

"I beg to differ with you there," offered a voice from directly behind Lady Alice. "Any number of things cannot be accomplished no matter how hard one tries."

"Mr. Duncan, I did not hear you enter," Alice said, turning in her chair to look up at him.

"No. Spelling had bewitched you with his conversation. You were lost in the very depths of his eyes. I cannot imagine what he said to so enchant you, though I envy him the ability. I should like to enthrall you so myself. Instead, I seem to find myself the one bewitched by your lovely face."

"Oh, Mr. Duncan!"

"Rubbish," mumbled Spelling.

"Pardon, Mr. Spelling?" asked Alice, turning back to face him. "I did not quite hear."

The Duke of Sotherland stared open-mouthed at the passageway before him.

"You have got to light a lamp," urged Delight, tugging at the hem of his coat. "I am not allowed to light one and Becky and Jem an' Jackie willn't, because Mr. Jenkins told them not to and they are frighted to disobey, aren't you?"

"Uh-huh," said three little voices simultaneously.

Sotherland looked down at the four children gathered about him and then back at the passageway. "Are you certain this is the staircase we want?" he asked.

"Uh-huh," replied all four at once.

"Very well then. You there. Jem? Fetch that lamp for me."

"Right away, yer graceness," the potboy said, much impressed with the dour-looking duke.

"And you, child," Sotherland began.

"Becky," provided Delight, poking the little scullery maid in the ribs, thus eliciting a very unbalanced curtsy.

"Becky," amended Sotherland, "have you no shoes? Freeze your feet right off going up those granite stairs without shoes."

"M'sister has borrowed 'em, yer hightness," explained Becky. "She couldn't not go off wif Mr. Jenkins in 'er own shoes. They was torned up."

"I tried to give Becky mine," explained Delight, "but her feet is too little and there is not a pair will stay on."

"They goes flop-flop-flop an' then flies across the floor," giggled Becky.

"Does Lord Wickenshire know that you and your sister must share a pair of shoes between you?" Sotherland asked.

"It were his lor'ship what sent Mr. Jenkins an' Maryrose ta Swiftinwhold taday, yer honor," Jackie offered. "Maryrose an' Becky jus' comed 'ere four days ago an' Cook couldn't not turn 'em away even though we didn't need no more help. She thought as ta hide 'em. But Mr. Jenkins, he founded 'em. So now we gots extra help. An' 'is lor'ship said as Mr. Jenkins is ta git 'em some clothes this very day. Aye, he done said 'zactly that. Clothes an' shoes. They is orphuns, Becky an' Maryrose, an' don't got but one coat atween 'em neither."

"I see," murmured Sotherland. "And you are?"

"I be Jackie the fireboy, yer honor. I be the one what builds all the fires in all the whole house. At least, I will be when I be a bit older. Mr. Jenkins 'elps right now, but he don't let on about it to no one."

"The butler helps you to build fires?"

"Aye. 'e be a sport, Mr. Jenkins be."

"Mr. Jenkins says it is our verimost duty to help people whenever we discover them to be in need," Delight explained soberly as Jem came with the lamp and the duke proceeded to light it. "An' sometimes the need is building a few fires."

"Well, up the stairs we go then," the duke said gruffly, scooping Becky up in one arm. "There, now your feet will not freeze. Lead on, Delight. Can you see well enough? All of you?"

"Aye, yer graceness," answered Jem. "We kin see good."

It was the oddest thing to think of himself surrounded by urchins, climbing up a hidden staircase. It was not at all what Sotherland had expected when he had suggested that Delight take him with her the very next time she ascended to Glorianna's special room. Nor could he imagine what awaited them at the top of the stairs. "Bewildering house," he muttered under his breath.

"Bless ye," offered Becky at once.

"I did not sneeze, goose."

"Soun'ed like a sneeze."

"We're almost there," called Delight from ahead of them. And then she and Jem stepped out from the circle of the lamplight.

"Delight? Where the deuce are you?" Sotherland bellowed.

"Shhhhhh," Delight replied, stepping back into his sight. "We are right in here."

It was indeed a special room. Sotherland recognized that at once. Not a storage room, he thought, setting Becky down upon a piece of worn carpeting. "Is that the trunk?" he asked, placing the lamp on a dressing table made of fine cherrywood.

"Uh-huh," nodded Delight. "But someone has put it back up on its table again."

"Most likely Wickenshire. I dare to imagine, m'dear, that he has discovered your secret room."

"Oh. Well, just so he does not come in while we are practicin'," Delight said. "That would ruin ever thing. Can you lift down the trunk so we can see what is inside of it, duke?"

"Certainly." Sotherland crossed the room, lifted the heavy sea chest and set it on the floor. The lock had been broken and the top swung easily upward and back. Sotherland stared into the chest as tiny figures pressed around him. He pulled out an ancient dress, a uniform jacket of a kind he had never seen, a purple shawl and an interesting garment of lace and whalebone.

"We can use every one of those," cried Delight gaily. "Oh, Becky, I must only get my needles and threads and we will have the most beautiful people!"

"People?" asked the duke.

"Ain't actu'l people," offered Jackie, running a piece of black silk through his hand. "They be stockin's, actu'ly."

"They are almost people," declared Delight. "And now they will look proper, too."

"Well, but mebbe we ain't s'posed ta use none of these fine thin's," voiced Jem, who had stuck his hands deep into his pockets to keep from touching any of the fabrics. "They b'longs ta someun, Miss Delight. Don't ye thinks they b'long ta someun, yer graceness?"

Sotherland nodded and continued to empty the chest. "I expect they belong to someone who lived here very long ago, Jem, m'boy. Someone who will not care any longer what becomes of them." He took a leather pouch from near the bottom of the chest, untied it and poured the contents into the palm of his hand. "Here, what are these?"

"Jewels!" exclaimed Delight.

"Naw, them ain't jewels," protested Jackie. "I has done seed jewels, I has, an' them ain't none."

"Uh-huh," Becky declared, nodding a head covered in reddish curls. "Jewels."

"They sparkle like jewels," said Delight, considering the pretty stones that spilled out into the duke's hand.

"But they ain't 'tached ta nothin'," Jackie pointed out. "Jewels is always 'tached ta somethin' like a chain what ye kin hang aroun' yer neck, er a pin, er somethin' what makes em stick on ladies' ears."

"I seen a lady wif pins on 'er ears oncet," giggled Jem. "She were funny."

"Are they jewels, duke?" Delight asked, touching a finger to one of them.

"I cannot say, m'dear. They certainly look like jewels, but why they should be unmounted and lying up here in a sea chest—well, perhaps they are simply gemstones, kept in memory of someone. We must get a jeweler to look at them to be certain."

"Ain't no jew'ers in Swiftinwhold," Jackie declared with conviction. "Was one las' year, but he died."

"He did?" asked Delight. "Why?"

"Some fella run 'im through wif a sword. Squish! Right through the middle. Gruesome, it were."

"Yuck!" exclaimed Delight and Becky simultaneously.

"Exactly so," Sotherland agreed. "Yuck."

At the precise time that the duke was lending his aid to the children, Sayers was riding slowly across Willowsweep's lower pasture. When he came in sight of the double stone row, he dismounted, tethered his horse to a tree and walked to the large but incomplete circle at the northern end of it. Deep in thought, he made his way carefully along the path between the stones until he reached the far end. He stood for a long while gazing back the way he had come at the incomplete circle, then strolled rather dazedly a few hundred feet east of the row to the well house that lay half-buried in the ground, its broken steps leading beneath a worn portico down to a sweet-smelling pond, fed, he was certain, by an underground spring. There were letters carved into the granite of the portico. With Spelling beside him yesterday, he had ignored them. But now . . .

Sayers removed a glove and gently passed his bare fingers over what remained of the engraving. He closed his eyes and concentrated only on the touch of the cold stone against his ungloved hand. His breath came slowly, evenly, as he caressed the portico. Then he inhaled deeply and sighed. Surely, surely this was meant to be an E, this oddly shaped indentation that his fingers lingered over so lovingly. It must be. It had to be. It was. He was certain of it. Here, in this pasture, brown and frosted with cold, Sayers' soul fluttered inside of him like a wild songbird struggling to be free.

"And there is an old barn," he muttered to himself as, at last, he took his fingers from the granite and tugged his glove back on. "Spelling said he discovered the coin in an old barn. That will be the giant's hut the villagers at Idleoer tell tales of to frighten the children. I wonder can I find the place?"

It was midafternoon when the Wickenshires and their guests donned coats and hats, scarves and gloves, and climbed into the rear of the old farm wagon, which had been filled with straw, heated bricks and blankets to protect them from the chill. John Coachman smiled widely as he gave the two great plow horses the office to start, and off they rolled, gravel crunching beneath them, along the drive and through the gates, along the road for a mile or so, then north on a rutted trail toward the woods to pick themselves a Yule log. Wickenshire held a thoroughly happy Sera close in his arms; Delight giggled and wiggled excitedly against Spelling; Duncan sat beside Lady Alice at a quite proper distance, as Sotherland, who found himself in the far corner of the unorthodox vehicle with the dowager beside him, kept a close eye upon his daughter and that particular gentleman.

"Does the scoundrel move one half-inch closer," the duke muttered grumpily, "his head will roll."

"As if you did never wish to sit close beside a pretty young woman," replied the dowager. "Are you so old, Nathaniel, that you do not remember what it was like to be young?"

"Alice is not pretty. She is fair but plain. And he does not so much as know his own name," grumbled the duke. "Likely as much a nodcock as Spelling."

"Nathaniel!" exclaimed the dowager softly.

"And who gave you permission to address me by my Christian name, madam? I have not been so addressed since I was in skirts."

"Rubbish."

"It is not rubbish."

"Only you think it is not rubbish. Do you tell me your duchess did never utter your Christian name one time?"

"Well, but that—"

"Makes your previous assertion nothing but rubbish. And I will call you Nathaniel if I please. I am much too old and too impatient to be always concerned with the proprieties."

"No," replied Sotherland, feeling a quick stirring of something deep within himself. "Madam, you are neither too old nor too impatient. You are too independent." His eyes sparkled in the sunlight as he said it. His lips curved upward the slightest bit. And though he turned away from her, neither the sparkle nor the upward curve eluded the dowager countess' sharp gaze.

"Look how his grace smiles now," Alice observed, watching the changing expressions on her father's face. "I do believe that Lady Wickenshire is good for him."

"As you are good for me," replied Duncan softly. "You are the only medicine, I think, that will make me well again."

"Mr. Duncan!"

"What? Ought I not say it? But I have always been one to tell the truth, whatever it may be. And the truth of it is, Lady Alice, that when I am anywhere near you, my heart soars heavenward and I am not afraid."

"Not afraid?"

"Not afraid," repeated Duncan, unbending his knee and straightening his leg, which brought it down upon the straw very near Lady Alice's own. "You cannot know—I hope you never know—how frightening it is to awake one day and not remember the first thing about yourself. There is the greatest fear inside of me at every dim dream, every recollection, every lack of recollection. What if I am not a gentleman? What if I am some thief who has stolen a gentleman's clothes? Or what if I am a gentleman, but one sadly debauched and without the least saving grace? Why do I not remember who I am? Is it because, perhaps, I have done something so dastardly that I do not wish to remember who I am? Always, every waking moment, my mind finds something to fear. Unless—unless you are near to me."

Alice nibbled at her lower lip. She could not think what to say. To have a gentleman confess to her that she was the one person who drove such horrendous fears from him, that he depended upon her to ease his mind and provide him comfort, what could she say in reply to such as that?

"If only you will grant me a smile from time to time, or take my arm and allow me to escort you to somewhere you particularly wish to go. It is enough," sighed Duncan. "To be anywhere near to you is enough."

"It is merely because you are in such an awkward position, Mr. Duncan," Alice said at last. "Once you remember who you truly are, your fears will depart. You will discover that you love some lady and that she waits for you, and you will be off to gather her into your arms at once."

"I do love some lady," whispered Duncan. "I find I love a particular lady with all my heart." He looked at her, his eyes clearly brimming with emotion, his lips quivering the slightest bit. His face shone like an angel's as the wagon passed through the winter sunlight, and Alice thought him the most handsome, the most romantic gentleman she had ever met; but she could not for pennies nor pounds understand why he should speak so to her.

"Nodcock," muttered Spelling under his breath as he glared at Duncan. "Piece of tripe."

"Who is a piece of tripes?" Delight asked, balancing on her feet in the moving wagon by clinging to Spelling's shoulders.

"Duncan."

"Our Mr. Duncan?"

"He is not our Mr. Duncan. Must you make everyone part of the family, infant?"

"I taked you into the family, an' our duke, an' Lord Bradford, an' Lord Peter."

"You did not take me. I was a member of this family before you were even born. And as for the rest, well, I expect you did not do too badly with the rest, but this Duncan fellow—"

"Is pertendin' to be in love with Lady Alice."

"What makes you think he is pretending?"

"I jus' know," replied Delight confidently. "I am the verimost best pertender in all the whole world next to Nicky an' I know when someone is pertendin'. Just like our duke."

"What do you mean, just like our duke?"

"Well," Delight explained, her arms clinging tightly to Spelling's neck as she swung around him to land with a plop in his lap. "Our duke is a'ways pertendin' to be crochedy, but unnerneath he is not."

"He is not?"

"Uh-uh. Cannot you tell?"

"No. He seems peevish enough to me. Are you certain that Duncan is merely pretending to be enamored of Lady Alice, Delight?"

"Yes," replied the child. "I am positive."

Ten

It was in the midst of dragging the cheerfully bedecked Yule log home that the party came upon Sayers, who saluted the log quite as he was expected to do. He then rode up to the wagon and bid the entire lot of them a good afternoon, though his eyes lingered upon Lady Alice.

"Sayers," said Wickenshire, "lost again, are you?"

"Lost? Oh, no, not at all. Simply out for a ride. I seem to have come a bit far and ended up on your land again, eh? I hope you don't mind."

"Mind? No, not at all. Come home with us and help us to welcome the Yule log into the house. Stay for dinner," Wickenshire added at a whispered word from his lady. "Just family. Most informal. Be pleased to have you."

"I should be honored," Sayers replied.

"Good. Glass of hot punch awaits us the moment we squeak that log in through the parlor door. Cold day for a ride."

Without the least hesitation, Sayers turned his horse's head in the direction of Willowsweep and kept pace beside the wagon. Spelling's gaze fastened upon him with great misgivings. What the deuce did the man think he was doing hovering about Willowsweep like some haunting spirit?

"If I may be so bold as to say it, Lady Alice," Sayers ventured, "you are looking just the thing with your cheeks all pink from the cold. Like roses on snow, they are."

"Th-thank you, Mr. Sayers," Alice replied. "I— It is a pleasant surprise to see you again."

"Indeed," Duncan agreed, moving surreptitiously closer to Lady Alice so that he might touch her gloved hand with his own.

Spelling said nothing. He merely glared at Duncan and Sayers from over Delight's head and tightened his arms around the child.

"Good gawd, now there are three of them," murmured Sotherland from the far corner of the wagon. "Not bad enough that Duncan and Spelling must always be staring at the gel, now this nodcock must come trailing after her spouting utter nonsense."

"Shhhh, Alice will hear you," cautioned the dowager. "And it is not nonsense."

"It is. Pink cheeks like roses on snow. Utter nonsense!"

"Nathaniel, if you do not hush, I will discover a cramp in my leg and kick you quite soundly. She is a young woman. Allow her to enjoy being so. I should have enjoyed to have had three gentlemen dangling after me, let me tell you."

"Bah! You had three dozen and more or I miss my guess."

"You miss your guess," frowned the dowager. "Now hush."

"Are you not goin' to say nothing?" asked Delight, bending backward to stare up at Spelling.

"Say what?"

"Something pretty about Lady Alice."

"No."

"Why not?"

"Because I am not. Not here. Not now. Change the subject, minx, or I shall dump you into this straw."

Delight giggled.

"Think I am jesting, eh? Well, just try and see."

"No! No! Please do not!" cried Delight in melodramatic glee.

"Delight, what on earth?" asked Lady Alice, her eyes widening with concern for the child.

"Cousin Neil will not say nothing pretty about you like Mr. Sayers," giggled Delight. "He is 'barrassed to do it, an' he has threatened to dump me into the straw for bringing it up, too."

"Devil! Now you are going to get it," declared Spelling, leaning back and tipping them both.

"Mr. Spelling!" Lady Alice exclaimed. "Delight! Mr. Duncan, do something. They—"

"They have both gone mad, my lady," Duncan observed as Spelling and Delight rolled about, laughing heartily. "I dare say Spelling has taken a nip or two from that silver flask he carries in his greatcoat pocket."

"Mr. Spelling? Carries a flask?" asked Alice.

In a gown of blue velveteen with gold trim at collar and cuffs, Alice allowed herself to be escorted into dinner that evening by Mr. Sayers. Though she had hesitated to take his arm when he had offered it, not to do so would have caused any number of eyebrows to rise, and so she had done the thing. As he helped her to sit and then took the seat to her right, she blushed and wished herself across the way beside Mr. Spelling.

Through the entire first course, she spoke pleasantly to Mr. Duncan on her left, but when the second course appeared and she found herself compelled by propriety to engage Mr. Sayers in conversation, she could not bring herself to do it. She turned to him quite properly, smiled, and turned away at once.

"You truly ought to speak to me," Sayers whispered. "The entire party will take note if you do not, my dear."

"Do not call me your dear," hissed Alice, spearing a piece of roasted hare with her fork.

"I see. Now that you have become a titled lady, you can find no use for me, eh?"

"You know very well, Mr. Sayers, that it was you who could find no use for me."

"Oh?" Sayers reached for his wine glass. "I am sorry you took my actions to mean that. I was stupid, of course, to think you would take them any other way, but— Are you going to eat the hare, Alice, or glare at it for the remainder of the meal?"

Alice snapped the bit of meat from her fork, chewed it angrily and swallowed. "Do not call me Alice. Someone will hear."

"And if they do?"

"It is much too familiar."

"No. Is it? After all we have shared together?"

"We have shared nothing," protested Alice, feeling herself grow excessively warm as she attempted to sip her wine without spilling it. How my hand shakes, she thought. Anyone would think I have the palsy. And why? Simply because of this wretch!

"I thought we had shared a great deal," responded Sayers. "Certainly we shared dreams, Alice. I went so far as to confide in you my passion for the witches. There was nothing I feared to tell you in my letters, just as you never feared to tell me all you wished for in life."

Alice stared at him, her eyes wide.

"I have kept every letter you ever wrote to me, my dear," Sayers said. "Did you not know that I would? I could not destroy them, Alice. Never. They are quite the most wonderful letters I have ever received."

Alice thought she would die on the spot. Her wine glass tipped in her hand as she set it aside and tiny red drops like blood splattered down the side of it and onto the tablecloth.

Spelling, who had the pleasure of dining with Delight to his right and the dowager countess to his left, sat with his attention focused on Lady Alice and Sayers. What the devil does he say to her? he wondered as droplets of wine splattered from Alice's glass. "What?" he asked, feeling a tug on his coat.

"It is me tuggin'," Delight informed him.

"Somehow I did not think it was my Aunt Diana. It is not acceptable to be tugging at gentlemen's coats when you are eating dinner beside them, infant. You are far too young to be out of the nursery."

"I am not. I am very growed up. An' I have been invited to eat dinner with everyone else this evening. *Sera* invited me."

"She is your sister. She ought to know better. Now what does he say to her? Her hands are fluttering about like flutterbys."

"That is just what I want to talk to you about," declared Delight in a determined whisper.

"Flutterbys?"

"No, Lady Alice an' Mr. Sayers. He is botherin' her."

"Yes, so I see."

"An' she is goin' to cry."

"No, I do not think she is going to cry."

"Uh-huh. Thank goodness it is time for the minced pies."

Spelling's gaze left Alice and Sayers on the instant. "What have minced pies to do with anything?" he asked, astounded. "You are the oddest child."

"No, I am not, an' minced pies means that dinner is almost over an' now is the perfeck time."

"The perfect time for what?"

Delight got to her knees on the chair and whispered into Spelling's ear, drawing everyone's attention down on them. Spelling and Delight, however, took no note of it; and as she ceased to whisper in his ear, he pushed back his chair, set his napkin upon the table and rose to his feet. "I do beg your pardon," he addressed the rest of the party, "but Delight and I have just now thought of something that must be attended to. You will excuse us." And with that, he helped Delight from her chair and the two of them hurried from the room.

"I wonder what that can be about," said Duncan quietly, claiming Alice's attention. "My lady, are you not feeling just the thing?" he added solicitously. "You are pale as bleached muslin. Do you feel faint?"

"I am fine, Mr. Duncan. I am a bit warm. Nothing more."

"Are you certain, my lady? Perhaps you would care to leave the table and take a brief stroll through the garden. I should be pleased to accompany you."

"Truly, it is not necessary, Mr. Duncan. I shall be fine in a moment. I ought not to have worn this particular gown. It does make one feel rather breathless."

"It made me feel breathless," whispered Duncan softly, "the very moment I saw you in it."

The Duke of Sotherland took note, at once, of the perfectly astounded look that crossed his daughter's face as Duncan spoke to her, just as he had noted her uneasiness with Sayers. "Ought to have seated m'gel beside that dunderhead of yours," he muttered at the dowager. "She will starve between those two featherbrains. They stir her up to such a point that she has barely eaten a bite."

"I thought you did not wish her to become attached to Neil," the dowager responded.

"That has never stopped you from getting them together before, madam."

"There is something very odd occurring between Mr. Sayers and Alice, Nathaniel. Did you see how upset she became at his conversation?"

"I did. And I will look into it once you ladies withdraw. Have Sayers' guts for garters does he think to ever upset her so again, and I will tell him precisely that, too. Danged stallions, sniffing about the gel as if she were some prize filly."

The dowager Lady Wickenshire's lips curved most temptingly upward. "She is a prize, your grace. Surely you realize that. And a beauty as well."

"She is not a beauty, my Alice. Too much of me in her features. Nothing of her mother's delicacy about her."

"But she is sweet and gentle and intelligent, and her eyes sparkle in the most splendid way when she is happy. Any number of gentlemen will be drawn to her when she makes her curtsy."

"Bah! She is my daughter, you mean, and any number of gentlemen will see the sparkle of jewels and the gleam of gold in those eyes."

"Some will," the dowager nodded. "Some will. But that is not at all what my nephew sees. Neil sees something else entirely."

"And those two?"

"I do not know."

"Awwrrrk!" interrupted Lord Nightingale as he entered through the doorway on Spelling's arm. "Yo ho ho, Sarry Knistmass! Waswrening. Mornin' Nicky."

"Now what the deuce is this?" the duke asked, as he looked up. Then Delight attempted to wink at him and his eyes began to twinkle with great good humor.

At the servants' entrance to the dining room, Jenkins raised a hand and halted the delivery of the minced pies to the table. James, Hobbs and Mackelry, grinning, shuffled about so that they all might get a glimpse of the marvelous sight that set the generally placid Jenkins to chuckling.

"I tole you," Delight whispered up at Spelling. "Lady Alice willn't cry now. She is overcomed by how splendid Lord Nightingale looks."

Alice surreptitiously dashed away the sting of tears from her eyes with the back of her hand and then abandoned all thought of Mr. Sayers and Mr. Duncan both and replaced those thoughts with puzzled contemplation of Mr. Spelling. Whatever is he doing? she wondered as Spelling smiled at her and then winked. Oh! Oh my! Only look at Lord Nightingale. Her eyes began to bubble with laughter; her hands came up from her lap to clap softly as Jenkins hurried to procure another chair and set it between those of Spelling and Delight. Quickly the butler moved plate and silver aside and set an extra cover. "We were not expecting you, sir," he said, as soberly as he could, bowing before the macaw and then strolling back to his place behind Lord Wickenshire.

With a tiny wreath of ivy and mistletoe upon the crown of his head, held tight by embroidery thread tied beneath his chin, with gleefully fluttering wings beneath a mantle of puce velvet hemmed in fur, the macaw shuffled down Spelling's outstretched arm onto the back of the chair.

"Ho, ho," whispered Delight at Lord Nightingale.

"Yohoho," squawked Lord Nightingale in return.

"Ho, ho, I be," whispered Spelling, going to one knee beside the chair on which Nightingale sat. "You can do it, old fellow. You did it on the way here. Ho, ho, I be Old. . . ."

"Yohohoho Ibe OlFather—Chrismiss Ibe comedtashare—tashareyer—piepiepie PIE with ye."

"To share yer pie with ye?" chuckled Wickenshire from the head of the table.

At the foot of the table, Sera was laughing so hard that tears blurred her vision. There was not, in fact, one person gathered around that table who was not chuckling, smiling or laughing softly as Lord Nightingale strutted proudly in his finery, back and forth along the chairback. "Pie!" he squawked, fully aware of the pleasant sensation he caused. "ShareyerpiePie PIE Ol'Father Chrismiss!"

This being, in Jenkins' opinion, a perfect moment, he signaled the footmen, and James, Hobbs, and Mackelry marched into the room and around the table, each carrying a minced pie and each attempting not to join in the laughter.

It was Jenkins himself who cut the pies and placed a slice before each of the diners. The one he set before Lord Nightingale had pine nuts and cherries decorating the top of it.

Very late that same night, Alice discovered that she could not possibly sleep. All evening long Mr. Spelling and Mr. Duncan had been most attentive to her. What one did not propose, the other did. They had played at jots and jumbles, attempted to cut each other's silhouettes out of paper, strung bright wooden beads and decorated Lord Nightingale's cage with them. Mr. Spelling had found the largest bead, set it upon the carpet in the Gold Saloon and set the feathery Father Christmas in all his finery to rolling it about. Everyone had placed wagers on how far Nightingale would roll it and in which direction. And all the while, no matter what she happened to be doing, Mr. Sayers had watched her with near-unblinking eyes.

I must have been mad, she thought as she paced the floor of her little sitting room. How could I ever have trusted such a man as Mr. Sayers? I have only now begun to rejoice in having a father and he would take all that joy from me for his own benefit. "Because it is money he desires," she whispered to the walls of the chamber. "It is money he desires and he will threaten his grace with a public betrayal of my foolishness in order to get it. I am certain he will."

She would have cried from the pain of the memory of Sayers' first betrayal of her if she had not been so very angry about this present betrayal. But she was angry and tears were far from her. "What can I do?" she asked the flames upon the hearth as she settled into the wide leather chair before it and curled her legs up under her. I could simply shoot Mr. Sayers, she thought. "No, I cannot," she said then. "That would be most improper, particularly at Christmastime."

But I must do something, she mused, nibbling distractedly at a fingernail. I cannot allow him to blackmail me. Besides, I have no money to speak of. Perhaps he intends to force me into marriage with him. As the son-in-law of the Duke of Sotherland, he would have money and power both. "Wh-what?" she sputtered, as something slithered against the wall behind her. She turned, knelt upon the chair seat and peered over the back. Her mouth opened into a wide *O* as something moved in the shadows. The wall was opening! The panels of oak were somehow swinging away and a cold, damp chill came gushing through the room toward her.

"Where the devil am I?" hissed a frustrated male voice. "Of all times for the damnable lamp to run out. Obmigawd!" exclaimed Spelling hoarsely, catching sight of Lady Alice staring at him in wonderment from over the chair back as the door swung closed behind him.

"Mr. Spelling?"

"I shall go right back and you must pretend you never saw me," sputtered Spelling. "I h-had no idea that— I did not realize how long I—and the lamp— It was so dark I could not see my fingers before my face. I could not tell where I was."

"You are in my bed-sittingroom, Mr. Spelling."

"Y-yes, I see. I am leaving."

Alice abandoned the safety of the chair and crossed the carpeting to where he stood. "Is it a secret passage?" she asked, studying the paneling.

"Old servants' stairs," managed Spelling, his heart thumping with misgivings and his eyes fastened on her every movement as she touched the wall—first high, then low, then here, then there—searching for the doorway through which he had come. "You are not screaming," he said blankly.

"Screaming?" Alice turned to look at him. "Oh, because you are in my chamber? But you have no evil intent. Do you?"

"No! Never!"

"Just so. Where is the door? I cannot see it now."

"Here," Spelling replied, shoving at the section of paneling through which he had arrived. "You cannot see it even in daylight. You cannot actually see any of them."

"Any of them?"

"All over the house," murmured Spelling, as she stared up at him, her long black hair loose and curling to her waist, her flannel gown clinging to her every curve, and her eyes—those incredible blue eyes—lit with something . . . with some emotion. . . . "What is it?" Spelling asked without so much as realizing that his lips had parted and his tongue had moved. "What is it I see in those beautiful eyes?"

"Mr. Spelling!"

"What? Damnation, I did not actually say— I did!"

"You most certainly did. This is neither the place nor the time, sir, to be speaking of my eyes."

"No. I ought to go at once. Ah, might I borrow your lamp? I cannot see my fingers before my face in there without one."

"You may. What are you doing in there? Or ought I not ask?"

"I am— I have— I promised Sayers that I would, and—"

"Mr. Sayers? What can you possibly have promised Mr. Sayers? You are not one with him in his despicable escapade?"

Spelling, who had taken the small oil lamp from the top of the covered bookcase and set his own in its place, turned and faced her, a frown creasing his brow. "Wh-what escapade?"

"You know very well what escapade if you are involved in it, and if you are not, it is none of your business."

"Oh. You are going to do that again."

"What?"

"Accuse me of something without giving me the least

opportunity to explain, *and* advise me that I have no business questioning you about Sayers."

Alice glared at him and then a tear rose to the corner of her eye and made its way quietly down her cheek. Another followed. And a third. In a moment more, Lady Alice was sobbing, though she had not the least wish to do anything of the sort.

Spelling set the lamp aside and gathered her into his arms. "No, do not cry," he whispered, his hand smoothing her hair as her tears dampened his cravat. "I ought not have reminded you of either thing," he whispered, his lips barely touching the sensitive skin near her temple. "It was cruel of me. You have every right to assume evil intent of me without the least evidence, and your association with Sayers is not a bit of my business. It certainly is not. Please do not cry, Alice. I have not the first idea what to do when a woman cries."

"I c-cannot h-help it," sobbed Alice. "It is all so im-impossible. Mr. Sayers is the d-devil himself."

Eleven

"Women cry over the oddest things," Spelling observed softly. He was sitting in the enormous leather chair that Lady Alice had previously abandoned and he held Alice on his lap, neatly tucked within his arms, her head resting against his shoulder. "Letters. What are a few letters? I thought you had done something seriously wrong when you began to speak of blackmail."

"You do not understand," Alice protested. "A young woman does not write to a gentleman—not without p-permission."

"Even so, a few letters—"

"Love letters," interrupted Alice. "They were not at first, but then— I thought I had come to love Mr. Sayers. From the things he wrote to me, I imagined him a kindred soul."

Spelling smiled a bit despite the wobbly feeling her words produced in his stomach. "You decided that you loved him because of the letters he wrote? You never met him? Not once?"

"Not once, but I believed that I knew him, you see."

"And what if he had turned out to be a one-eyed gnome?"

"I do not particularly care what a person looks like. It is what goes on inside of a person that matters. It is heart and soul that make a person what they are, not beautiful eyes or curly hair or a charming smile. I am not a belle and yet, I fancy that someone will come to truly love me. S-someone. S-someday."

"Someone already has come to love you," murmured Spelling, so softly that the lady upon his lap did not catch his words.

"What?"

"Nothing, m'dear. So, it is the fact that these letters are love letters, eh? But the duke will not care about something as simple as that. He is a fierce old gentleman. Not easily scandalized, you know."

"But in one of them I agreed to run away with Mr. Sayers. Oh, I am so ashamed! I actually planned to run off with him from school and be married over the anvil. I would have done it, too."

"Yet you did not."

"N-no, but only because he did not come. He said he would come for me in a closed carriage. I was to meet him at the gate to the school and he would sweep me off with him to Scotland, but he did not come. I stood there before the sun had even risen. I was so cold—so very cold—waiting and waiting—but he never came. In the end, I was forced to sneak back into school."

Spelling shivered at her words. "Poor child," he whispered, his arms tightening around her. "Poor little girl. To place your life in someone's hands and to be so betrayed. I will black both Sayers' eyes for that. See if I do not."

"Oh!" Alice abruptly sat straight up and stared at him. "Mr. Spelling! What are we—what am I doing? I am sitting on your lap! Oh!" She scrambled out of his arms and off of his lap at once and stood with her hands pasted flat against her cheeks, her lips parted in surprise. "I did never mean to— I am a regular lightskirt! Mr. Spelling, I have compromised you!"

Spelling had never seen a more ravishing sight in his entire life than Lady Alice standing before the hearth in her nightclothes, her hands to her cheeks, her cheeks flushed with embarrassment, her mouth open in a perfect *O.* He stood and took a step toward her, but when she took a step back, he ceased his advance at once. "Only give me your hands to hold," he said then, offering his own. "What do you know of lightskirts? A proper young lady like you. You were upset and required someone in whom to confide and that is all. If I am compromised, then it is my fault for tumbling so unexpectedly through your wall."

"That was an accident."

"Yes, it was. And no improper thought brought you to sit on my lap, either. But if you wish me to be compromised, I will certainly be. I will go to his grace first thing in the morning, explain what has happened and request your hand in marriage."

"No, you ought not, Mr. Spelling."

"No, I do not think so, either." Spelling smiled, giving her hands a squeeze. "All you did, m'dear, was speak and all I did was listen. And I will tell you this, my dear. Even though Sayers threatens to show those letters around, it will not happen. He will not do it."

"He will not?"

"No, m'gel, he will not. I shall see that he does not. He will return the letters to you and you may burn every one of them. You do not—you do not still love him, do you? What I mean to say is, if you find that you do—"

"Love him? After he wrote to me in such a fine manner and then abandoned me? I am not such a gudgeon as to believe anything Mr. Sayers says ever again, much less love him."

Hope rose inside of Spelling like a flutterby winging its way to the next highest flower.

"Did you note how much attention Alice gathered tonight, Nicholas?" Sera asked as she leaned back against the pillows and took Wickenshire's hand into her own. "Mr.

Sayers did not take his gaze from her the entire evening. And Mr. Duncan— I have never heard such flowery compliments flow so easily from a gentleman's tongue. Poor Neil has considerable competition, I fear."

"You are enjoying every moment of this, are you not? You and Bedazzler?"

"Yes," Sera admitted, smiling as she played with Wickenshire's fingers, stroking them one by one. "I find myself liking Neil a good deal more than I ever have and Bedazzler certainly wishes him success. I can tell."

"Can you? And what does Bedazzler think of our Mr. Duncan?"

"Do you know, Nicholas, we are neither of us quite certain of Mr. Duncan. He is most handsome and polite and charming, but neither Bedazzler nor I quite trust the fellow."

"I rode to Hadley's this morning. Hadley is of the opinion that we have taken in a rogue. No one about will lay claim to the fellow. Ought I to send him riding off to Swiftinwhold and the Northstar Inn? He has a considerable sum of money with him. We discovered as much when we put him to bed that day."

"Send a gentleman who does not so much as know his own name off to Swiftinwhold and the Northstar Inn? At Christmas? Oh, Nicholas, I do not think we ought."

"No, I expect not," sighed Wickenshire, tucking his arm neatly around Sera's shoulders and bestowing a kiss upon her ear. "If we are to be murdered in our beds, it is most likely Neil who will do the thing, not Mr. Duncan."

"Nicholas!" Sera cried, disengaging herself from him and grabbing for one of the pillows. "What a thing to say! Neil is family!" And she whopped him teasingly over the head.

"Think you are safe because of your condition, do you?" laughed Wickenshire, pulling the pillow from her and tossing it to the floor. "You and Bedazzler think you are beyond reprisal? Well, my lady, you and the scamp are very wrong!"

"Nicholas, do not," giggled Sera. "Oh, you beast! Do not!"

With the lamp shaking the merest bit in his hand and Lady Alice, who had changed hurriedly into an old round gown and a shawl, clinging tightly to his arm, Spelling returned to the passages. "You ought not have come," he whispered.

"I wish to help," she replied. "It is important to you to discover these journals. You said so yourself."

"Yes, but it is not just the thing for you to be jauntering about inside of Nicky's walls with me."

"I do not care. You are going to force Mr. Sayers to give my letters back. It is little enough for me to help you in return. Lord Wickenshire has said you may have these journals if you can find them, has he not?"

"Nicky has no need of them. Never thought to go searching after them himself."

"And you will give them to Mr. Sayers?"

"Yes. And in return, Sayers will give me my Aunt Diana's wedding ring and your letters. The letters were not part of our original bargain, but he will give them to me because he is determined to have the journals at any price."

Alice ceased walking and turned to him in the shadows. "Your Aunt Diana's wedding ring? How in the name of goodness does Mr. Sayers come to have—no, do not tell me. I do not wish to know."

"Believe me, you do not," agreed Spelling. "It is a very long story and not worth the effort of repeating. That will be the room Nicky, Jenkins and I found the other night," he added, lifting the lamp. "There is an old sea chest in there which might just prove to be the hiding place. I hope it does. I have looked everywhere else."

Spelling led Alice into the room, placed the lamp carefully on the dressing table, located the sea chest and opened it.

"What an amazing thing!" Alice exclaimed softly.

"What? What is amazing?"

"This room. That such a cozy little room should be hidden away between the walls of a house."

"Oh. There may be something beneath all these old clothes. Let me just see if—what is this?" Spelling asked, tugging out a small leather pouch. He untied it and emptied the contents into his hand. "Stones."

"Stones?"

"Look here." Spelling carried them to the dressing table and held them beneath the lamp light. "Pretty things."

"Perhaps they are unset jewels," offered Alice.

"I doubt it. M'uncle would have sold them long ago. Gambling man, m'Uncle Evelyn. Turned every jewel in his household to paste. Left m'Aunt Diana and Nicky with nothing. M'Aunt Diana's jewels are scattered all over London. Have been for years."

"He sold her wedding ring as well?" Alice looked up into Spelling's deep brown eyes. They are like melted chocolate just now, she thought. I have never before been able to sink so deeply, so pleasantly, so cozily into a gentleman's eyes.

"Yes," sighed Spelling, pouring the stones back into the pouch. "Turned Aunt Diana's wedding ring to paste as well."

"And Mr. Sayers has come into possession of the real one?"

"Um-hmmm. Quite beautiful. A ruby, surrounded by diamonds. I offered to purchase it from him, but he knew I had family at Willowsweep and so refused to take anything but the journals for it. Heirloom, that ring, though it did not manage to remain in the family long once Uncle Evelyn got his hands on it."

"Surely your Aunt Diana protested—"

"No," interrupted Spelling, stuffing the pouch back into the sea chest. "I do not believe she protested anything Uncle Evelyn did. He might do as he liked as long as he took time now and then to speak kindly to Nicky. Did not like being a father, Uncle Evelyn. Jenkins was more a father to Nicky than his own papa."

"What will you do with the ring when you get it?"

"Do with it?" Spelling looked up to discover Alice staring at him with the most serious expression upon her face and her hands clasped uneasily before her. "Well, I—" He did not finish the sentence. He stared at the proud little face in the lamplight and what he imagined he saw there came very near to making him cry out in protest. But he did not.

She is correct to question my motives, he thought with shame. She has been building a home for herself in my heart every moment of every day. And from the moment I first became aware of how deeply she has burrowed, I have promised myself to change my ways. Yet, here I have come into Nicky's house to steal his Aunt Elaina's journals so that I can obtain his mama's wedding ring and bestow it on Miss Helena Ducane as payment for not telling her brother, Richard, a lie that would make it impossible for him not to call me out and shoot me dead.

"What will you do with the ring?" Alice asked again, the merest shiver in her voice. "You do not say."

"I will return it to Aunt Diana," Spelling answered.

A smile rose from Alice's lips all the way to her eyes, and such warmth radiated from those eyes to Spelling that he would have sworn summer had come to Willowsweep.

What does it matter, he thought, if Richard Ducane shoots me dead one fine morning soon? I shall have this Christmas, this woman, this smile to light my way into the nether world, and I shall meet my Maker with at least one good mark to my name.

* * *

Duncan sat before the fire in his sitting room and stared into the flames, pondering, a glass of brandy in one hand and an unopened volume in the other. His thoughts lolled about his brain like honeybees dosed with laudanum—languid, lazy, without direction. At one point, his lips turned upward into a pleasant smile and then his eyelids fluttered closed. They opened again just before the glass of brandy began to tip from his hand. He set the glass safely aside and did likewise with the volume.

I have never felt so very comfortable anywhere, he thought to himself, or so welcome. Never in my own home or anywhere else. The cold outside, myself warm as toast and actually welcome inside. No bellowing, no gossiping, no one vying for attention, everyone merry most of the time. A fellow could grow accustomed to such a place as this. Even the old duke is not as bad as I imagined. Made me smile four or five times this evening whether he intended it or not. And the child—to come begging for my stocking so prettily and to bring that marvelous bird to table. Not at all like my own nieces, who do nothing but glare at me and then walk off with their noses in the air as though I had an odor about me.

Duncan gazed for a long moment into the flames of the fire on his hearth. A smile encompassed him all the way from the bottom of his feet to the top of his head. "I think I would sell my soul to keep my life as pleasant as it is this moment," he whispered. "I have never before thought such simple pleasures worth much, but I think I would sell my soul to live pleasantly in such a place as this, with people such as these."

Now what the devil can that be? he wondered, starting at a scrabbling sound behind the paneling. Rats in the wall? Mice scampering about behind the paneling? Well, a place as ancient as this is bound to have rodents wandering about somewhere.

"Bound to," he whispered with a chuckle. "Rats in the wall, a parrot in the Gold Saloon, a dog and a cat meandering about anywhere they please, and a child with an unfortunate blemish but the most appealing innocence. And I am drawn to all this like a fox to his den." He levered himself up from his armchair, went to the armoire and collected his own coat—the one he had worn when first he had set out for Willowsweep, the one that Carson had attempted to resurrect, but which, for all practical purposes could never be worn in company again—and he quietly departed his chamber.

In the Gold Saloon, Lord Nightingale pecked and tugged beneath Aunt Winifred's shawl. He had not been housed in this cage for so very long without learning how to open the cage door. He was well on his way to doing it, too, urged gently on by a "mmmphing" Stanley Blithe at the bottom of the stand and a "rrrrwing" Sweetpea who from time to time leaped up to bat at the shawl's fringe as it wiggled about. With one last, mighty peck, the door swung open and Lord Nightingale edged his way downward, grasping tightly to the bars of the cage, until his bright red head poked out from beneath the shawl, one vagrant knotted fringe hanging rakishly between his wide amber eyes.

He nodded his head, studying the dog and the cat most thoughtfully. Then he swung himself about with his beak, clambered down the remainder of the cage, and fluttered to the floor. There he shuffled back and forth before the two animals for all the world like a tiny, pigeon-toed Napoleon. "Knollsmarmer," he muttered as he shuffled. "YohohoI minced piepiepie. Ol' Father restyemerry Chrismiss. Shareyer. Shareyer. Minced minced minced pie."

Stanley Blithe and Sweetpea, engrossed by this interesting speech, sat quietly down on their haunches and waited for more.

"Heytheremist er. Sawkiss. Sawkissyer. Kissyer piepiepie," Nightingale rattled off as he began to rock backward and forward on his two fine feet. "Mornin' Nicky, yohohoknooollsmarmer!"

Lord Nightingale cocked his head to the side. Stanley Blithe and Sweetpea did likewise. "Rrrrmph," said Stanley Blithe. "Mrrrrrow," declared Sweetpea.

With grave decision Lord Nightingale ruffled his chest feathers, gave a tentative flap of his great wings, and then flapped them again with meaning and soared upward near to the ceiling. He flew once around the chandelier, lowered his angle a bit and exited the saloon just beneath the top of the door frame. Stanley Blithe and Sweetpea dashed after him.

The kitchen at Willowsweep was large and lay at the very rear of the house on the ground floor. It was divided into myriad nooks and crannies, one of which, especially late at night with the oven fires banked and the moon shining in through a window, always seemed especially cozy. This night a large Venetian glass lamp rested in the center of the small table that stood in the very middle of that particular little nook. A piece of minced pie and a tankard of ale sat upon the table as well. And to the other side of the minced pie and the ale sat the Duke of Sotherland.

"I thought I heard someone wandering about," declared the dowager Countess of Wickenshire, stepping from the shadows of the doorway into the lamplight. "May I join you, Nathaniel? Or do you prefer to sulk alone?"

"Sulk?" asked the duke, rising quickly to his feet. "Me? Why would you think I am sulking, madam?"

"Because you look so serious. I thought perhaps you

were upset by all the attention Lady Alice received this evening."

"No. Come sit down with me," he urged, crossing to a corner and bringing a chair to the table for her. "Would you like a piece of pie? I have got it out."

"Yes, so I see," the dowager acknowledged with a smile. "However, I do not think I require a piece of pie. Perhaps some ale. I do so enjoy ale."

"You do?" queried the duke with the cock of an eyebrow.

"Yes, and always have. Do not peer at me as though I am some odd bug sitting upon your horse's ear, Nathaniel. Any number of ladies enjoy ale now and again."

"They do? Well, they must enjoy it in secret then, because I have never seen a lady in my life drink down a tankard of ale, and I have lived a very long time."

"Nathaniel, you speak like an old man. You are in the prime of your life," the dowager replied, taking a seat and watching him as he fetched another tankard from one of the cupboards and stepped through a door at the rear of the kitchen.

"I take it your son enjoys a bit of ale now and again, eh? Pleasant place to keep a keg, so near to hand."

"Nicky only keeps it there during the Christmas holidays. The rest of the time one must go down into the cellars. Thank you, Nathaniel," she said, as he set a full tankard before her. "This will help me to sleep the night away. Did you speak to Mr. Sayers after dinner as you said you would?"

"Indeed. Told him I would not tolerate his upsetting my Alice with his conversation ever again. Claimed he had no idea what he had said to make her so overwrought. He thought perhaps it was because he spoke of witches."

"Witches?"

"Apparently the featherbrain has a passion for witches. Knows about this particular aunt of your husband's, too."

"Elaina Maria."

"Yes, her. Longing to know more, I think."

"So, that was why Mr. Sayers was lingering in our park the night of the fire," murmured the dowager.

"He was lost, I thought."

"You and my Nicky share a certain innocence, do you not?"

"No, but I do not follow you. Why would Sayers linger in that storm if he had not lost his way?"

"In hope of spying the Witch of Willowsweep. There are those who say she has appeared from time to time in the fourth-floor windows of this house. Of course, Nicky boarded over those windows years ago and only unboarded them recently. She must be a witch indeed to have appeared in any one of them."

"A witch?" asked a voice from the threshold. "You will pardon me, I hope. I did not intend to disturb you. I was going to simply turn around and walk away. But, a witch?"

"Mr. Duncan. Is there something you require?" asked the dowager pleasantly.

"Well," Duncan replied, "the minced pie did seem to be haunting me and I thought perhaps I might—"

"What a place," grumbled the duke. "Haunted by dead witches and minced pie. There, Duncan, on that counter. Tankards above you and ale on the other side of that door to your left."

"I rather think I will leave the two of you in peace, Nathaniel," offered the dowager.

"No. You have barely touched your ale."

"I will take it with me. You may make use of my chair, Mr. Duncan. Do enjoy yourselves."

"I do apologize," Duncan said from the vicinity of the cupboard once she had departed. "It was gauche of me to interrupt your assignation, your grace."

"My what?"

Duncan looked down at the pie, picked up the knife that

lay beside it and prepared to cut himself a piece. "Your, ah, assignation?"

"You young scamps! Must everything be passion and assignations with you? Cannot two ancients meet quite by accident in the kitchen of an evening and share a bit of ale and a bite to eat? Of all the nonsense!"

Duncan barely heard a word. He stood there, staring down at the knife in his hand. His eyes, as tawny as a barn cat's back, glittered like a midnight predator's in the lamplight. One thrust, he thought, and I am out into the night and no one the wiser until morning. Avoid the nonsense of luring the girl off with me alone, overpowering her and carrying her to m'brother's little cottage at Lydepool. With the Duke of Sotherland dead, Lady Alice must necessarily return to Auntie Fiona, must she not? Auntie is the girl's grandmother, after all. How swiftly and easily then is all accomplished. And everyone will lay the deed at the feet of some curious Mr. Duncan who does not exist.

He turned his head to gaze back over his shoulder at the duke, who was just then attacking his piece of pie. The old scapegrace does not so much as look my way, Duncan thought. One thrust merely and my bargain is complete. Much faster and more certain this way. Less fuss as well. A good deal less fuss.

Twelve

The Dowager Countess of Wickenshire came close to spilling her ale as she reached the eighth step of the staircase to the first floor. "What on earth!" she cried softly, juggling the tankard as she ducked beneath Lord Nightingale's wings and stepped hastily aside at one and the same time to avoid the ungainly but hasty descent of Stanley Blithe, followed closely by Sweetpea. "And they are all bound for the kitchen," she whispered, watching as the lot of them turned into the corridor, Stanley Blithe overshooting the turn just a tad and setting the vase on the vestibule table to rocking precariously. "They are," she smiled. "The charge of Wellington's pie brigade. Well, they are lucky enough to have Nathaniel and Mr. Duncan there to give them each a piece. They would be forced to fend for themselves else. I wonder if they could fend for themselves?" With a grin and a sigh, she continued her journey back to her chambers, the ale once again calm within the tankard.

I shall be forced to speak to Nicky again about that cage, she thought as she rounded the landing and began her ascent to the second floor. It does no good to confine Nightingale to a cage which he can open at his own whim. "Now what was that?" she said aloud, coming to a halt. She stared ahead of her into the shadows cast by the lamp at the head of the stairs. "Hello?" she called quietly. "Is someone else still up and wandering about?"

A whispering of cloth reached her ears and muffled footsteps from the corridor just above her, but no one answered her soft query or stepped into her sight.

Well, what on earth, she wondered, stepping quickly up the remaining stairs and gazing down one corridor and then up the other. "Hello?" she called again. "Is someone here?"

"Ladyship? Be that you?" asked a quiet voice from the shadows on her right. "Oh, thank goodness!"

"Mr. Carson? What on earth are you doing wandering about at this hour? Come out. Come out from the shadows, Mr. Carson. I will not bite you."

"N-no, of course you will not, your ladyship," managed a trembling Mr. Carson as he stepped into the pool of light spread by the lamp on the cricket table. "I do apologize, your ladyship, for not speaking up at once, but I thought—I feared—that is, I did not expect—"

"You did not expect anyone else to be up and about and thought me to be the Witch of Willowsweep, is that it?"

"I am afraid so, your ladyship."

"Really, Mr. Carson, you must get over this silly notion that there is a dead witch wandering the hallways of Willowsweep. You will feel so very much more comfortable here if you do."

"J-just so, your ladyship. It is merely that—that—my master, your ladyship, has disappeared."

"Disappeared? Mr. Spelling has disappeared, Carson?"

"Y-yes, your ladyship. Not in his chambers, he is not. I entered his dressing room, your ladyship, to return some handkerchiefs to the clothespress. I peeked in to see if Mr. Spelling might require anything of me, and he was not in his sitting room, your ladyship. So I peered into his bedchamber, just to be certain, you know, that all was right with him, and he was not there either."

"Perhaps he has gone down to the study to find something to read, Mr. Carson?"

"I went to the study. There is no one there."

"Well, I know for a fact he is not in the kitchen for I have just come from there." A scowl took up residence on the dowager's face. "He would not dare," she murmured to herself. "Mr. Carson, stand right in this very spot and hold this tankard for me until I return. Do not move," she added as she swept off down the corridor to her left.

I had best be mistaken. You had better not be where I fear to find you, Neil, she thought to herself. Nephew or no, I will not have an innocent girl compromised in my home. Especially not this girl! With a soft knock upon the door and a quick lifting of the latch, the dowager let herself into Alice's chambers.

"Yohoho. Ol' FatherChris missIbe!" squawked Lord Nightingale, zooming in through the wide kitchen door, around one corner and into the nook where Sotherland and Duncan lingered. With the greatest precision he swooped over Duncan's head once and then again, coming near to parting the gentleman's hair by the breeze he produced. Bounding behind him came Stanley Blithe, who paused to place his forepaws on Sotherland's knee and give the duke's cheek a thoroughly sloppy lick, and then pranced merrily up to Duncan and sat properly down before him, tongue lolling. Sweetpea hopped daintily up into Sotherland's lap and sat quite like a statue, her pea green eyes staring at Duncan and the knife he held in his hand.

"Sharepie, sharepiepiepie. Yohoho villain!" demanded Nightingale, landing on Duncan's semi-extended arm, digging his claws into Duncan's coat sleeve and giving Duncan's wrist a tentative peck.

"I should surrender to the invading forces if I were you, Duncan," declared the duke, turning a bit in his chair to meet Duncan's bewildered gaze.

"What the devil?" Duncan murmured, and stared at the

macaw balanced on his arm, midway between his elbow and the hand that held the knife.

Lord Nightingale gazed back at him sideways, through one large eye that was only a bit more amber than Duncan's own. "Herewe comeawasailing villain," muttered Nightingale.

Duncan stood frozen, flabbergasted. The bird cannot possibly know, he told himself. It is a dumb fowl. It cannot know what thoughts enter my mind. Nor can it have come sailing down here to— No, no, a coincidence is all.

"Rrrrrrffff," Stanley Blithe said, taking the hem of Duncan's coat in his teeth and tugging at it urgently.

"Scuttle theblackguard," Nightingale suggested to Stanley Blithe encouragingly.

Duncan's mind reeled. They did know. Not only the bird, but the dog as well. And then he gazed in Sotherland's direction and met Sweetpea's disdainful glare. "I was not actually going to do it," Duncan whispered fearfully. "It was a thought. Nothing more than a thought."

"Not going to do what, Duncan?" asked Sotherland.

"Wh-what?"

"I hope you do not mean that you were not going to cut a slice of pie, eh? That is what they have all come for, these rapscallions. A bit of minced pie. At least I should imagine that to be the case. Nightingale, Duncan cannot make use of that knife with you upon his arm. Come," the duke commanded.

Lord Nightingale blinked one amber eye with grave consideration at Duncan, shuffled farther down his arm to his wrist, took one of the fingers wrapped around the handle of the knife into his beak, nibbled it lightly and then freed it.

"Nightingale, come!" demanded the duke again, and the macaw, with nary a backward glance, took to the air and landed on Sotherland's shoulder. "Well, get on with it, Duncan. Slice the pie. It has been haunting you all evening and likely haunting these three scoundrels as well. Time to put the knife to it."

"I am so very sorry to have disturbed you, my dear," murmured the dowager as she discovered Alice just entering her bedchamber from the adjoining sitting room.

"Lady Wickenshire. Is something wrong? Do you require my assistance?" asked Alice.

"No, no, it is not that. I came in because I feared that— Well, but it is of no consequence. You are perfectly safe, are you not? I mean to say, there is no one— Oh, for goodness sake," the dowager countess said with a sigh. "I am not at all equipped to speak in any but a straightforward manner, I fear. You must pardon me, my dear, but my nephew is not hidden away anywhere in your chambers, is he? He has not strolled in and forced himself upon you or anything equally as ludicrous?"

"Mr. Spelling? Forced himself upon me?" Alice attempted to look appalled, but the high drama of her expression was quite ruined by the smile that kept rising to her eyes.

"Just so," murmured the dowager. "Now that I stop to think, it is a most ridiculous notion. Neil is so petrified of doing the least thing to set you against him that he would never— I do apologize for appearing to be so very eccentric, my dear. I am not generally so."

"Of course you are not eccentric, my lady," Alice offered, extending her hand to the dowager. "There is yet a fire in my sitting room. Come and sit with me for a moment. There is something I wish to tell you."

"There is?" asked the dowager.

"Oh, yes," Alice nodded, taking the dowager's hand and leading her into the adjoining chamber.

No sooner were the two settled comfortably near the dwindling fire than Alice began to doubt the impulse that had led her to wish to confide in the dowager. She opened her mouth, closed it again, nibbled at her bottom lip with indecision. "You will not tell his grace?" she asked at last. "There would be a dreadful row if you were to tell his grace."

"Is it something quite serious, Alice?"

"No. That is to say, it was not serious, but his grace may see it quite differently."

"Then I give you my word that I shall not say a thing."

Alice smiled with relief. "Mr. Spelling was here," she said, causing the dowager to sit straight up upon the edge of her chair. "Not purposely," Alice added quickly. "You must not think that he came to me with any illicit intentions, for he did not."

"Neil came here, into your chamber? This evening?"

"Yes, my lady. Actually, he stumbled into this chamber through the wall. His light had gone out, you see, and he—"

"What on earth was Neil doing in the old passageways?" interrupted the dowager.

"That is just it. He was searching for Elaina Maria's journals, and his light went out and—"

"Journals? Elaina Maria's journals?"

"Yes. Lord Wickenshire said that Mr. Spelling might have them, could he but find them, and it has occurred to me— Do you perchance know where they might be, my lady? Or has Mr. Spelling asked you already?"

"Nicky said that Neil may have Elaina Maria's journals? Without so much as approaching me on the subject? Well, of all things. And why would her journals cause a row should your father hear of them?" the dowager Lady Wickenshire added with a perplexed frown. "Your father is not so very old, you know, that a lady living in the sixteenth century would have mentioned his indiscretions in her scribblings."

"It is not the journals would cause the row, but the fact

that I accompanied Mr. Spelling to search for them," Alice confessed softly.

"You did what?"

"I—I went with Mr. Spelling into the passageways to search for the journals."

"Oh, my heavens," groaned the dowager. "Alone? You and Neil were alone together inside our walls? This very evening?"

Carson could not decide what he ought to do. He had been standing alone in the middle of the corridor for a good twenty minutes and still her ladyship had not returned. Perhaps she had forgotten all about him? Yes, he thought, most likely she has. The ladies have sat down to have a coze and my very existence has faded from her ladyship's mind. I am not very memorable, especially to such a one as the dowager Lady Wickenshire.

With hesitant steps, he made his way toward the turn in the corridor that would take him back to Mr. Spelling's chambers. He walked slowly, so as not to spill what was in the tankard, and softly, so as not to call the least attention to himself. One never knows, he thought as he stepped into and out of the shadows along his route. One never knows when there is a witch about or when there is not.

He glanced back over his shoulder and to his right and to his left, his head ever in motion, to be certain that no long-departed lady would rise up to greet him out of the dark places or no Witch of Willowsweep be trailing along in his wake. When at last he reached Mr. Spelling's chambers, he very quietly, very carefully lifted the latch and eased himself silently around the door, his gaze fastened upon a curiously altering bit of shadow behind him, his back entering the chamber before his front.

"What the devil are you looking for out there?" asked Spelling of his valet's backside.

Carson straightened, turned, gasped and tipped the tankard all at one and the same time. "Oh," he gasped, his hand going to his heart as he backed against the door and slid slowly down to the floor as it slammed shut behind him. "Oh, my heavens."

"Carson? What is it? You are not ill?" Spelling inquired, crossing the sitting room to kneel down beside his valet. "Why do you hold your hand to your heart so? You are not thinking of dying, are you, Carson?"

"N-no," gasped Carson. "No, Mr. Spelling. It is merely that I was n-not expecting—you were n-not here and now you are and I— Oh, Mr. Spelling, I imagined for a moment you were *her*."

"Her? Her who? Glory, what a mess! What the devil was in that tankard? Ale?" Spelling asked, his eyes widening as he touched a finger to the spilled liquid and tasted it. "Carson, you are foxed!"

"N-no, Mr. Spelling, I am not. I was merely holding the tankard for the dowager countess, Mr. Spelling. I did not drink one drop of it. Not one. I—I th-thought you were *her*, sir, and I felt my heart stop."

"You thought I was my Aunt Diana? And your heart stopped? You *are* foxed, Carson. Top-heavy. Why would my Aunt Diana be in my chambers? Or did you imagine these to be her chambers? You intended to sneak into my Aunt Diana's chambers with a tankard of ale in your hand, Carson? What the deuce has got into you?"

"Oh," moaned Carson in despair, Spelling's words whirling about in his mind and he so distraught as to be able to make no sense of them. "Oh, Mr. Spelling, I am dead. I am frightened to death. Such a fate *is* possible. I shall expire in a moment."

Spelling grinned. Ordinarily, he would not have done, but he could not help himself. A few moments ago he had been bluedeviled because even with Lady Alice's help, he had been unable to discover Elaina Maria's journals. For a week and more he had been searching through the passages at odd hours of the day and night in hopes of finding them, but had found nothing. It was only when he and Nicky and Jenkins had located the secret little room that his hopes had risen to a high state again. And then, he and Lady Alice had found nothing. Now, when the stakes had risen to include Alice's peace of mind over those foolish letters, he had run out of places in which to search. All had combined to make him most dispirited. But he discovered that he could not remain so with his valet sitting flat on the floor, legs straight out before him, covered in ale and threatening to expire.

"You are not going to expire, Carson," he said. "Not any time soon. Let me help you up."

Against all of Carson's protests, Spelling helped the man to his feet, trundled him across the floor and bundled him into an armchair before the fire. "There. Now, take a very deep breath, Carson. Take two or three, if you like. Very nicely done. And now tell me, can you feel your heart beating again?"

"Oh, oh, Mr. Spelling. I vow to you, sir, I am not foxed. I do not drink ale. I am a lover of tea, Mr. Spelling. And it was not her ladyship I imagined you to be, Mr. Spelling, it was—"

"Who?" asked Spelling, tugging a straight-backed chair over to where his valet sat and then straddling it. "Come, Carson, you may be honest with me. Did you think to have an assignation with one of the maids, perhaps?"

"No! Never! I thought you were the witch, Mr. Spelling, come to grab me up and lay a curse upon me!"

"Not the witch again," Spelling sighed.

"You might have been her," Carson protested excitedly. "I came to see did you require anything more of me, sir, and you were not here. I searched everywhere for you and I could not find you. I stood in the corridor near the staircase forever, waiting for her ladyship. You did not come up the stairs, sir, nor did you come down from above. You did not come by way of the servants' staircase. I did not expect anyone at all to be here, especially you! H-how do you come to be back in your chambers?" added Carson with an abrupt frown. "You did not pass me in the corridor and you cannot have got here without passing me." Carson's eyes opened wide and his mouth formed a round little *O*.

"Do not for one moment start that again!" demanded Spelling with a chuckle. "I am not the Witch of Willowsweep disguised as your master, Carson. No, and I am not a haunt either."

"But how did you—"

"I entered through the wall, Carson."

"Through the wall, Mr. Spelling?"

"You can do likewise. I will show you how. But I do not recommend it. It is dark and cold as the winter of sixty-five in there."

Duncan huddled in his bed, his eyes wide open, his thoughts blowing about like mad robins in a windstorm. No matter how hard he tried, he could not dismiss from his mind the idea that those creatures had come running to the kitchen to protect Sotherland. "It is preposterous," he muttered to himself over and over again. "Such things do not happen. They came to fetch themselves some pie and nothing more."

But how the devil did they think to fetch pie? If we had not been there just at that time, the lot of them would have gotten nothing. No, they came because they knew someone was in that kitchen. The dog likely heard us, or the cat, and in they came hoping for a handout. And when that blasted bird saw the knife in my hand, he came directly for me. But why? Does he know what a knife is for? What it can do? No, I cannot believe that.

With a groan and a sigh, Duncan rolled over onto his stomach and plopped a pillow atop his head. He did not wish to think about it anymore. He had been thinking about it for hours and hours and he had no clearer sense of what had happened than he had had at that precise moment. "I would not have killed the duke regardless," he mumbled into the sheet below him. "I knew directly after I thought the thing that I would not do it. I may speak of doing murder and think of doing murder, but I have never actually murdered anyone in all my life."

No, and I have never kidnapped a lady either, but I came here to do precisely that, he thought. I took my great auntie's money and agreed to return the girl to her one way or another—even if it be over Sotherland's dead body. Why did I do that?

"Because I am a blackguard," he told himself. "I have been a blackguard from the day I was breeched."

No, that is not true at all, he corrected himself, shoving the pillow from his head onto the floor and turning over to stare up at the ceiling. I am always claiming it to be so, but there is no truth in it. There was a time when I was not a blackguard. There was a time when someone was accustomed to call me a fine fellow. We would laugh and sing and dance together and I was as far from being a blackguard as any other lad.

"But it was so very long ago," he said softly, "that I cannot remember her name or even the color of her hair." Tears attempted to assault him, to come slipping and sliding down his cheeks. He closed his eyes and fought against them. He pretended the tears did not exist, that he was not crying now nor was he ever likely to. "Blackguards do not," he whispered hoarsely. "They never give in to tears for any reason." And then he rolled over, buried his head in his arms and sobbed himself to sleep.

Thirteen

"I kinnot b'lieve it is made," Maryrose said, studying the odd formation of wood and cloth that now stood in the very middle of the special little room just off the ancient passageway. "Mr. Jenkins an' Mr. Tripp are wonnerful, ain't they?"

"I should think so," agreed Delight, smiling gratefully up at Jenkins. "It is beautiful."

"Hurrah fer Mr. Jenkins an' Mr. Tripp!" shouted a long white stocking which strutted merrily behind a wooden shelf, a patched linen sheet painted to look like the night sky at its back. It sported two green button eyes, a nose of black embroidery silk and wide, red wool lips. "An' hurrah fer Miss Delight, too!" it shouted excitedly.

"Hurrah for me?" asked Delight.

"Uh-huh," the stocking replied. "On accounta ye painted the backthin's so purty an' made sich fine clothes."

"An' no one caught ye doin' of it," added a blushing pink stocking with most becoming curls of yellow yarn, quite properly decked out in a long dress of faded blue silk, with a tiny purple shawl and a most extraordinary bonnet of sprigged muslin and lace. "Oh!" exclaimed the puppet abruptly and bounced its chin against the shelf, then disappeared.

"What happened?" asked Delight, rushing behind the stage.

"Becky fell off 'er tippy-toes," grinned Jackie, helping the little girl up from the floor. "It be too high fer Becky. I think it be too high fer Jem an' you, too, Miss Delight."

"But it has got to be this high to cover you and Maryrose," Delight replied, attempting to reach the shelf. "I know just the thing!" she exclaimed. "Maryrose, come with me an' we will get my special books."

"The ones what we hid unner yer bed, Miss Delight?"

"Uh-huh. They are verimost big and thick. Becky and Jem and I can stand on them. That will fix everything."

"I be goin' with ye," said Jackie with some authority. "Miss Delight, you be carryin' the lamp an' me an' Maryrose'll carry them there books."

They were back within minutes, having taken the old passageway down and back again.

"Now we kin practice properly," Maryrose declared. "You will see, Miss Delight. We will do ever'thin' perfeck now."

"An' ever'one will be 'mazed at us," added Becky. "An' we will git to see the ladies in their Chris'mas clothes. It will be the bestest Chris'mas in all the whole world."

Jenkins found himself quite inclined to agree with the little girl. Certainly it would be the most entertaining Christmas that Lord Wickenshire had ever had. And quite likely, it was destined to be the most memorable Christmas of all time. "Are you quite certain that there is room enough for all of you behind there?" Jenkins asked, sending Delight and Maryrose scurrying behind the stage where Jem, Jackie and Becky already hid from sight. "We cannot make it much larger, but if there is not enough room, we can easily extend the sides outward a bit."

"We is fine, Mr. Jenkins," called Jackie amidst a good deal of giggling. "Be ye ready ta start?"

"Perfectly prepared," Jenkins responded, taking a lantern fashioned from a hatbox and setting it upon the shelf. "Are you all ready back there?"

"Uh-huh."

"All right then. Once upon a time," Jenkins began in stentorian tones.

"No, no, you have got to do it from the verimost beginning," Delight exclaimed from behind the stage. "Please, Mr. Jenkins?"

"Very well, Miss Delight. From the very beginning then." Jenkins walked away from the stage, then strolled back and bowed most regally. "Good day to you, ladies and gentlemen," he said. "We welcome you to the home of the Willowsweep Thespians—"

"Sespeens," giggled a little voice from behind the stage.

"Shhh," hissed another.

"The Willowsweep Thespians," Jenkins resumed, "as they present their extraordinary drama, Lord Nightingale's Christmas."

"Now," whispered Maryrose, out of sight.

"Uh-huh," Delight responded, and up went her arm with a stocking upon it covered in myriad feathers, some from old bonnets, some from Lord Nightingale himself, and a goodly number from the Willowsweep hens. With gold buttons for eyes and a beak made of paper and paste, the parrot puppet hopped across the stage to stand beside Jenkins.

"Once upon a time," Jenkins began most seriously, "in the land of Egypt, which was merely a hop and a skip from Willowsweep . . .

Spelling sat forward in the chair in Wickenshire's study, his arms resting along his thighs, his hands clasped, his head bowed. "I did not think you would mind," he said quietly. "They are nothing but old scribblings."

"They are as much a part of this family as this house and these lands, Neil," admonished the dowager Lady Wickenshire. "And I am certain Nicky did not say you might help yourself to them."

"I never said that he did. I told Lady Alice that he had no use for them and had not so much as thought to go searching after them himself. All of which is perfectly true. I did not actually say that I had asked him if I might have the things."

"You planned to steal them," the dowager observed sadly.

"No! I—I—merely discovered that the journals could be of help to me and decided to have them. I did not think of it as stealing precisely."

"You never do think at all, Neil. You never consider anyone besides yourself."

"I do!" exclaimed Spelling, raising his gaze to meet his aunt's. "I have been attempting very hard of late to consider others. I am just not accustomed to it, Aunt Diana, and so it is difficult to remember to do it all the time."

"I see," nodded the dowager. "I stand corrected."

"You are not going to tell Nicky?"

"No, I am not. Nor am I going to tell his grace that you spent last evening wandering about inside our walls with his daughter. But I should do both."

"But you will not? I was not going to take the journals merely for my sake, Aunt Diana. Truly. Well, I was to begin with, but now, I have given up my own plans and the journals will be used to purchase Lady Alice's freedom."

"What?" The dowager countess stared at him in wonder. "Purchase Alice's freedom? Her freedom from whom, may I ask?"

"From Sayers."

"Oh, great heavens! There is more to this story?" asked the countess, rising and beginning to pace the room. "Out with it then, Neil. Tell me all."

Spelling gulped. "I have no right to tell all," he replied. "My story is a very simple one, Aunt Diana, and quite like every other bumblebath I have ever got myself into, but Lady Alice's story is hers alone and I will not betray her confidence in me."

"You will not?"

"No."

"Not even if I call Nicky *and* his grace into the study this very minute and tell them all I know?"

"No. I cannot. It is Alice's secret and I cannot think she wishes me to make it public."

"Not even if I agree to look the other way once you discover the journals and allow you to take them for your own, Neil?"

Spelling considered his aunt's words gravely. Was it possible? Would she actually give them to him?

"It would make me feel a deal better to have them with your blessing, Aunt Diana," he replied softly. "But I cannot. It is not my place to tell Alice's story to anyone."

The dowager Lady Wickenshire ceased her pacing as she reached the chair in which Spelling sat. She reached down and smoothed an errant curl back from his brow. "I do believe you love that girl, Neil," she whispered. "I have never known you to be so honorable before. I am amazed at it."

"Yes, but without the journals, I cannot help her," Neil sighed. "There is nothing else Sayers wishes from me. He will not take my money or anything else I have thought to offer him."

"Once they were tucked away in the little room off the old passageways, but they have since disappeared, I understand."

"We looked in that room only last night."

"Have you looked in the barn?" asked the dowager.

"In the barn? In the old barn, do you mean? Yes. We discovered the coin there, Aunt Diana. I told you as much."

"But that was merely in a chink in the wall. There is more to the old priest's hole than that."

"I know, but—"

"Perhaps you ought to take out the stones one by one, Neil, until you uncover the full extent of it. The coin must have fallen from somewhere. I have no doubt it was wrapped in oilskin or such because it was not much tarnished. Perhaps someone thought to stow the journals away in the same place, in the same manner. I have not seen them for years now, after all. Perhaps, for some reason, your Uncle Evelyn wished to hide them."

Lady Alice strolled into the breakfast room, a bright and shining young woman in burnished gold velvet with a smile in her eyes and a sprightliness to her step. "Good morning, Mr. Duncan," she greeted the only other person present. "You are up and about early this morning."

"It is near ten of the clock, my lady."

"No, is it? As late as that?"

"Indeed. How glorious you look, like the rising sun," he added, pulling out a chair for her at the table. "No one is about. May I have the pleasure of serving you myself?"

"I shall have merely tea and toast," Alice replied.

"Done!" With a competent hand, Duncan procured the toast from the sideboard and set it before her together with a dish of butter and another of preserves. He asked what she would have in her tea and attended to her cup. "You shine like the dawn in that dress," he said, as he set her tea before her.

"Why do you say so, Mr. Duncan?"

"Because it is true."

"It is not true," Alice protested quietly. "Ever since you have come, you have been overflowing with compliments for me and they have every one of them been false."

"I protest!" exclaimed Duncan taking his seat.

"No, it is I who protest, Mr. Duncan. I am not so pretty as you would have me believe. I see myself in my looking glass every morning and I am nothing if not plain."

"To some, perhaps."

"To almost everyone. Were I a man, I should be handsome like his grace and my brothers. But I am not a man, and the features I share with the men of my family are discouraging to womanly beauty to say the least."

"You do not believe that a gentleman could find you beautiful, my lady?"

"I believe that one particular gentleman finds me beautiful, Mr. Duncan, but you are not he."

Duncan took a sip of the coffee that had been cooling before him and studied Lady Alice with some chagrin. "You think I offer you Spanish coin, but it is not so."

"Hah! Mr. Duncan, I may look to you like a veritable peagoose, but I assure you, I am not. Mr. Duncan? Goodness, Mr. Duncan, what is it? Are you not feeling just the thing? You have gone white as a ghost."

"Howdedo m'pretty," drawled a most familiar voice, and Lord Nightingale sailed above Alice's head, banked and returned to land on the chair at the head of the table. "Mornin' Nicky. Mornin' Genia. Mornin' villain. Ol' FatherChris miss Ibe. I."

Gads, the blasted fowl is stalking me, thought Duncan. He does know I'm a blackguard. He knows I intend his people harm and he is determined to prevent it.

"Do not tell me that Nightingale frightens you, Mr. Duncan?"

"N-no. He—I—I was not expecting him, is all."

"Herewecomea was sailin'," sang Lord Nightingale jauntily, stomping one way and then the other across the chair back. "Amongthe leeeeeeaves sogreen."

"Oh," grinned Alice. "She has got him to sing it in proper order at last."

"Who has?"

"Delight. She thinks he will sing in church for the Christmas service."

"He will not, will he?" queried Duncan, pleased to have a change of topic, even if it must be Lord Nightingale.

"I do not believe so. If Christmas came in summer, perhaps Lady Wickenshire would allow herself to be talked into it. But it is much too cold outside for a parrot to go anywhere."

"How lucky for all of us." Duncan smiled.

"Ah, Duncan, just the fellow I'm looking for," said Wickenshire as he strolled into the room. "Nightingale? Now what the deuce are you doing here? I vow, Mama has got the right of it. We will be forced to find some way to close your cage door so that you cannot learn to open it. Good morning, Lady Alice."

"Good morning, Lord Wickenshire."

"No hurry, Duncan, but when you have finished, I should like to speak with you for a moment or two. I will be in the stables—after I have delivered this pirate back to his brig. Come, Nightingale," Wickenshire commanded and Lord Nightingale flew directly to his shoulder.

"He certainly understands the word 'come'," observed Duncan when Wickenshire and Lord Nightingale had departed.

"Lord Wickenshire and his grace would have it that Lord Nightingale understands more than that, Mr. Duncan," replied Alice. "A great deal more."

Duncan nodded as his hands began to tremble.

"Charlie Osgood 'as delivered the new tack, m'lord," called Bobby Tripp as Wickenshire entered the stable.

"Has he? And what do you think of it, Bobby?"

"I thinks m'lady an' Miss Delight will be overcomed by it," grinned Wickenshire's head groom. "It ain't goin' ta matter, m'lord, that there be'ant no snow fer ta take out the sleigh. Thrilled they will be, regardless."

"I do hope so. They are accustomed to snow on Christmas. And this is the second Christmas in a row that we have had none."

"It don't gen'raly snow much 'ere, m'lord."

"Yes, I know. But a bit of it at Christmas would be nice."

"Have a foot of the stuff at Northridge by now," offered Sotherland, peering around the backside of an enormous black. "Rather pleased, myself, that it has not made an appearance here. Grown much too old for such winters as we have in the north."

"Have you seen the new harness, Sotherland?"

"Indeed. And I am in full agreement with Mr. Tripp here. The ladies will be overcome. The trip to church will prove a merry one, Wickenshire. I have been thinking," continued the duke, stepping from the stall and strolling to where Wickenshire and Bobby Tripp stood. "I have been thinking that it might prove desirable to hitch my blacks with your grays to that quaint old vehicle you keep hidden away at the rear of the carriage house."

"My grandfather's traveling coach?" asked Wickenshire, his eyes dancing with merriment.

"Is that what it is? I did wonder. You have done a fine job of keeping it up. Shines like the stars inside and out."

"Refurbished it, Bobby and the lads and I, but I never thought to actually drive the thing. It is extraordinarily large and extremely heavy, Sotherland."

"And therefore just the thing for what I am about to propose. Only think how elegant it is, Wickenshire. Like something from a faery tale. Just the thing to give the ladies a thrill since we cannot drive the sleigh for Christmas."

"Well, Mama and Sera would be vastly entertained. Delight would imagine herself a regular faery princess. And your Alice might find it exciting as well, but it is so heavy, I cannot think how my grandfather ever found horses to pull the thing."

"An eight-horse hitch," Sotherland suggested with great enthusiasm.

"No, do you think?"

"Of course. Which is why I have been pondering the efficacy of hitching my blacks with your grays, Wickenshire. It can be done and what a sight it would be. A gray in golden bells and red ribands beside a black in silver bells and ivy, and behind the black, a gray, and behind the gray, a black."

Wickenshire grinned at the thought. "Sera would like it above all things. But my coachman cannot drive eight-in-hand."

"No, no, mine cannot either, but I can," announced the duke. "I have done. And not so long ago as you might imagine. Life at Northridge is a trifle boring," he admitted with a quiet smile. "Bradford and I once hitched ten horses together and had a go at driving them. Ten are a handful, but eight are a cordial group when you have got a feel for them."

Wickenshire stood undecided, licking at his lower lip. "There is no fear of that old coach tipping, do you think?"

"Never. Solid, and not the least top-heavy."

"Because I could not take a chance of anything happening to Sera and the baby, Sotherland."

"Nothing will happen but smiles and laughter and a song or two. I am certain of it."

"Well, then. We will do it, eh? But can it be done by day after tomorrow? Do the horses require to be made accustomed to such a hitch?"

"Tripp and your lads and I will begin at once. A few times up and down the drive and perhaps a mile or two up and down the road and they will work together as if they have always done. Accustomed to being hitched two across, all of them. It is only one leader from each team must become accustomed to following instead of leading."

Wickenshire nodded. "And you will not mind to play the coachman on Christmas?"

"I shall enjoy it no end. Morning, Duncan," added Sotherland as that gentleman entered the stable.

"Your grace."

"Mr. Duncan. I thank you for coming so promptly,"

Wickenshire greeted. "Come and stroll with me around the paddock, eh? There is something I should like to ask of you."

They left the stable behind and walked out into the sunshine. "Christmas is day after tomorrow," Wickenshire began.

"And you wish me gone by then, do you?" asked Duncan.

"Gone? Have you remembered where it was you were bound?"

"No, but—"

"Then I certainly do not wish you gone. What a thing for me to do, put you out on the very eve of Christmas. No, it is something else entirely about which I wish to speak to you."

Duncan looked at him questioningly.

"It is about the rooster."

"The—rooster?"

"Yes. Our rooster. It seems that our rooster has had an unfortunate accident, and just at the worst time, too."

"Your—rooster?"

"Indeed. Fox nosing about the henhouse. Met the rooster. The rooster is dead."

Duncan blinked his tawny eyes in confusion.

"Well, most definitely you are not from hereabout. You would realize else. A rooster is required on Christmas morning, and we only had the one."

"I know they are required for—to make chickens, but—" stuttered Duncan.

"On Christmas morning all the unmarried ladies in the household are expected to walk to the henhouse and knock on the door. And if a rooster crows at their knock, it means they will be married within the year."

"Truly?"

"Well, it does not always prove to be the case, but it is

a great deal of fun for the ladies, you know. And Christmas is the day after tomorrow, and our only rooster is—"

"Dead," provided Duncan.

"Just so. And I wondered if you would—if you feel up to it, that is—if you would ride into Swiftinwhold and purchase another rooster for us."

"Swiftinwhold?"

"It's the nearest village. Directly down the main road about twelve miles. You need merely stop at the first cottage you come to. That will belong to Harvey Lamb. You need only say that Wickenshire has asked you to purchase a rooster, and if he does not have one for sale, he will know who does. I would send one of the stablehands or one of the household servants, but with the holidays so close they are all—"

"Say no more," interrupted Duncan. "I shall be more than happy to fetch you a rooster. I should be a veritable ingrate to decline to do so after all you have done for me."

Fourteen

"Are you certain, Spelling?" asked Sayers as he chiseled cautiously at the ever-widening opening to the priest's hole in the ancient barn.

"No, I ain't," Spelling replied testily. "It was my Aunt Diana's suggestion, but a suggestion merely. She could be correct. That coin came from somewhere and it was enclosed in something or it would have been black as night. Keep working, Sayers, or we shall never open the entire thing.

"Yes, of course, but about Alice's letters—"

"What about them?" growled Spelling, sitting back on his haunches to rest and wiping a deal of sweat from his brow with his coat sleeve. "You will not go back on your word, Sayers. You will return her letters, each and every one. If you do not, I do not give you the journals."

"I hesitate to point it out, Spelling, but you ain't got the journals to give me as yet."

"I will have. And I will tell you this, Sayers. Do I not find the journals before the holidays are over, you will return Alice's letters to her regardless. Before she leaves Willowsweep. You do have them with you, do you not?"

"As a matter of fact, I do. I enjoy to read them over from time to time."

"Very well. You shall keep the ring until I deliver the

journals, but you shall return the letters to Alice. If you do not, Sayers, I will call you out."

"Call me out? Why?"

"You know very well why. The letters are to be returned or I will meet you across a piece of grass on a dew-drenched morning."

"No!" exclaimed Lady Alice from somewhere below the loft in which the gentlemen worked. "Neil Spelling, you will not fight a duel on my behalf. Not ever!" With a swish, a swirl and a stomp of riding boots, Alice made her way up the ladder and into the loft itself. "Your Aunt Diana said that you would be here. But she did not say that you would be here calling Mr. Sayers out."

"I am not calling him out," countered Spelling, crossing to help her up the last few rungs into the loft. "I am merely telling him what will happen if he does not return your letters to you. Rackety thing to do, Sayers. Despicable."

"Do ye be needin' help up there, m'lady?" called Dick, the youngest of Wickenshire's grooms. "Ought I be comin' up?"

"No, Dick, I am perfectly fine," replied Alice. "You must simply wait outside and keep a close eye on the horses."

"Yes, m'lady."

"And you, Neil Spelling, will speak no more about duels."

"It does not matter if I promise to meet him," Spelling grumbled. "Makes no difference to me if I am killed by Sayers or by the legendary Ducane. I will be dead all the same."

"Ducane? Who is Ducane?" Alice asked, taking Spelling's arm. "Neil, do you mean to say that you are already bound to engage in a duel? But why? What have you done?"

She called me Neil, thought Spelling, letting all else slip by. She called me Neil twice! He stared down at her, his eyes so filled with wonder and with love that Alice gasped to see them.

"I thought our entire bargain was struck to *keep* Ducane from calling you out," Sayers said, observing closely the silent, but most intimate exchange between Spelling and Lady Alice. "You provide me the journals; I give you the ring which you bestow on Lady Helena; and poof! the threat of Richard Ducane's prowess with a pistol is gone by the wayside."

"You intend to give that ring to some Lady Helena, did he say?" asked Alice, taking a step back from Spelling.

"That was my plan at first," Spelling acknowledged, abashed. "But then you asked me, you know, what I intended to do with the ring, and I knew what it was that you expected of me. I knew it was the proper thing to do, too. I will return the ring to my Aunt Diana as soon as I come by it."

"You will do what?" asked Sayers, aghast, as a satisfied smile sweetened Alice's visage. "Spelling, are you mad? Lady Helena will accuse you to Ducane of seducing her, ruining her and then abandoning her and you will be dead the following morning!"

Alice's eyes widened. Her heartbeat thrummed in her ears. "You seduced this Lady Helena, Mr. Spelling?" she asked in a tiny voice as the loft seemed to whirl around her. "You ruined her and abandoned her?" And then she gazed deeply into Spelling's eyes and the loft ceased to whirl at once. "No," she said, taking his arm, "you did not. I shall not make the same mistake again. There is something left unsaid here. Some explanation. I will not believe this tale is true unless you tell me it is true."

"An enormous Canterbury Tale," offered Sayers over his shoulder as he went back to prying at the stones. "Spelling's rich as Croesus, Alice, and Lady Helena laid a trap for him. Thought to force him into marriage. When he would not be forced into it, she threatened him. When he said his heart belonged to someone else and he would rather die than marry Lady Helena, she gave it a bit of thought and then said very well, he would die—unless he got a particular ring from me and presented it to her."

"You knew all this?" Alice asked, staring at Sayers, appalled. "You knew, and still you would not sell him the ring?"

"How the devil!" exclaimed Spelling. "Who told you, Sayers, of the entire episode?"

"Lady Helena, of course. Never met her brother Richard, though. You have never met him either, eh?"

"No, but I have heard of Ducane."

"As have we all. At any rate, Spelling, Lady Helena and I have acquaintances in common. We meet from time to time. How do you expect she knew of the ring in the first place if she had not seen it in my possession? Showing it off, I was, the night I won it from Connelly. Boasting, you know. Later, she came to boast to me of how *she* intended to acquire my little prize."

"And you still would not sell it to Neil?" asked Alice again. "When you knew he might be killed? I cannot believe I ever thought you to be a desirable gentleman, Mr. William Sayers!"

"No, I cannot either," sighed Sayers, ceasing his work and staring up at them both. "I would not just stand there, Spelling," he said. "I would put both my arms around Alice now, if I were you. She loves you, you know. Can see it in her eyes. And any fellow willing to die merely to live up to a lady's moral principles—even though they do not particularly match his own—yes, you should definitely put both your arms around her."

"William!" exclaimed Lady Alice.

"Well, you do love him. It is not merely a schoolgirl's tendre this time, as it was with me."

"It was not a schoolgirl's tendre with you, William," protested Alice.

"Yes, it was. And when I finally came to my senses and realized what I had done—realized that I had persuaded an innocent girl, no more experienced than my sister, Cecilia, to elope with me, I was thoroughly ashamed of myself. I could not go through with it. My only excuse is that I was young, lonely and quite carried away by your letters. You did write the most wonderful letters. I will wager you still do."

"About those letters, Sayers," Spelling began. "Now that we have come full about, I will have them whether we discover Elaina Maria's journals this holiday or not."

"No, you will not have them, Spelling. Alice will have them. They go from my hand to hers. Though why you wish to have them back, my dear, I cannot think. I saved them because they are so pleasurable to read and make me smile to remember how innocent we both were—but I cannot think you would enjoy to remember that particular time at all."

"I will not be blackmailed with my own letters, Mr. Sayers," Alice declared, her eyes grown dark with fury.

"Blackmailed? Well, by Jupiter, what sort of a man do you think I am? I would not sell Spelling the ring because I desire the journals more than all the money in the world. Perhaps I caused him some hardship on that front, but I am not some evil dastard who would think to blackmail a young lady over a schoolgirl's indiscretion!"

"Alice? I thought you told me that Sayers had threatened to—" began Spelling, somewhat bewildered.

"Oh, devil!" Alice interrupted and then covered her mouth at the use of such a word, turned away from Sayers, and buried her face for a moment in Spelling's neckcloth. "I have done it again," she told the fine white muslin softly.

"What?" asked Spelling, his arms going tentatively around her. "I did not hear you, Alice."

"I have done it again," Alice repeated, looking up at him sorrowfully. "I am very much afraid that I assumed the worst of Mr. Sayers without the least bit of actual proof. I—the manner in which Mr. Sayers spoke to me of the letters—and—and the mere fact that he was so unexpectedly present—I assumed that he intended to—"

"Well, by Jove," Spelling said, cutting her off in midsentence. "You have got to cease doing that, Alice. You cannot go about expecting the worst of everyone. You will be in a state of turmoil your whole life long if you do."

"Do be still, bird," Duncan muttered. "You will be free shortly and have a new harem of hens all for yourself." A rooster, he thought. I am grateful above all else that Alan and Helena are not present to see me riding with a rooster tied in a sack to my saddle bow. How they would point and laugh at me. I would never live it down. Likely become a tale passed on in the family for generations. "Not that I care," he muttered to his mare. "I do not care what either Helena or Alan thinks of me, Candle, or what they think of the things I choose to do."

Still, I must care, he thought. I would not always attempt to pass myself off as such a devilish rogue, else. But I ought not to care! Not a fig! They think themselves so perfect, when anyone can plainly see what a stuffy, self-satisfied, self-righteous fellow Alan is and what a spoiled, snobbish harridan Helena has become. Why should I allow such wretched people as they have grown up to be to determine how I conduct myself?

Her name was Mary, he thought then, astonishing himself. Where the deuce did that come from? But it is true. I am certain of it. Mary Dalrymple. Of all things, that I should remember her name now! And her hair was a fine reddish brown and her eyes blue and she had the sweetest way of pursing her lips before she said anything at all significant. By Jove, I can see her face as clearly as if she were standing before me. And I thought I should never be able to call her to mind again!

He brought Candle to a halt and sat staring off down the road, remembering the only time in his life that he had been truly happy. With a wobbling heart he envisioned a young nursery maid with pretty pink cheeks and a manner as gay and compelling as a frisky breeze on the finest spring day. "Mary," he whispered. "Mary Dalrymple. Wherever did you go? I would have grown to be a far nicer fellow had you not gone off and left me all alone."

But you did go off, and without so much as a word to me, he thought. And I cried for days and days. Of course, I was merely four. A fellow may cry for a lost love when he is four.

"After you left, Mary," he said softly, "rivalry and jealousy broke down my nursery door. I have tasted nothing but snobbery and bitterness ever since."

With a trembling lip and an angry shake of his head for what he might have become, Duncan set his mount into a trot and then a gallop. Forgetting completely his helpless passenger, he held the reins tight in his fist, urged the mare off the roadbed, up a hill and straight at a hedgerow. He threw his heart over and Candle followed just as Duncan knew she would.

He continued his mad ride across the pasture until the poor fowl's petrified squawking at last commanded his attention. "Oh, m'gawd," he muttered, drawing Candle to a halt. "Oh, m' gawd, I hope I ain't ruined Wickenshire's blasted rooster."

"It is not some plaything for Stanley Blithe?" Sera queried, looking up from the basket she was packing.

"No," Wickenshire answered. "Guess again."

"I cannot, Nicholas. I have guessed every guess I have

in me. All that is left to me is to believe that you have gone mad."

"Is that basket for Jebediah and Julia?" asked the dowager as she entered the quiet nook in the kitchen where Sera and Wickenshire had taken refuge.

"Indeed it is."

"Then these are to go in it," the dowager said, giving seven packages wrapped in silver paper into Sera's hands.

"How very pretty. What is in them, Mother Diana?"

"Mother Diana?" asked Wickenshire. "Where did that come from? You make my mother sound like the abbess of a nunnery."

"Nicky!"

"Well, you do."

"But I must find something permanent to call your mama. I cannot be dilly-dallying about, trying this and that, for much longer. The baby will be here soon."

"Grandmama," Wickenshire offered easily. "You will not mind to be called Grandmama, will you, Mama?"

"By everyone?"

"Um-hmmm. Even I will call you Grandmama, eh? Then Bedazzler will get in the way of it quickly."

"Bedazzler?" The dowager countess stared at her son aghast. "Nicky, you would not! You could not possibly name your own child Bedazzler?"

"No, no, Mother Diana. It is merely a—a—"

"Nom de plume," Wickenshire provided. "Except the poor child has no plume as yet."

"Nicholas!" cried both ladies simultaneously.

"Well, but Bedazzler does *not* have a plume as yet," repeated Wickenshire. "Does not have a nom as yet either. We cannot decide on one. But I am almost positive that every one of us ought to begin calling you Grandmama, Mama. Especially Sera, since she is the one cannot settle on anything else."

"The boy is mad," proclaimed the dowager countess.

"Yes, I do believe he is," Sera agreed. "He has been standing here with his foot on the seat of that chair, fiddling with that silly bit of wood for ten minutes and more."

"Fiddling with . . . ?" The dowager frowned until Wickenshire held up a fat fagot of ash and then she smiled heartily. "Nicky! For Lady Alice?"

"For Lady Alice and Delight and you, madam."

"Oh, no. Not for me, Nicholas. I am much too old."

"Age has nothing to do with it."

"Age has nothing to with what?" asked Sera, looking from one to the other of them. "Will someone please tell me? You cannot both have lost your minds at one and the same time."

"It is merely a stick from an ash tree with bands of green ash tied around it. Nothing more," declared the dowager.

"And this is the ninth band. Finished," Wickenshire said. "Which band will you choose? I have been watching, Mama. You and Sotherland are not so formal as you once were."

"What," asked Sera, "has a stick of ash to do with the Duke of Sotherland? Oh, please tell me."

"It is merely a game, my dear," the dowager replied.

"A game? It is much more than a game, Mama," Wickenshire insisted. "It is a veritable Devon tradition. Works every time. Except, it does not work for gentlemen," Wickenshire informed his wife soberly. "Rotten luck, that. I might have been more confident of winning your love, Sera, did it work for gentlemen and had I burned it the Christmas before we met."

"Every unmarried lady in the family chooses one of the bands of green ash for her own," explained the dowager countess blithely. "Then the fagot is burned on the fire at midnight of Christmas morning."

"And if yours is the first band that catches and bums free of the fagot, Mama, you will be the next in the household to marry," finished Wickenshire for her. "And I do not think either I or Sera have a doubt who it is will marry you."

The dowager countess actually blushed and both Sera and Wickenshire laughed to see it. "What are you sending the Tomlinsons, Mama?" Wickenshire asked, setting the fagot aside.

"Well, there is a military cap for Tim. He does so love to play soldier, Julia says. And a pair of red slippers for Margie, who has been praying to God for them every night for a year. And there is a mechanical frog for Zacharias, a spinning top for Talley, a ruffled cap for Ellen, a toy horse for Anthony and a tiny doll of cloth and yam for baby Emma."

"Mama is in love with baby Emma," observed Wickenshire. "Bedazzler will be forced to be adorable or lose out to the Tomlinsons' youngest."

"Bedazzler will be adorable," Sera assured him sweetly. "I will see to it myself. Have you found a present for Mr. Duncan, Nicholas? Or Mr. Sayers?"

"Sayers? We are having Sayers here for Christmas?"

"Well, I spoke to Mrs. Hadley," Sera responded, "and she said that they did not plan to invite him."

"No, neither did we."

"I know we did not, Nicholas, but Squire and Mrs. Hadley's household is filled to overflowing. They have not a single room unoccupied, Mrs. Hadley says. Family and friends and even a completely unexpected guest. They cannot possibly make room to include Mr. Sayers with so very many. And a gentleman ought not to spend Christmas day alone. You would not like to do so. I sent Hobbs this afternoon with an invitation. I told Mr. Sayers that we would be attending at St. Mary's in Swiftinwhold. Perhaps he will join us there and ride back with us."

"Since we have Mr. Duncan, we may as well have Mr. Sayers," agreed the dowager countess. "And since we have decided to bestow presents on everyone else, we must think of something to give each of those gentlemen as well. It need not be anything truly significant, Nicky. Just a small remembrance of their Christmas at Willowsweep."

Duncan chose to ride slowly, along the tree line, rather than return to the road. The sound of the wind in the trees, the stream burbling merrily along among them and the warmth of the sun shining brightly down upon him lifted his spirits considerably. His anger had evaporated by the time he came upon the ancient barn and noted the horses gathered before it with the little groom sitting on a rock nearby.

"I say," called Duncan, "you are one of Wickenshire's grooms, are you not?"

"Aye," answered the boy, hastily gaining his feet and tugging a forelock.

"Is Wickenshire in the barn?"

"No, sir. Her ladyship be in the barn wif the two gen 'linen."

"Lady Wickenshire?"

"No, sir. The young ladyship, sir."

"Lady Alice?"

"Aye, that be 'er."

"With two gentlemen? Ought you not be inside with her, boy?"

"Oh, no, sir. Said as she would not be awantin' of me. Said as I was ta watch the horses. She be safe, sir. Mr. Spellin' be wif 'er, an' the gen'leman what be livin' at Dwyer Cottage."

Duncan's eyes narrowed in consideration. Lady Alice, Spelling, and the second gentleman would be Sayers. Was he not the one lived at Dwyer Cottage? Yes, indeed he was. The rooster in the sack on his saddle bow crowed and the young groom stared at the sack, astonished.

"Yes, well, it's a rooster in the sack," offered Duncan.

"Your master asked me to fetch him one. I wonder, boy, would you consider carrying it home to Lord Wickenshire for me?"

"Yes, sir," nodded Dick. "But I kinnot go 'til her ladyship be ready, sir."

"No, that will not do at all," mused Duncan aloud. "Lord Wickenshire is waiting upon this fellow even as we speak. What is your name, boy?"

"Dick, sir."

"Well, Dick, I wish to have a word with Lady Alice, but I cannot think it advisable to delay the delivery of this fine fellow in my sack for much longer. If you will ride off to deliver this rooster, Mr. Spelling and I will take your place and escort her ladyship safely back to Willowsweep."

"I be'ant s'posed ta leave her ladyship's side, sir."

"I am quite certain those were your instructions, m'lad. But you have already left her side, have you not?"

"She be safe wif Mr. Spellin', sir. An' I be right here."

"Just so, and she will still be safe with Mr. Spelling and have me to keep her safe as well, Dick. I cannot think that Wickenshire would find it necessary for you to remain since there are now two of us to get her safely home. And I am certain that your master must have this rooster. He will be pleased with you, I think, should you deliver him this bird and advise him that Lady Alice remains in suitable company."

"D'ye think, sir?"

"Indeed, Dick. I can find no fault with it. His lordship merely wished the young lady not to be riding about the countryside alone, eh? She will not be alone. I vow not to allow her to ride off without myself beside her."

The young groom studied the gentleman most seriously. Like Mr. Spelling, this gentleman had come to abide at Willowsweep for the holiday. Apparently, he was then to be trusted. And his lordship *did,* it seemed, be requiring of the rooster. "Right," Dick nodded at last. "I will be atakin' o' the bird. But ye willn't let her ladyship out o' yer sight, will ye, sir? I'd be in thick briars if anythin' happened ta her."

"I will not let her out of my sight, Dick," Duncan assured the boy. "I give you my word on it."

Fifteen

Duncan watched the little groom depart and then entered the barn. From overhead the sound of movement and voices drew his attention at once to the loft. He crossed to the ladder and called up. "Lady Alice? It is I, Mr. Duncan. I must speak to you for a moment."

A clatter of boot heels, a murmur of velvet, and Lady Alice was peering down at him from above. "Mr. Duncan?"

"Can you descend for a moment, your ladyship? His grace has sent me with a word for your ears alone."

"His grace? Well, for goodness sake! Mr. Spelling, I must go down and speak with Mr. Duncan," Alice called back over her shoulder. As Duncan stepped back from the ladder, she descended. "What is it, Mr. Duncan?" she asked as she reached the main floor. "His grace is not ill?"

"May we step outside?" Duncan asked quietly.

"Yes, of course," replied Alice, leading the way. "I cannot think what his grace would—where has Dick gone?" she asked abruptly. "I told him to wait right here and keep watch over the horses. His horse is gone as well."

"I have sent him to await us at the road, Lady Alice. I am ashamed to say it, but I lost one of the fobs Mr. Spelling furnished me as I was riding here to fetch you and Dick is to search for it until we reach him."

"Oh. You came by the road, Mr. Duncan?"

"Most of the way. I hesitate to admit it, but I could not

screw up the courage to come across the pasture after my fall."

"You must not feel badly about that. It was a frightful accident. You merely wish to be careful for a while."

"Just so. At any rate, his grace has requested that we ride into Swiftinwhold this afternoon, Lady Alice. He wishes you to purchase a gift in his name."

"A gift? But we have brought Christmas gifts for everyone. Well, except for yourself, for we were not expecting to find you here. But he did discover something he wishes to present to you. What can his grace be thinking?"

"He thinks of Mr. Sayers, Lady Alice. Lord Wickenshire intends to invite that gentleman to join us on Christmas day."

"He does? Yes, I expect he would. He would feel obliged to invite Mr. Sayers to join us if it has reached his ears that Mr. Sayers might spend Christmas day alone."

"Just so. Wickenshire's thoughtfulness and generosity are incomparable. This I say having experienced the benefit of both. His grace says that he has a gift for me— I cannot think what, or even that I am deserving of one just for falling off my horse like some fool. But he frets over Mr. Sayers and wishes you will hurry to his aid. And I must have your advice on my own purchases, for I shall not be content to merely sit and receive gifts, you know. I have money to purchase gifts of my own."

"Well then, I shall be of aid to you and his grace both," replied Alice with a determined nod. "Will you help me into the saddle, Mr. Duncan?"

"Indeed. And then I will step inside and advise Mr. Spelling that we are off on an errand, eh? So he will not fret over our disappearance?" With the sureness born of years of helping his sister into the saddle, Duncan saw Alice settled and then strolled back into the barn. He climbed the ladder and stuck head and shoulders up through the entrance to the loft. "Spelling, Sayers, Lady Alice and Dick and I are off to Willowsweep. There is a surprise to be prepared. You are to keep on about your business here until you have finished, eh?"

"A surprise?" asked Spelling.

"Just so, and you are not to know of it as yet. Carry on, gentlemen," he said, smiling, and then he descended the ladder.

And just as quickly and easily as that, Duncan thought to himself, a gentleman may abduct a lady from hearth and home.

"Is it not a beautiful day, Mr. Duncan?" Lady Alice asked as she rode companionably beside him. "I do never remember a December as lovely as this. Of course, I have never before spent a December in Devon. Perhaps it is the place that influences the weather? The place and the company."

"The company, Lady Alice?"

"Oh, yes. The people with whom one spends the holidays make every difference. We could be in the midst of a regular blizzard, Mr. Duncan, and still I would discover it to be a very fine day. You will think me a complete innocent, but I did never before realize how great a difference the company makes to the holiday. Christmas has always been a rather dreary and indifferent celebration in my life. Well, but there was only Grandmama to share it with and though she did her best to make it enjoyable, she was never a jolly sort of woman. I have always thought that, despite my presence, Grandmama could not be fond of any holidays. I cannot think why."

"Perhaps she found them lonely?"

"I do not think so. Grandmama had other family. If she had been lonely, would not she have invited some of them to join us? Or would we not have gone to join them? You will find this remarkable, Mr. Duncan, but I have never met any of my grandmother's family or my grandfather's either.

I did not so much as know my own father until a few months ago."

"I do find that remarkable. I cannot think why she should keep you apart from u—all of them."

"No, and neither can I. She is a madwoman, his grace says, and though I did never think so before, I fear he may be correct. At any rate, I find Christmas is much more enjoyable than I ever thought it could be, and all because of the people gathered here at Willowsweep, yourself included."

"Myself included?" asked Duncan in surprise.

"Oh, yes! Since you have ceased to praise my nonexistent beauty, I am most delighted with you. You are the very best at all the games we play after dinner, you know, and you have a wicked sense of humor."

"I do?"

"Indeed. I cannot help but feel a great sympathy for your family, Mr. Duncan, and for the particular young lady who certainly must love you, to have lost you so suddenly and completely and at Christmastime as well. But you must not worry. Your memory will return. And if it does not, we will search until we discover where you belong."

"We will?"

"Oh, yes. His grace and Lord Wickenshire have determined to do so. Even Mr. Spelling has promised to lend his aid to the cause." She smiled the most wonderful smile at him. "Mr. Spelling has relented toward you a great deal, I think. He was growing quite jealous of you, you know. He feared your intention was to win my heart."

"Your heart is not to be won, I think," Duncan replied softly. "It is already set on its true course. A course not to be altered."

"You are correct, Mr. Duncan. I did think, at first, that alteration of my course might be possible. We have not known each other for so very long, Mr. Spelling and I. And though he was most kind and considerate of me when first we met, he is not the most noble of all gentlemen. He has several . . . eccentricities that might well discourage a properly raised young woman—a woman who wishes more from a gentleman than his money and a bit of attention now and then—I mean—a woman with definite ideas of what is acceptable and what is not and expects those dearest to her to live up to such principles as she knows exist."

"And Mr. Spelling?"

"Is not accustomed to—living by certain principles."

"But there is something in him calls to you nonetheless?"

"Precisely. There is a gentleness, a vulnerability and a particular sensibility. I find I cannot help but love him. And he is sincerely attempting to change the way in which he sees the world, Mr. Duncan. And the way in which he reacts to it. I see him making that attempt day by day for my sake."

"You do?" asked Duncan. "Can it be done, do you think? Can a gentleman change his outlook and his attitudes? Can a man overcome his faults for the love of a woman?"

"Yes, I do believe so, as long as it is *his* idea to do it. And I believe that a gentleman can change for other reasons as well—for himself, his own well-being; for the hope of a better and more pleasant life with the ones he loves. We are not helpless creatures, Mr. Duncan, like leaves buffeted about by the wind. We have the ability to pick and choose. To make our own decisions and form our own lives to an enormous extent."

"Perhaps, but life is not always kind nor the choices easy," mused Duncan, as they approached the road.

"True," Alice agreed. "One must only look to his grace to know that. You do not realize to see him now, but my father sacrificed his own happiness and his family as well on behalf of my mother and grandmother. It was a dreadful choice for him to make, and I think he chose wrongly. But even so, he has got all of his children back once again and has begun to take his life in a very different direction. He is such an altered gentleman."

"He is?"

"Oh, I know he seems a grumpy-grouch to you and to most people, but to hear Edward and others speak of what he once was—well, he is so very much more gentle and happy and satisfied with life. Mr. Duncan? I do not see Dick at the side of the road. You do not think that something has happened to him?" Alice asked, bringing her mount to a complete halt.

"No, no, nothing has happened to the boy," Duncan responded, stopping his own horse beside hers, his tawny eyes seeking her own blue ones. "Speak truly to me, Lady Alice. Is there hope that a gentleman may change his own life from one of loneliness and sorrow and anger into a life like that of Lord Wickenshire's, say? A young man? Not one so old as your father?"

"There is always hope for love and happiness, Mr. Duncan," Alice replied, an enormous sympathy for that gentleman rising up within her. "You are remembering at last, are you not? And what you remember is not pleasant, I think. I am so very sorry. Is there anything at all that I can do to help you?"

Duncan could not think what to say. They were at the road. Here it was that he had intended to overpower this slight girl and force her to accompany him to the cottage in Lydepool. The opportunity had come so abruptly and yet so effortlessly that it had appeared to him to be fated. And yet—and yet—

"Mr. Duncan? Are you not well? You look so discomforted of a sudden. Are you in pain? Is it your ankle or your wrist? Oh, where is Dick? Dick! Dick! Do come at once! Mr. Duncan is in pain and needs our help!"

"Do not call for him," Duncan murmured, reaching across to touch the hand with which Alice held to her saddle bow. "Dick is not here. The boy is at Willowsweep by now."

"At Willowsweep? But you said he was to meet us here at the road, Mr. Duncan."

"I lied, Lady Alice. I have been lying to you and to everyone else from the moment you found me upon the ground in Wickenshire's pasture."

"Well, where is she?" bellowed the Duke of Sotherland, stomping out of the stables as Spelling dismounted in the yard. "Do not look at me as if you are deaf and dumb, you dunderhead. My Alice rode out to that wretched barn to speak with you not an hour ago and Duncan sent word back that you and he would escort her home. How dare you return without her. Without either of them. Spelling! What have you done with my daughter?"

"D-done? With Lady Alice? Not a thing," replied Spelling, squaring his trembling shoulders and turning to face the duke. "You have forgotten, your grace. She has gone off on the errand you set her, with Duncan and Dick, just as you requested."

"Just as I requested? I requested nothing!"

Spelling's heart began to quake the merest bit. When he spied Dick peering out from around the stable door, his poor heart came near to shaking itself to death. "What the devil are you doing here, Dick? You did not let Duncan take her off alone? You were to accompany him and Lady Alice."

"N-no, sir. You was ta 'company 'em. I was ta bring the rooster home."

"Good gawd," whispered Spelling. "Duncan and Lady Alice have gone off together alone."

"Never!" bellowed the duke. "My Alice would never ride anywhere in the company of a gentleman with no groom to stand propriety for her. Never! I knew there was something havey-cavey going on. I knew it the moment this boy appeared toting that damnable rooster!"

"S-something havey-cavey? Havey-cavey? You do not for one moment think that Alice has—that she has—run off with Duncan?" Spelling could not bear the thought of it. He came close to sitting right down upon the ground. But he did not. He stood taller instead. As tall as he possibly could. "Balderdash! She would never do such a thing as that," he declared with certainty. "Something has happened to them. They are lost, or there has been an accident. She would not run off with Duncan, not my Alice."

"She is not your Alice!" howled the duke. "She is *my* Alice!"

"Hush," demanded a most feminine voice as the dowager Lady Wickenshire strolled meaningfully into the stableyard. "Nathaniel, do control yourself," she urged, walking directly up to the duke and seizing his arm with both hands. "You are terrifying everyone within hearing distance. What is it that has happened? Tell me slowly and quietly, my dear."

"Lady Alice is missing," offered Spelling when the duke appeared unable to respond at once. "She and Duncan both. I shall ride out immediately to search for them."

"No, do not go, Spelling," Sotherland managed as Spelling swung back up into the saddle. "Do not go alone, at any rate. Duncan was to bring the rooster here, but sent this boy home with it instead. Then he lied to you about my sending a message to Alice. All to get Alice alone, I think. No telling what lies he told her to get her to accompany him. It is some devious plot."

"You are correct there," nodded Spelling, who had evolved more than his share of devious plots in his lifetime. "And for that reason alone, the sooner it is ended the better. What is it you imagine Duncan to be about, your grace?"

"I fear he has abducted my daughter," responded the duke. "And if he has, that particular dastard will not live to see another dawn! Dick, saddle the fastest horse Wickenshire owns for me. Lady Wickenshire—Diana, my dear—

you must release my arm, eh? Alice will be terribly frightened by now. Spelling and I must discover her whereabouts as quick as quick can."

"But why?" asked the dowager, nibbling worriedly at her lower lip. "Nathaniel, why would a complete stranger abduct Alice? It makes not a bit of sense."

"She is the daughter of a duke, Aunt Diana," Spelling offered. "Likely the blackguard means to hold her to ransom. But he will not have that opportunity. I will black both his eyes for him and draw his cork as well before he has time to turn around."

"And if he has a pistol, Neil?" asked Wickenshire, having overheard the last of the conversation as he was dashing to them across the stable yard. "If Duncan has a pistol, what then?"

"Then he will shoot me, but not before Alice is safely in her father's arms," Spelling declared. "I will see she is safely with his grace before I die. I vow it."

"Oh, dear," said the dowager softly.

"What, Mama? What is it?" Wickenshire asked. "If you will wait a moment, gentlemen, I will send for my pistols and join you in the hunt. It is my home from which the miscreant had the nerve to take her."

"Nicky, do not send for your pistols," the dowager said.

"I must, Mama. If Duncan has armed himself, we dare not go up against him with mere fists."

"No, it is not that, dear boy."

"What is not that, Mama?"

"Aunt Diana, we are taking much too long with this discussion as it is," declared Spelling. "The longer we wait, the farther away that wretch will have time to take her."

"No, no, the closer he will bring her, Neil."

"The closer— What the deuce are you saying, Aunt Diana?"

"Only look over there. Coming around the paddock."

"Well, by gawd!" exclaimed Sotherland. "Alice!" he bellowed, setting every nerve in every person within hearing distance to shuddering. "Alice, are you all right, my dear? Come straight to me, no matter what that jackanapes says or what he threatens. He will not dare to harm you in my presence. Ride straight to me, gel, like the brave young woman you are. And you, Duncan, do not you advance any farther or I will shoot you from your saddle."

"Cannot do that," advised Spelling. "Have not got a pistol among us."

"Yes, but he does not know it," growled the duke. "He does not know it."

"No, your grace, do not shoot him!" cried Alice as loudly as she could. "You do not understand at all what has happened. You must give Mr. Ducane the opportunity to explain."

"Mr. Ducane?" asked Spelling, his eyes widening considerably. "Nicky, did Alice say Mr. Ducane?"

Sixteen

"Ought to have sent Ducane packing," sighed Wickenshire as Sera went to help him tie his neckcloth. "I cannot think why I did not. A regular serpent in our midst."

"Oh, Nicholas, Mr. Ducane is not a serpent. It was despicable of him to come here under false pretenses and to think to abduct Alice, I know, but were he a true serpent, he *would* have abducted Alice, not accompanied her straight back to us."

"I know, but it does seem as though I ought to do something to—to show my distaste for his intentions at the least."

"You did. You and the duke both. The two of you gave him such a dressing down that I doubt the poor gentleman's ears will cease burning for months. Dearest, do not wiggle about so. I am almost done."

"Why must Lady Vermont set Ducane upon us at this time of the year? Can she not allow Alice to have even one Christmas with her father?"

"I expect she is bitter and jealous and lonely, Nicholas."

"And mad. Sotherland claims she is mad as a hatter."

"Likely so. Your mama says that she has always suspected there were a few cracked cups in Lady Vermont's cupboard. Lady Vermont and your Uncle Ezra grew up together, you know."

"No, I did not know."

"Yes. And your mama says that Lady Vermont and Ezra have always been the very best of friends."

"Lady Vermont and Uncle Ezra?"

"Um-hmmm. And you know what that means."

"That Lady Vermont must be a lunatic because Uncle Ezra is the most demented person in all of England. Not that a reasonably sane person cannot be fond of Uncle Ezra most of the time, because any number of us are, but to be his very best friend—"

"Precisely, Nicholas. There, you are quite presentable. Do smile, Nicky. It will prove a most distasteful dinner if you, the duke, Neil and Mr. Ducane are all sullen. Oh! Oh, my!" exclaimed Sera, one hand going suddenly to her stomach.

"Sera, what is it?"

"Oh, Nicholas, Bedazzler is most upset, I think. He is kicking me something fierce and I am having such a pain!"

With a worried frown, Wickenshire scooped Sera up into his arms, carried her into the sitting room and set her down upon the old fainting couch. "Perhaps you ought not go down to dinner. Perhaps you ought to remain here and I will have a tray sent up."

"No, no, he is growing calmer now, and the pain is lessening. I cannot think why he should start to fuss so. He is a puzzlement, your heir."

"She is hoping to make an appearance soon."

"No, he is not. He is not due to present himself until mid-January at the very earliest. That is what Mrs. Parkins said."

"Midwives have been wrong before. We ought to have a physician here with us, Sera. A physician or a surgeon. Someone who knows more than Mrs. Parkins."

"You know very well there is none such to be had anywhere about. And Mrs. Parkins is most dependable and merely a quarter-hour away. She has birthed hundreds of babies, Nicholas. And she is pleasant and confident and I trust her."

"Just so," nodded Wickenshire. "You trust her."

"Yes, I do. And Bedazzler trusts her as well. It is nothing, Nicholas. We are fine now. Perhaps he did not like to stand still for as long as it takes to tie your neckcloth."

Wickenshire studied his young wife seriously and then smiled. "Perhaps so," he agreed. "I do not like to stand still for as long as it takes to tie my neckcloth either."

Spelling sat upon the love seat beside Alice and held tightly, but inconspicuously, to her hand once the gentlemen had joined the ladies in the Gold Saloon after dinner. Wickenshire and Sera shared a sopha; the dowager took up residence in the lyre-backed chair; Sotherland stretched his long legs out before him as he settled into the armchair before the fire. Only Ducane did not sit. Ducane paced uneasily around the room. He looked up and his tawny eyes caught at Alice's sympathetic blue ones. He lowered his head. He looked up again and discovered Neil glaring at him. He spun on his heel and paced the other way. When he paced back again, he lowered himself to the very edge of the seat of a ladder-backed chair. With arms resting on his thighs, his hands clasped tightly between his knees, he took a deep breath and then another. "I really ought to leave first thing in the morning," he said softly. "I do not belong in this house. Never have."

"Well, perhaps you did not belong at first, young man," the dowager replied, "but now you do, I think."

"No. It is only because you are kind that you ask me to remain. And such kindness is—well, it is beyond my comprehension. I have never—no one has ever— I have made my way in life by pretending to be hard, clever and evil. Those are the things I understand."

"You said that to me when we were riding back to Willowsweep, Mr. Ducane," Lady Alice replied, her thumb playing across the back of Spelling's hand. "What I do not understand is why you thought you must pretend to be so."

"Because I could not have survived in my household without such pretensions," Ducane answered softly. "At least, I thought I could not. It is all very complicated and—"

"And all merely an excuse for behaving badly," inserted the duke testily.

"Yes, I expect you are correct," Ducane sighed. "I cannot say how sorry I am, Lady Alice, for what I almost did. There are not enough words in the entire language to excuse me. I was a fool. I have been a fool for most of my years. But this—this is the most foolish I have ever been. And Wickenshire, I cannot think how you bear to look at me after all the advantage I have taken of your good nature. I—I ought to be taken out and—"

"Scuttle the blackguard!" provided Lord Nightingale loudly from his place on his cage at the far end of the room.

"Yes," Ducane agreed, a vague, haunted expression rising to his handsome face. "Just so, Lord Nightingale. Truly, you are a seer of the soul."

"Balderdash," muttered Sotherland. "He is a scurvy pirate of a bird and nothing more."

"Ol' FatherChris missIbe," Nightingale reminded the duke forcefully. "Cometashare yer piepiepie withye!"

"Yes, but you are not Father Christmas at the moment, old fellow," Sotherland replied. "At the moment you are nothing more than what you were born to be."

"And I am nothing more than I was born to be either," said Ducane softly. "Merely a second son with no prospects. Once word gets 'round that I have turned coward and failed Lady Vermont, I shall have lost all hope of any sort of future at all. Alan will laugh in my face and propose to send me off to foreign shores to outlive my disgrace and

Helena will stick her nose into the air and never mention my name again."

"Your disgrace?" asked Sera in surprise. "Why, Mr. Duncan, I should think to have done what you set out to do would have been the disgrace."

"No, no, the puppy is right," interjected Sotherland. "When one builds a reputation as a cruel, evil villain and then fails in such a simple task as Alice's grandmama set him, there are some will see it as a disgrace. I ought to know. I have spent years as the Devil Incarnate, after all. And now look at me. Look at me, Ducane," he demanded, gruffly. "What do you see?"

"A contented gentleman sitting before the fire."

"Just so. Am I wallowing in disgrace at having been proved a fraud? No, I am not. I do not choose to see it in that way at all. Rather, I am enjoying the lack of a considerable weight that I once carried upon my shoulders."

"A considerable chip that he once carried upon his shoulder," the dowager restated. "In this house, you have been forgiven, Mr. Ducane, if not thoroughly understood. Can you not accept that? In this house, we are none of us perfect—except, perhaps, for my pending grandchild."

"Do not believe her, Ducane," said Spelling. "In this house, everyone is perfect except me. I do not know how I shall ever forgive you."

"Neil!" cried Alice in a tiny voice.

"Well, it is true. I do not understand how all of you can forgive him. I should still like to beat him black and blue with my bare fists."

"Neil, do not say so!"

"It is merely that— I do not understand how to forgive him, Alice! I am willing to make the attempt, but I do not know how to go about it. I have always assumed that to forgive people must be the simplest thing in the world. But it is the most difficult thing I have ever attempted. I cannot understand now how Nicky ever forgave me one-tenth of the things I did to him. But as for your sister, Ducane," he added, glancing up to meet Ducane's interested gaze. "I should not give a fig for what she thought of me. And if your brother is at all like her—well, then I should be happy to be shed of him as well."

"You know Helena?" asked Ducane.

"She does not pretend to be evil. She *is* evil. Your sister, Ducane, is a harridan of outrageous proportions. I find it a testament to you that she did not succeed in murdering you while you were still a babe in the cradle."

"You *do* know Helena."

"She promised to tell you that I had seduced her, compromised her and then abandoned her. Promised me that you would call me out and shoot me dead. I believed her, too. Your reputation is such that I dare not disbelieve her."

"My reputation is sadly lacking in fact," Ducane provided, his lips twitching upward.

"Five men you killed on her behalf. I have heard it said any number of times in any number of drawing rooms."

"Five? And all for Helena? I would not go out of my way to tap a gentleman on the shoulder for Helena. And she knows very well that were she to come crying to me with such a Canterbury Tale as your seduction of her, that I would be much more inclined to believe the opposite. Helena has been attempting to compromise her way into a title for years. You must be incredibly rich for her to lower her sights and decide to settle for your fortune, Spelling, without so much as a Sir before your name."

"Perhaps she saw something in Mr. Spelling beyond riches," Lady Alice whispered. "Perhaps she discovered the possibilities that lay deep within him."

"No," Ducane replied. "You, my lady, are the sort to unearth and to treasure hidden possibilities, but Helena treasures only power, position and great prosperity."

* * *

It was quite late and the entire household bound for bed when Lady Alice donned her sable-lined cloak and walked out into Willowsweep's winter-ravaged garden. She shivered as a biting wind touched her cheeks. She tugged her cloak closer around her as she paused on the garden path and gazed upward at the clouds stroking across a glowing moon. "I wish," she whispered to the moon. "I do so wish."

"What do you wish, my dear?" queried a deep voice from the shadows of the elm near the kitchen door.

"Your grace?" Lady Alice turned, peering into the darkness.

"Here," he said, strolling toward her. "I did not feel much like sleeping. Thought that perhaps a breath of air— What brings you outside, my dear? That lovely moon? Your mama used to love the moonlight when she was young. It is one of the few pleasant things I remember about her. Do you love it as well?"

"Yes, I fear I do. I can rarely resist such a moon as that."

"Just so," nodded Sotherland. "And what is it that you wish, Alice?" he asked as he paused beside her.

"Nothing. It is nothing."

"Rubbish! Of course you wish for something or you would not say the words so plaintively. Are you unhappy, Alice? Do you wish that Ducane *had* taken you to your grandmama?" he asked, turning his gaze from her as though he could not bear to hear her answer.

"No, I do not. For her to go so far as to hire Mr. Ducane to kidnap me! And she told him to take me over your dead body if necessary. He did not tell you that, but he told me and I was thoroughly appalled by it. She is mad, Grandmama, just as you said. But even if she had not done this outrageous thing, I would still wish to be here with you, Papa," Alice replied, and then she felt her cheeks flame.

Sotherland's gaze returned to her on the instant. "It was a mistake, I assume," muttered the duke, studying Alice's face in the moonlight. "A mere slip of the tongue."

"No," Alice replied thoughtfully. "No, it was not, Papa."

"There you have said it again."

"Indeed. You are my papa, are you not? I admit that I did not know at all what to think of you at first. Grandmama had filled my head with such tales of the demonic Duke of Sotherland, that to meet you was very much like meeting a hobgoblin. And then, to discover that you were truly my father! But all that Grandmama told me of you is the stuff of nonsense. I know that now and I have come to—to love you."

"Me? You have come to love me, Alice?"

"Yes, and come to recognize that Grandmama is your cruelest enemy. I cannot walk about forever with my eyes closed and my brainbox stuffed with rags. As much as I long to understand Grandmama and to help her arise from the demented world in which she lives, I cannot doubt that she has been your most formidable enemy from the very day that I was born."

"For longer than that; from the day I married your mother."

"For so very long? Oh, Papa! And what a cruel enemy she has been—to never mention your name to me at all, to pretend that my father was some shadow of a Mr. Daily. If Edward had not come to see me—"

"I sent Edward to see you. I have watched you many times, m'dear, from afar. I knew Edward could not deny you once he took note of the family resemblance. I trusted, should anything happen to me, that Edward would look to your welfare."

"It was Edward forced Grandmama to admit that my father was not this Mr. Daily. It was he who forced her to say that my father was the Duke of Sotherland."

"And still she continued to lie—to you and to Edward both. She lies to this day."

"Yes, but she cannot help herself, I think. Grandmama is a sad and pitiable person. She has made you into the

Devil Incarnate in her mind. All the tarradiddles she created about you and Mama over the years, she has come to believe."

"Just so. She was willing to struggle to the death for you when you were born. Her death, your mama's death, my death, it seemed not to matter. And so, to save us all, I gave you to her."

Alice nodded sadly. It was all so very new to her, this truth of her birth, the travesty of lies that had been her upbringing.

"But I did not force myself upon your mama, Alice. Never. Nor did your mama take her own life. Well, Peter told you that. Your mama became as mad as your grandmama over time, but we were man and wife, Alice. Man and wife."

Alice could not bring herself to reply. For eighteen years she had thought her mama and papa dead, Lady Vermont her only living relative. Her heart cried out now against the madness and villainy that had ripped apart the Duke of Sotherland's family and left her without knowledge of her mother, her brothers or this man who was her father.

"I *am* the Devil Incarnate," murmured the duke in the face of her silence. "I have destroyed every life I have ever touched. I ought to hide away at Northridge forever, not come jaunting down to Devon to spend Christmas with my recent in-laws. They are quite nice in-laws, not deserving of the likes of mw."

"Balderdash, Papa," Alice said in the most gentle of tones, raising her hand to brush a dark curl back from his brow. "You have made mistakes, but mistakes do not make you evil. As you forgave Mr. Ducane, you must forgive yourself. No one chooses correctly all the time."

"Still, we are responsible for our choices."

"I know, Papa. But Edward forgave you all; Peter forgave you; and now, I forgive you for whatever you think you have done to me. Does not that help to set your mind at ease?"

The Duke of Sotherland took his daughter's hand shyly into his own and holding it tightly, stared up at the sky. "What were you wishing for, Alice?" he asked softly, his voice husky with unshed tears. "Only tell me what it is, and if it is within my power, I will give it to you."

"I wish to marry Mr. Spelling, Papa, if he should ever gather the courage to ask, and to have your blessing when I do."

"But you could do so very much better, my dear. There are any number of gentlemen would long to have you to wife once you make your curtsy. Good men, too. Spelling has a strong touch of the scoundrel in him. He is a dunderhead to boot."

"I know, Papa. He is proud and selfish as well. But I love him. I love the touch of scoundrel in him. I love the bit of him that is dunderheaded, too. And pride can be a very good thing if one simply points it in the proper direction."

"And selfishness, Alice?"

"He has never learned to think of others first. But already he attempts to do better. Can you not see it in him, Papa? See how he tries? And he will do better. I have every confidence in him. And he does love me, Papa. I know that. His eyes glow with love for me, just as they overflow with grief when he thinks he has disappointed me. Oh, Papa, I love Mr. Neil Spelling with all my heart."

The Duke of Sotherland took his daughter into his arms beneath the light of the moon and held her there, silently, tenderly. The sheer presence of her seemed to fill a great void within him. "I have allowed my heir to marry a plain miss and Peter to marry a parson's daughter," he whispered in her ear. "And if it is truly your wish to marry a dunderheaded scoundrel, I will not stand against you, Alice. You shall have Spelling with my blessing."

"Oh, Papa!"

"But does he harm you or bring you to the edge of disaster with some scheme of his, I will chop off his ears and have them with eggs for my breakfast and I will tell him precisely that when he comes to me to apply for your hand."

Seventeen

The day before Christmas at Willowsweep proved to be a busy, giggly and secretive day. Everywhere hushed voices discussed what was to be done and how and by whom. Bits of colored paper and bright ribands traveled to this room and that. All the gentlemen of the household, at one time or another, found it necessary to ride off to have a look at the sheep or to see if Harold, Willowsweep's sole ram, was safe, or to check on Mr. Sayers, and when they returned, one after the other, they made their ways immediately to their own chambers with pockets or arms full of packages and without so much as a word to anyone. In the kitchen, Cook, Cook's helper, the scullery maid, Maryrose, Becky and Jem appeared and disappeared and appeared again. They trudged to the icehouse, hurried to the cellars, scurried down to the well house and back up to the main house. The footmen and the maids, like Mr. Jenkins, were everywhere and nowhere all at one and the same time. Even Jackie, the fireboy, could not be found for an entire quarter-hour and when asked where he had been, he could not say, explaining that he must have hit his head just like that Mr. Ducane fellow.

In the stables, horses were being combed and brushed, their tails and manes braided so that in the morning there would be lush curls. The new tack was lovingly rubbed and polished and combined with the always exquisite tack of the Duke of Sotherland. Excited voices discussed the dawning of the next day and the elegance of an eight-horse hitch. Those who had witnessed Sotherland's practice sessions with precisely that hitch could not keep from exclaiming at the prowess and power that such an elderly gentleman possessed. The duke's own coachman could not help but glow at the honorable phrases bestowed on his master by the grooms and stableboys. "A reg'lar Jehu he is," he agreed time and time again, his chest puffed out with pride. "Could drive the mail blindfolded and with one hand tied b'hind his back."

It was no great wonder then that the arrival of a smallish traveling coach in the front drive, which halted merely a moment or two, then followed the curve around and drove back toward the road, went quite unnoticed by those who ought to have been at their posts but were not. Nor was it frightfully odd that a tiny woman should find it possible to walk around to the kitchen door and slip inside, purloin one of the lanterns used to travel down to the stable by night and scurry unobtrusively around a corner and into the old passageways.

Everyone at Willowsweep was so thoroughly preoccupied, in fact, that even when the tiny woman stepped out of the passageways for a moment and into the Gold Saloon to gain some idea of where in the house she was, only Lord Nightingale took note of her. Most curious as to whom this new addition to his household might be, Nightingale took flight and landed at her feet. "Scat," she adjured him grumpily and stepped back through the hidden door in the paneling. She did not once look down to see Lord Nightingale shuffle hurriedly in behind her.

Late that very afternoon, Carson was most contentedly polishing his master's shoes over a large cloth spread atop the carpet in Spelling's little sitting room. He was rejoicing in the quiet he had at last obtained. The staff at Willowsweep was not so very large, but they never spoke, it seemed, below a bellow. And they always spoke. Did two of the Willowsweep staff come together, no matter where, conversation ensued. And apparently, the mere thought of Christmas Day tomorrow had made them giddy besides. Not until Mr. Jenkins had taken pity on him and suggested that he might do better to polish Mr. Spelling's shoes upstairs in Mr. Spelling's sitting room, provided he was careful of the carpet, did Carson ever think to be alone and cozy with his own thoughts again.

"I will present Mr. Jenkins with the extra bottle of scent I have brought along," Carson murmured to himself. "Indeed. That is precisely what I will do. I shall say it is a Christmas gift and bestow it on him tomorrow morning."

"Mornin'," responded a voice from beyond the wall.

Carson ceased to polish for a moment and listened closely. Had he actually heard someone speak? No, of course he had not. That was absurd. On this most peculiar day, not even the upstairs maids were about.

"I have been spoke to so much for so long that my ears are still hearing words from the day before yesterday," he told himself. And then he heard the most hideous mutterings, as if a madman had come up behind him. The shoe in Carson's hand thumped to the floor. A flurry of movement answered the thump, followed by a sinister gasping and shuddering at Carson's back. Very slowly, attempting to move as few muscles as humanly possible in the process, the little valet set his blacking down upon the floor. "Who—who is th-there?" he queried as the hairs at the back of his neck prickled. "Mr. Sp-Spelling? Is it you, s-sir? Do not be p-playing games with me if you p-please."

"Ol'Father Chrissssssmiss Ibe," replied the voice.

"No, no you do not!" Carson exclaimed, leaping up from his chair, perspiration drenching the back of his neck as he turned to stare at the wall behind him.

"FatherChrisssmiss," the voice repeated.

"The W-Witch of W-Willowsweep," Carson whimpered and began to back slowly toward the door.

"Halt!" commanded the voice loudly.

Carson halted on the spot.

"Scuttle the blackguard. Hangemfrom t'yardarm. Pirates!"

"Oh, oh my gawd!" Carson gasped.

"Villain! Rapscallion! Son of a seawitch!"

With one hand clinging to the doorlatch, Carson took three very deep breaths. "Villain?" he whispered. "Pirates? Son of a— L-Lord Nightingale? Is it you?"

A flurry of flutters, scratchings and tappings answered Carson's brave sally.

"You are n-not h-her pretending to be you?" asked Carson, attempting to get his fingers to let go of the latch.

"Herewecomea was ailiiiing amongtheleaves so greeeeen."

"It is you," sighed Carson. "Somehow you have got into the wall. Be easy, my lord. I will rescue you. You will not bite, will you, my lord? I should not like to be bitten. Now, exactly where is the door that leads into the passage? Do not be frightened, Lord Nightingale. I am coming."

His meager courage summoned and wrapped securely around him, Carson located the door and pushed it open. Lord Nightingale, his feathers ruffled, his tail spread wide in agitation, scuttled right over the toes of Carson's shoes and into the room. For the length of the wiggle of a cat's whisker, Carson heard the whisper of long skirts and saw a flicker of light above him in the passageway. A bit of material disappeared up the highest of the steps. His heart came near to stopping. But then there was nothing. No light, no sound but Lord Nightingale fluttering his wings, and Carson scolded himself for possessing a too-active imagination. "There is no Witch of Willowsweep," he said aloud.

"There are no such things as witches." Hastily, he stepped back into the sitting room and the door closed behind him.

Very late that same evening, after a quiet dinner, the Wickenshires settled down with their guests in the winter parlor. The wassail bowl appeared; the approaching Christmas Day was toasted; and a number of letters to Father Christmas were burned in the fire on the hearth. "Now, where the deuce has Sotherland got to?" asked Wickenshire as he sipped at his wassail. "He was here a moment ago."

"Yes, and Delight has wandered off as well," acknowledged Sera, her eyes glowing with love for her handsome husband. "There is definitely something afoot with Delight and Jenkins, Nicholas, and the duke is now involved in it."

"My!" exclaimed the dowager from her place beside the hearth. "Did you hear that? What on earth could make such a scraping, thumping sound as that inside our wail?"

"And how do there come to be footsteps in there?" asked Alice, laughing softly as she sat comfortably beside Spelling on the settee.

"Faeries," offered Wickenshire nonchalantly, stretching his long legs out toward the fire.

"Uh-oh, they have dropped something else," Spelling observed, his eyes lit with good humor. "Clumsy faeries. An entire battalion of them. Why do you look so perplexed, Ducane? Do you not have faeries in your walls at home?"

"I am certain he has not," smiled Sera. "Ours is an odd household, Mr. Ducane. We do not actually have witches, of course, but we do have faery passages. And it does sound as if every faery in Devon is in there at the moment. On their way to the Gold Saloon, I should think."

"Ah, so that is why the doors to the Gold Saloon have been closed to us and we are forced to use the winter parlor. The faeries are busy in the saloon," Wickenshire said.

"Speaking of faeries and things," Spelling ventured. "Do

you still have that frightful purple cloak that you wore to the opera when Eugenia made her curtsy, Aunt Diana? Is it here at Willowsweep, perhaps?"

"At the very rear of my armoire, Neil," the dowager replied. "I am attempting to forget that I ever purchased the horrid thing, much less wore it in public."

"Might I have it, do you think?"

"Have it? Neil, you certainly do not intend to wear—"

"No," interrupted Spelling hastily. "It is—it has to do with Christmas and since you despise the thing—you would not mind, Aunt Diana, if I were to—to—cut a piece or two of the sable lining out?"

"You may snip away at it all you like, Neil. Though why you should wish to do so, I cannot think."

"Like the noises in the wall, it has something to do with faeries," Spelling replied. "Two rather small but perfectly charming faeries. Will you have some more wassail, Lady Alice?" he asked. "It only appears once a year, you know."

Alice nodded and watched him as he carried her cup off to the bowl to refill it. "Not quite a full cup, if you please," she said, standing and crossing the room to come to a halt beside him. "Thank you." She took the cup from his hands, gazing up at him, her fine blue eyes alight with unspoken love for him. "You will accompany us to services tomorrow, Mr. Spelling?"

"Indeed. Are you happy tonight, Alice? You are no longer worried about—anything?"

"I have never been as happy as this. This is the nicest Christmas of my entire life. If ever I should marry, I will see my house filled with my family and friends at this time of the year, just as Sera has done."

"You will?"

"I will. Or if it cannot be, then I and my husband will travel to Papa at Northridge or to one of my brothers' houses. But we will not spend our Christmases alone."

"You do not think it would prove romantic to spend the

holiday with only the man you love just as your brothers and new sisters-in-law must be doing now on their wedding trips?"

"Another holiday, perhaps, but not Christmas. Can you not see, Mr. Spelling, how it is here at Willowsweep? Oh, surely, Christmas is intended to be a celebration of families and for families. And I have gained such a large and merry family in the past few months."

"You have," nodded Spelling. "Do you know, you are not at all the same Miss Daily I met in Kent."

"I am not?"

"No. When first we met, I thought you beautiful and interesting and quite the finest young woman—"

"You thought me beautiful?" interrupted Alice, her eyes wide. "You thought me beautiful?"

"Yes. The most beautiful woman I had ever seen."

"Oh, my. Let me look into your eyes, Mr. Spelling. Is there a glaze upon them?" She set her wassail aside and put her hands on his cheeks and stared directly into his eyes.

"What do you see?" Spelling asked softly.

Alice's lips parted in wonder. "I see myself," she whispered, "and I am—"

"Beautiful," breathed Spelling.

"Have you got the toothache, Cousin Neil?" cried Delight excitedly, poised on the parlor threshold like a little sparrow frozen in flight. "Oh please, do not have the toothache. It will ruin everything."

"I doubt he has got the toothache, m'dear," the Duke of Sotherland replied. Lord Nightingale sat contentedly on the duke's shoulder as Sotherland stood, frowning, behind Delight, his hands resting upon the child's shoulders. "My Alice's hands do not touch his cheeks in such a manner for that particular reason, I think."

All eyes thus directed toward the two at the wassail bowl, Alice's hands left Spelling's cheeks immediately to hide behind her back and she blushed prettily while the crystal cup in Spelling's hand came near to losing its wassail over one side.

"We have broughted everything, Nicky," announced Delight proudly, turning her attention to her brother-in-law. "Is it midnight yet? It is ever so late; it must be midnight."

"Good heavens, the child is correct!" exclaimed the dowager, glancing at the watch pinned to the bodice of her gown. "Where has the time flown?"

With a grin and a giggle, Delight skipped across the carpeting and presented Wickenshire with the ash fagot he had prepared in the kitchen and with a second, partially burned piece of wood, as well. This second bit of wood Wickenshire offered to Sotherland. "Sera and I should like it, your grace, if you would light our Yule log."

"I have not lighted a Yule log since my lads were in the nursery. Is this what remains of last year's?"

"Indeed. Not much, but enough. We cannot possibly have as much good fortune next year as we have had this, neither one of us, your grace, but we shall hope for it, eh?"

Sotherland, a gleam in his eye and a smile on his lips, knelt before the hearth and set the bit of wood alight from the fire already burning there. Then, with the other gentleman's aid, he moved the new Yule log into place and used the old bit of Yule log to light the new. "Now, what is this other thing Delight has fetched for you?" he asked, staring interestedly at the ashen fagot Wickenshire held out to him.

"A game," the dowager replied. "Alice, you must pick one of the bands tied around the fagot for your own, and Delight, you must do the same."

"And then you must pick one, Mama," asserted Wickenshire.

"No, I will not."

"Why will she not?" Sotherland asked, still kneeling before the fire, accepting the ashen fagot from Wickenshire's hand. "What is it that your mother fears, Wickenshire?"

"That her band will burn through first. Means she will be the next lady in the household to marry."

"Is that so?" asked Sotherland, as he smiled up at the dowager countess who sat in the wing chair just to the right of where he knelt. "Say which band will be yours, Diana."

"It is for *young* ladies, Nathaniel."

"And you are as young as springtime this evening. Do pick one. It will be fun to see what happens."

"Very well. The one on that end."

"And Delight, my gel, which will be yours?"

Delight joined him before the fire and pointed.

"Alice?" he called, his gaze returning to the dowager.

"Ol' FatherChris missIbe," cried Lord Nightingale, ruffling his chest feathers as he stretched on the duke's shoulder.

"Papa, let Lord Nightingale pick for me," Alice replied from beside the wassail bowl. With her father's back to her, her hand had firmly taken up residence in Spelling's.

"Just so," agreed the duke. "Release my daughter's hand, Spelling," he added. "He was holding the gel's hand, was he not, Diana? Yes, just as I thought. Pick a band, Nightingale," he ordered, lifting the fagot up before the macaw.

With great curiosity Lord Nightingale studied the thing, then reached out and pecked at a green band.

"Yours is the one directly beside Diana's, Alice. We will put it on the fire, eh? And see what happens?"

Spelling smiled as he slipped between the sheets that night—a wistful, hopeful smile. Never in his entire life had he thought to discover himself grateful to Lord Nightingale. And yet, this very evening, the old feather duster had picked the precise ashen band to first catch fire and burn free of the fagot. How Alice's eyes had brightened to see it. She had gazed up at him with the most incredible hope, the most incredible heat in those once-cool, blue eyes. He had not the least doubt that she loved him.

"But will she marry me if Sotherland is opposed to it?" he whispered into the night. "She has only now found her father. They are just coming to know each other. If I cannot gain his consent to the marriage, will she— No, I will not so much as ask it of her. Force her to decide between us? Never. That would be most unfair."

I will go to Sotherland first, he decided, and find some way to cajole him into giving his consent. And only when I have got it will I ask Alice for her hand. Not one to be easily cajoled, though, Sotherland. Doubt it will be an easy task. Invulnerable to charm, I should think. My sort of charm at any rate. Perhaps it would be better to demand his daughter's hand in marriage.

No, I cannot do that, he thought, tossing about the bed in an attempt to discover a comfortable position. I cannot demand that Sotherland allow us to marry. That is precisely the way to sink the entire thing. Raise his hackles and make him even more inflexible than he is. Stupid idea. Will not attempt to cajole him or demand it of him. Simply ask him properly and plainly for the privilege of asking Alice to marry me. That will not set his teeth on edge too terribly much. He will find nothing to offend him in that. What can he say?

"He can say no," groaned Spelling. "He can say I am a scoundrel and a dunderhead and do not have so much as a *Sir* before my name, and send me packing."

He would be correct, too. I am a scoundrel and a dunderhead and I do not have so much as the *likelihood* of a title. But he cannot send me packing, Spelling consoled himself. This is Nicky's house. Sotherland dare not order me out of my own cousin's house. That would be the height of audacity. Besides, Nicky is on my side. And so are Sera and Aunt Diana. They all want me to marry Alice. "Aunt Diana!" he exclaimed, sitting straight up in bed. "She will know how to approach the old tyrant. She is not the least bit afraid of the duke.

"Of course, I expect she is disappointed with me at the moment, because of my attempting to take those damnable journals without a word to anyone," he muttered, sliding back down under the counterpane. "Perhaps she is so disappointed that she will not like to help me. Why must I always be scheming and lying? Had I but asked Nicky and Aunt Diana for the journals and explained everything at the very first, they well might have wished to help me. Will I never learn?"

And now, I do not even need the journals, Spelling thought. Sayers has promised to return Alice's letters, journals or not; and I have nothing to fear from Ducane, so I need not worry about the ring. Still, it would be a fine thing to be able to return that ring to Aunt Diana. And Sayers' heart is truly set on having those journals. Great heavens, I am feeling sorry for Sayers, now! Still, he worked like a man afire at the barn and we discovered nothing but the pouch from which that coin slipped. Poor old fellow. Never saw such disappointment on a gentleman's face. I expect it is all right to feel sorry for Sayers. Never actually felt sorry for anyone before, but I expect it is all right to do it.

I will confess all to Nicky—that is precisely what I will do, Spelling decided. He will be angry that I have been involved in another plot, but he will understand once I tell him all. And perhaps he will have some idea where the journals can be found, and know how I may go about winning Sotherland to my side. Things are not near as bad as I am making them out to be. Truly they are not. Alice loves me and all else will fall into place if only I am honest and pluck up a bit of courage.

Alice tumbled into bed with a smile upon her face and a heart soaring toward the heavens. Of course, it had been only a game, the burning of the ashen fagot, but Lord Nightingale had picked the proper band for her.

I shall be the next young lady in this household to marry, she thought ecstatically. I shall marry Mr. Spelling. I wish to do so; Papa has said that I may; and so I will. I must only encourage Neil to apply to Papa for permission and all will be well with us. "This is the very best Christmas of my entire life!" she exclaimed to her bedchamber at large. "I shall remember it and our visit to Willowsweep forever."

Practically overflowing with joy, Alice rested her head against a pillow and closed her eyes. I must sleep now, she told herself sternly. Christmas Day is already upon us and we must all be up and dressed and off to church very early.

Though she expected it would take her hours to actually fall asleep, Alice drifted into a light doze almost at once and she was well on her way into dreams when a sound awakened her.

"What?" she queried, rolling over onto her back and listening intently.

The sound came once again, and though she could not put any sense to it, she nonetheless knew that it was something that ought not be there.

Now what can that be? she wondered, rising from her bed and searching about for her slippers. It cannot be Neil traipsing through the passages? No, I am certain it cannot. He said to me that he had covered every passageway and was not inclined to search through them again.

And yet, as she listened, there did seem to be a shuffling noise and a whispering of sorts inside the wall between her bedchamber and her sitting room. Donning her slippers and wrapping her flannel robe around her, she trudged to that particular wall and pressed her ear against it. "Mr. Spelling?" she whispered, scratching lightly on the paneling. "Neil, is it you in there?"

Myriad whispers and shufflings answered her.

"Whoever you are, you had best come out of there, and at once!" she demanded loudly. "Mr. Sayers? Have you sneaked in to have another look around? Neil, is it you? Answer me, do!"

Immediate silence arose in response to her questions. The night closed eerily about her and not so much as a floor-board dared to creak or one single branch to click against her window. A distinct shiver of foreboding slithered up Alice's spine.

"If you do not answer me," she said softly, "I shall come in there after you and force you to come out. See if I do not."

Most likely one of the servants has gone larking about in there and is afraid to be discovered, she thought. Either that or it is Mr. Carson's witch making an appearance at last. As a growing nervousness tingled in her fingertips and her toes, Alice took a very deep breath, lectured herself sternly for giving any credence whatsoever to Mr. Carson's witch and chastised herself for a paltry poltroon. Then, with chin high, she fetched her bedside lamp, turned up the wick, crossed into her sitting room and walked straight to the door through which she and Mr. Spelling had entered the passages. With an angry jab, she pushed the door open. And then she screamed and screamed again, her heart rising up into her throat as a gnarled, palsied hand seized her arm and dragged her into the passageways.

Eighteen

"Alice!" Spelling called. In robe and slippers, his nightcap madly askew, the ruffles of his nightshirt peeking out from the V of his robe, he made his way through the west wing of the first floor. Lamp in hand, he scrutinized each and every room from front to back and side to side. "Alice, answer me!" he called again. "I cannot help you if I do not know where you are!"

"The witch has got her," whispered Carson, close behind his master. "I just know it."

"If you mention the Witch of Willowsweep again, Carson, I will send you back to your chambers and continue on without you," threatened Spelling, stepping into the Gold Saloon.

"Yes, Mr. Spelling. I am sorry. It is merely that I ought to have mentioned—"

"What?" asked Spelling, coming to a halt and staring down at his valet. "You ought to have mentioned what, Carson?"

Above them and below them, in and through all the nooks and crannies of Willowsweep, the search for Lady Alice had commenced. Servants and gentlemen alike, frowning with concern, had divided the portions of the house among themselves mere moments after her screams had brought everyone rushing to the second floor corridor of the west wing and Lady Alice had been discovered to be missing. Now, as Sera and the dowager and Delight waited together in the master sitting room and the female servants huddled in the servants' dining room, all of Willowsweep blazed with light.

"You ought to have mentioned what, Carson?"

"Villain!" squawked Lord Nightingale raucously from his cage, beneath the shawl.

"Not speaking to you, Nightingale. Go back to sleep. Ought to have mentioned what?"

"What I glimpsed in the passageway, Mr. Spelling."

"You are not making a bit of sense, Carson. Which passageway? Glimpsed what? When?"

"Th-this very after-afternoon, Mr. Spelling. Lord Nightingale was caught in the passageways and—and—I opened the d-door to let him out and I saw—I th-thought I s-saw—"

"What, Carson?"

"A l-light, Mr. Spelling. And a bit of cloth dragging on a stair. And—I h-heard the swi-swishing of a lady's skirts. I th-thought I did. B-but then, I th-thought perhaps I d-did not."

"Villain! Scoundrel! Wassail!" shouted Nightingale from beneath the shawl, which wiggled and waggled most distressingly.

"You never said Nightingale was in the wall. How the devil did he get in there? By Jupiter, he may have followed someone in. Wickenshire and Sotherland are searching the upstairs passageways as we speak, Carson, and you did not think to mention to them that you had seen a light and heard skirts swishing in there?"

"No, sir. I thought it must be the w-witch, sir. And since I am not to believe in the w-witch—"

"Yo-ho-ho!" Nightingale interrupted, sticking his red-feathered head out from beneath the shawl. "FatherChris miss Ibe bitevillain!" And before Spelling could so much as comprehend that the bird had opened his cage and come out, Lord Nightingale was soaring around the room, squawking and banking at the corners, then sailing down so close to Spelling's head that wind whistled in Neil's ears.

"Now what the devil is that all about?" Spelling mumbled as he watched the macaw land on the floor and shuffle back and forth before a section of paneling, jerking his red head fitfully up and down and pecking here and there at the wood.

"Howdedo m'pretty. Howdo. Howdedo m' pretty." Nightingale ceased to peck at the paneling and began to scratch at it instead with his claws.

"Howdedo m'pretty?" queried Spelling as, somewhat in awe, he advanced to where the bird stood, handed his lamp to Carson and knelt down beside the macaw. "Nightingale? Howdedo m'pretty? Do you mean Alice? Do you know where Alice is?"

"Howdedo m'pretty. Howdo," Lord Nightingale replied, ceasing his scratching and staring up at Spelling through one amber eye.

"Is there a door, Mr. Spelling?" asked Carson. "Where his lordship was just now fidgeting about?"

Spelling reached out and gave the paneling a shove. It moved inward under his touch. He gained his feet quickly and shoved the door the rest of the way open.

"Howdedo m'pretty," Nightingale said most licentiously and strutted, much like a peacock, into the dark. Without a word, Spelling, with Carson and the lamp, entered behind him.

"I cannot for one moment believe that you are here," whispered Alice. "Grandmama, you cannot do this thing."

"I can," replied the ancient lady in a voice like crushed satin. "And I will."

Her own lamp having shattered on the stone steps seconds after she had been tugged into the passages, Alice now carried Lady Vermont's lantern. Except for Lady Vermont's gray hair, pale face and palsied hands, the old woman was a specter in black and might well have been the witch Alice had imagined her at first. But she is not a witch, Alice told herself; she is a madwoman. "Grandmama," she tried again, "you cannot simply grab me up and force me to run off with you. It is foolish beyond belief. Where will we go? How will we get there? What am I to wear? I am in my robe and slippers, Grandmama."

"No matter," replied Lady Vermont.

"But it does matter. It is cold in here and colder still outside. I will freeze to death before we go beyond the stables."

"Not going beyond the stables. Going under the stables."

"Under the stables?"

"And straight through to the old cave where John Coachman already awaits us. You will be a bit chilly perhaps, in these passages, but you need have no fear of freezing, my dear. And once we reach the coach, I will tuck you safely around with the carriage robes and you will be warm as toast. You may sleep all the way to Lydepool."

"To Lydepool? Whyever do you wish to go to Lydepool?"

"One of my great-nephews has a cottage in Lydepool. He will never notice do we make use of it for a time. Cannot return to Wilderly Crossroads at once, girl. It is the first place that the Devil Incarnate will look for us."

She is mad as a hedgehog turned inside out, thought Alice with a bit of fear and a good deal of pity. I expect I ought to scream again, but if I do, she may well hit me over the head with her cane just as she threatened. Though how she thinks she will get me out of the house when I am lying witless in a passageway, I cannot imagine. No, I must convince her to cease this nonsense, and quickly, too. Neil and Papa and the others certainly heard me scream and are searching for me even now. I must slow us down considerably and hope that we are discovered and Grandmama overpowered. Please, God, she added. Do not let it be Papa who finds us. But if it is, please do not let him have a pistol in his hand. Grandmama has been a dreadful person and done wicked things, but I could not bear it if Papa were to shoot her dead.

"Grandmama, we ought to rest, I think. For a moment or two. Just sit down here on these steps and give your legs an opportunity to regain some strength."

"There ain't nothing wrong with my legs, girl!" returned Lady Vermont sharply. "They are old. As old as I and that is all that bothers them. Come along. Do not dawdle."

"But these passageways are filled with steps that are steep and cracked and worn."

"I have been in these passageways and on these steps many times. I once strolled the entire maze of them with Ezra Spelling and Lord and Lady Wickenshire and the Hydes."

"With Ezra *Spelling,* Grandmama?"

"Wonderfully wicked gentleman, Ezra Spelling. Known him for years. Might have married him had he ever asked. Married your grandpapa instead. It was Ezra brought me here to make the acquaintance of his sister's husband. Lord Wickenshire that was. Evelyn, Lord Wickenshire. Dead now, that one. Broke his neck. I have always thought that Ezra helped him to do it."

"This Ezra *Spelling,* Grandmama. He is not related to-to—Mr. Neil Spelling?"

"Yes, indeed! The lad's uncle. Traveled the entire length of the passageways we did. Spent hours investigating them. I shall not allow them to defeat me now."

"We could go out into the house, Grandmama, and travel much more easily."

"Hah! Do you think I am a simpleton? Go out into the house? I think not. Where are your senses, Alice? We must cling to the shadows. Hark, girl! Already there are footsteps above us. Hurry. To the right and down, Alice," hissed the ancient. "To the right and down again."

"But Grandmama, if there is someone above us, then they suspect that we are in here. Is it not likely, if there is someone above us, that there will be someone below us as well?" Oh, please, let there be someone waiting below us, Alice added silently. I will be forced to overpower Grandmama and whack her with her own cane, else.

"If that is the case, I pity whoever it might be," Lady Vermont replied, loosing her grasp on Alice's arm and reaching beneath her cloak to produce what Alice thought an alarmingly large pistol. "I pity whoever it might be, for I will use this if our way is threatened." The enormous horse pistol shook and shuddered in the palsied old hand that could barely lift it into a useable position.

"Is it—loaded—Grandmama?" asked Alice with a small gulp.

"Put the powder and the ball in the thing myself. It will pop a hole in any heart. I did think to search out where that fiend Sotherland lay sleeping and pop a hole in his heart before I came looking for you, but I could not find the place."

"Grandmama, you cannot truly have intended to kill Papa!"

"Papa!" hissed Lady Vermont. "You call that devil Papa now? What else has he forced you to do? No, do not tell me. I shall hear all when we are safe in Lydepool."

"But Grandmama, we can be safe here. There is no one here intends us harm. If only you will give over and—"

"Ha! No one here intends us harm? Has Sotherland departed? No, he has not. Dropped you on your head and jumbled your brains is what he has done, the evil dastard!"

"Papa has *not* dropped me on my head."

"So you say."

"Grandmama," sighed Alice, coming to a halt. "Dearest

Grandmama, you cannot abduct me in such a manner as this. It is most—most—undignified."

"Would not be forced to do it had Richard done his job with greater expediency. But no, he would dawdle about until I could wait no longer. I was correct not to wait. Already you call Sotherland Papa. Another day or two and there is no telling what you might be forced to do by that—that—"

"Villain!" squawked Lord Nightingale above them.

"Precisely," nodded Lady Vermont with great complacency. "That villain! Wait! Who said that?" she added. "It was not you, Alice, and not me. Already someone is very near at hand. We must hurry. Move, child. Move!"

Spelling, with Nightingale clinging tightly to his shoulder, peered before him with considerable care. "Light flickers below," he whispered to a trembling Carson.

"Villain!" cried Nightingale again.

"Hush, you featherbrain. If this witch who stole Alice is below us, we do not want to warn her that we are coming. But then, it might not be a witch at all, Carson," Spelling added with sudden consideration for his valet's nerves. "Perhaps it is Nicky ahead of us, or Sotherland. I cannot make out who it is, but they are moving again. We shall attempt to catch them up, but as quietly as we can, eh?"

With careful steps, Spelling moved forward. His feet were beginning to chill through his bedroom slippers and his ankles were already frozen because neither nightshirt nor robe covered them. Yet he noticed the cold not at all. He was so intent on reaching those who traveled below him without making them aware of himself that he did not even note how his bedroom slippers tended to slide on the stone steps. Not, that is, until he reached the fifth step and his slippers slid down over the edge and set him off his balance. He reached out and knocked the lamp from Carson's grasp as he began to fall, sending the thing crashing into the wall. Lord Nightingale took immediately to the air. Carson jumped up and his heart ceased to beat for a full three seconds before he landed again and began to shout after his tumbling master.

"Mr. Spelling! Mr. Spelling, sir! Do not you worry, Mr. Spelling, I am coming!"

He could not see a thing without the light of the lamp, the light ahead of him having already faded, but Carson made his way downward nonetheless. One hand straight out before him, the other pressed against the wall, his feet touching cautiously before every step, Carson felt his way after the sound that was Spelling oofing and oohing and aahing his way down the ancient stairs.

With a grunt, a groan and a great exhalation of air, Spelling came to a dizzying but abrupt halt against a wall. For what seemed an eternity, he lay there, attempting to catch his breath and puzzling over what had happened to him. "Fell," he concluded finally. "Ouch!" He ached everywhere. His head, his shoulders, his back, his ribs all protested as he fought to rise to his feet in the darkness.

"I am coming, Mr. Spelling!" cried Carson from above.

"Pirates!" shouted Nightingale from somewhere below.

At the sound of Spelling's tumble, Lady Vermont ceased to descend and spun about as rapidly as such an ancient might be expected to spin. The mammoth horse pistol wobbled wildly in her hand as she aimed it unsteadily in the direction of the landing just above her.

"Grandmama, no!" Alice cried, setting the lantern down upon the steps and reaching with both hands for Lady Vermont's arm. "It is Mr. Spelling," she shouted. "Mr. Ezra Spelling's nephew. You remember Mr. Neil Spelling, Grandmama. You do not wish to shoot the gentleman you plan for me to marry!"

"Mr. Spelling?" asked Lady Vermont softly, lowering the pistol to her side. "All that racket was Mr. Spelling? Why does he cry 'Pirates!' in such a raucous voice, Alice? Why does he cry 'Pirates!' at all?"

"It was not Mr. Spelling who cried 'Pirates!', Grandmama," Alice responded, greatly relieved to see the pistol pointed downward. "That was Lord Nightingale. Oh! There he is. Lord Nightingale, come to me."

"Howdedo m'pretty," Nightingale responded at once, waddling across the step above the lamp and staring up first at Alice and then at Lady Vermont. "How do?"

"Eek! A hobgoblin!" screeched Lady Vermont, raising her wavering pistol to point it at Nightingale.

"FatherChris miss Ibe," Nightingale declared, considering the odd stick the lady held out to him.

"Father Christmas?" asked Lady Vermont, staring uncertainly at the macaw.

"Herewecomea wassailllllling," sang Lord Nightingale with great gusto, shuffling back and forth upon the step and riveting Lady Vermont's attention as, merely four steps above, Spelling, pressed against the wall, turned the corner of the landing and began to make his way, painfully but silently, toward the shadowy tableau below him.

"Perch," Nightingale decided aloud, as the pistol continued to waver before him. With a nod of his head and a flap of his wings, he launched himself at Lady Vermont, with every intention of landing upon her pistol. Startled, the ancient lurched to the side and sent Alice stumbling against the wall. The muzzle of the horse pistol jerked spastically about as she wavered, off-balance, until, with a flash and a pop that echoed and reechoed throughout the passageways—over and over until it sounded as if an entire battalion were firing—the pistol exploded and the ball ricocheted off the wall, off the ceiling and then off Mr. Spelling's shoulder.

Lord Nightingale, abruptly aware of his mistake, flew

away at once, squawking. Lady Vermont screeched. Alice grabbed for her Grandmama and sent the now useless pistol clattering down the steps. Her grandmother, terrified, shoved the girl away and screeched again. Spelling, disregarding the sting of the pistol ball, launched himself down the remainder of the steps, seized Lady Vermont by the collar of her cloak with one hand and pulled Alice to his side with the other. Just then, on the landing above them, Carson appeared and stared in awe at the struggling woman his master apparently held by the scruff of the neck. Unable to speak, Carson pounded in panic against the inside wall until, in a moment of clarity, he felt a latch beneath his fingers. He pulled it and tumbled out into the rear of the kitchen.

"Help!" he cried, spinning about in search of someone—anyone. "Help! It is the witch! Mr. Spelling has caught the Witch of Willowsweep and she will kill him for it!"

Jenkins skidded around the corner into the rear of the kitchen as fast as his feet could carry him. "Where are they? Mr. Carson!" he demanded, sliding to a halt on the stone floor and grasping the valet by both shoulders. "Where are they?"

"In th-th-there," stuttered Carson, pointing toward the door that had already closed. "Mr. Spelling has got the witch and Lady Alice! He has got them! But the witch will kill him!"

"Take me to them," Jenkins demanded.

"We need a gentleman to help us," Carson protested. "She will kill Mr. Spelling and Lady Alice else."

"Mr. Carson," Jenkins declared, giving the valet a solid shake, "there is no witch. I assure you that there is no witch. Likely everyone has heard the ruckus in the passageways by now, but you and I are the closest. We must go to Lady Alice's and Mr. Spelling's aid. But we cannot if you do not come and show me which way to turn." With that, Jenkins seized a brace of lighted candles, patted the pale-faced Carson's arm and urged him back through the door he had only just exited.

"How the devil did she get here?" Sotherland grumbled, pacing back and forth before the hastily laid fire in the morning room, his robe flapping around him. "And what the deuce am I to do with her? Ducane, I thought she had paid *you* to abduct Alice?"

Ducane nodded, pulling his robe tighter about him as he sat in one of the armchairs near the hearth. "Paid me a tidy sum."

"Then why is she here? Woman's mind is made of mush. Wickenshire." The duke acknowledged the earl's arrival with a nod. "Spelling will live, eh?"

"An enormous bruise."

"The ball did not enter?"

"No. Lost a bit of its power from ricocheting about."

"Good. Good. Should hate to see the dunderhead bleed to death or anything. How enormous a bruise can a ball make?"

"The ball did not make too great a bruise at all. What I intended to convey is that Neil is one enormous bruise from head to toe. Tumbled down the steps. Lucky he did not break his neck."

"Or bash his skull in," offered Ducane. "Brave gentleman, Spelling. Practically buys the farm from his fall, picks himself up and takes a pistol ball to the shoulder, and still he saves the lady fair."

"Yes, well, a gentleman must be willing to suffer for the woman he loves, eh?" Wickenshire replied quietly with a rather triumphant glance at Sotherland. "Put Lady Alice's safety above all else, he did, even above his own life. Thankful Carson was there to fetch Jenkins. No telling but Lady Vermont might have twisted out of Neil's grasp before he got her all the way out of the passages. We should never have gotten to them in time to be of any assistance, Sotherland, still wandering about in the upper regions as we were. Old woman might have shot Neil straight on, Lady Alice says, if Lord Nightingale had not distracted her."

From the chandelier above Wickenshire's head, Lord Nightingale purred in perfect imitation of a contented Sweetpea.

"Yes, you are proud of yourself, are you not, Nightingale?" Wickenshire asked with a smile. "Neil says it was you led him to the ladies as well."

"Old pirate is a damnable sight better at tracking than that wretched dog of yours," observed Sotherland, continuing to pace. "That puppy had us clomping about everywhere."

"Did he?" asked Ducane, grinning. "At least you were not following a cat, your grace."

"You followed Sweetpea?" Wickenshire lowered himself into the matching armchair and stretched his slippered feet toward the fire. "Are you mad, Ducane? You followed a cat?"

"I thought at first that the cat followed me, but then, in the end, I seemed to be following her. Had I known about the passages in your walls, I might have found Aunt Fiona and Alice. The cat kept hugging the walls and mewing fitfully at me, but I could not guess why. I cannot believe that the old terror did not tell me about those passageways. Pays me to abduct the girl and then forgets to tell me about what might well have been the best way to accomplish the thing."

"None of which is to the point at all," growled Sotherland. "How did she get here is what I want to know, and what the devil I am to do with her. I cannot have my own mother-in-law gaoled. I should enjoy it immensely. And enjoy to see her sent off to the colonies, but Alice—Alice is much attached to the woman."

"She is," nodded Wickenshire. "Apparently, Alice is as

worried about what will become of her grandmother as she is about Neil's condition."

"We could just shoot them both," grumbled Sotherland. "Shoot Fiona and the dunderhead and claim they shot each other."

"On Christmas?" asked Ducane. "Surely not."

Nineteen

"Fiona, you must cease this nonsense," declared the dowager Lady Wickenshire with a frustrated frown. "Of all things, to sneak into this house like a thief!"

"I did not sneak," Lady Vermont responded. "I walked right in through the kitchen door."

"You did?" The dowager stared at Lady Vermont, amazed. "And no one thought to ask you your business?"

"There was no one about. Running all over the place, your entire household."

"Yes, well, it was the day before Christmas," replied the dowager, settling into bed beside the ancient and tugging the counterpane up around them. "There, now we will be warm and cozy."

"Warm and cozy! Bah! In a few more moments, my Alice and I would have been perfectly warm and cozy in my traveling coach and well on our way to Lydepool. Safe from that demon, Sotherland."

"He is not a demon, Fiona. Nor is he the Devil Incarnate. Were he either of the two, he would have throttled you to death the moment Neil, Jenkins and Carson brought you kicking and screeching into his presence. Or, he would have sent one of the grooms riding for the magistrate at Swiftinwhold and had you taken away and gaoled. He would not have sent a man after your coachman to bring him safely here, nor entrusted you to my care."

"So now, because he did not murder me or have me gaoled, the man is a saint? He deceives you, Diana, as he did my daughter and as he now attempts to deceive my granddaughter. I am not mad! It is Sotherland is mad and evil besides!"

Lady Wickenshire sighed and hoped that the chest of drawers that had been set before the door to the passage entrance from this chamber really was heavy enough to keep Lady Vermont from moving it on her own. Since it had taken both Wickenshire and Ducane together to push and pull it across the floor, she had been certain it would hold, but with madness, she knew, came strength. Still, it was a monstrous old thing. It seemed likely it could not be moved aside by one ancient little lady.

And both doors to the bedchamber are securely locked, she thought with a sense of relief. And I have the key well-secured. There is no way at all that Fiona can escape this night.

"We must attempt to get some sleep," she said, reaching over to turn down the lamp. "It is already Christmas, Fiona, and the household will be up and about very early."

"Vile holiday, Christmas," muttered Lady Vermont, settling her head against the pillow. "Always attempted to make it nice for my Alice, but it is a vile holiday when a woman is alone."

"You are no longer alone, my dear," whispered the dowager. "You are surrounded by people this Christmas."

"Confined in the midst of a nest of vipers," Lady Vermont growled. "A nest of poisonous vipers."

"Rubbish. My Nicky is no more a viper than Alice or Neil or darling Sera or Delight. Nor am I, Fiona. Have you run so mad that you cannot even recognize your friends?"

"No. I know you are my friend, Diana, and have been ever since Ezra brought us together. But, you and Ezra are the only true friends I have yet alive."

"Well, then I warn you, Fiona, as your true friend. You

must rein in this madness and quickly, too. You must not plague Sotherland any longer, nor seek his death, nor ever again attempt to abduct your granddaughter."

"But—"

"No! You must not! You do not wish to be locked away in a madhouse, do you?"

"But—"

"Fiona!" the dowager declared sternly. "Neil wishes to marry your Alice. Is that not precisely what you wished for her?"

"Indeed, but Sotherland will not allow it."

"He will. And then I will become Alice's aunt and Ezra her uncle by law. Even if the duke should wish to harm her, do you for one moment think that Ezra or I or Neil would allow it?"

"No. Ezra would have that demon's guts for garters."

"Just so. And do you think for one moment that Neil or Ezra or I would keep Alice from you?"

"N-no."

"Then you must curb this madness. For your own sake, Fiona. You will destroy all the love that Alice has for you else. You will drive her from you rather than bind her to you. And for no reason. Once she and Neil are married, Sotherland must relinquish any and all power over her to the nephew of your best friends."

Lady Vermont cogitated on this discourse for what seemed to the dowager an extraordinarily long time. All through the grimaces, sniffs and mutterings that this cogitation produced in the ancient, the dowager sent intense prayers up to heaven. Please, she thought. Please, please, please allow her to see that what I say is true. Please give her a bit of rationality. Enough to keep her from the madhouse.

"Very well," mumbled Lady Vermont at last. "I will not do another thing until I see whether Mr. Spelling succeeds in gaining Alice's hand in marriage."

"And you will not grumble or frown or speak ill of anyone in this house in the morning. You will put on a cheerful face for Christmas Day. Because I do not care what you think of the Duke of Sotherland, Fiona. I promised Nicky that you would behave in a civilized fashion or I would keep you locked up in this room. I mean to keep that promise, so you will behave with good grace and good humor to everyone."

"Not to Sotherland."

"Very well, but neither will you attempt to gut him like a fish under the kissing bough."

"No. I will not," sighed Lady Vermont. "I will ignore him completely until I learn whether Alice and Mr. Spelling are to be married or not. But if they are not, I will lop off the devil's head with a dull meat cleaver. See if I do not!"

A weary Wickenshire tumbled into bed beside his wife and bestowed a tender kiss upon her nose. "Go to sleep at once, Sera," he urged softly. "Christmas is already upon us."

"But where did Lady Vermont come from, Nicholas? And are you certain that she will not harm your mama? I cannot like to have your mama locked into a room with a madwoman."

"Mama and she will get on very well together. I promise you. They have known each other for years."

"But Lady Vermont is mad, Nicholas."

"Yes, I expect she always has been. Yet, she and Mama have always gotten on. Mama is confident that Lady Vermont will cause no more trouble. She promised me as much. Now go to sleep, Sera, or we will all of us snore through Christmas services."

"I do not snore," replied Sera primly, her eyes alight with mischief. "You are the one who snores—you and Bedazzler."

"Bedazzler snores? I do not believe it. I have never heard a sound out of the little rapscallion."

"That is because you are busy snoring so loudly yourself."

"Ha! How could you possibly hear me over your own snores?" Wickenshire teased, pulling her comfortably into his arms. "Such a racket as you make, it is a wonder that Bedazzler and I can sleep at all. My gawd but you are so very beautiful, Sera," he added, his voice rough with sudden emotion, his lips tickling at her ear. "I did never think you could be more beautiful than when we wed, but of late, you outdo yourself. There is no lovelier woman in all the kingdom. The very sweetness of your soul shines in your eyes. Do you know how much I love you?"

"With all your heart," Sera whispered, 'lust as I love you. Merry Christmas, Nicholas," she added, melting into his embrace with a sigh and a smile as his lips found hers.

Alice, in a carriage dress of forest green beneath a cape of cherry red satin trimmed and lined in white ermine, with a matching ermine hat upon her head, stared at the lot of them, totally bemused. "You cannot mean it," she said. "I am to go out and knock on the henhouse door?"

"Oh, yes. You must," the dowager countess replied. "It is expected of you."

"An' me too," added Delight, resplendent in red and gold.

"And Mama," Wickenshire said.

"No, not me, Nicky."

"Yes, and I expect Lady Vermont must as well."

"Me?" asked that formidable lady.

"Well, you are in the household and unmarried," offered Wickenshire. "One never knows. Now, off you go. Delight, you are in charge and must report back to us all what happens, eh?"

"Uh-huh," Delight replied, standing as tall as she possibly could, her little chest puffing out with pride. "An' I will be certain that we all knock loud."

The others watched them go, the ladies treading carefully along the path in their Christmas finery. "It is a shame Sotherland cannot be present," Spelling observed, his dark eyes bright with happiness despite the aches and pains that plagued him after his fall. "He would like to see Alice so bemused and excited, I think. But I expect the mere sight of him would send Lady Vermont off again."

"He will get a glimpse of Alice's face nonetheless," Wickenshire replied. "He is already down in the henhouse."

"He is?" asked Ducane. "Why? To throttle the rooster lest it should crow when Lady Alice knocks?"

"Rather to tweak it into voice when Nicky's mama knocks," smiled Sera. "And he looks splendid. When your mama sees him in his Christmas best, Nicholas, she is like to swoon at his feet."

"Mama?"

"He is in blue and silver, his hair curling about his face like a cherub's. If you look even half as handsome on the Christmas morning that you are as old as he, Nicky, I might very well swoon at *your* feet."

It took a mere five minutes for the ladies to return, all of them laughing, even Lady Vermont.

"We did it!" Delight cried joyfully, "an' Lady Alice, an' Lady Wickenshire are both to be married within the year."

"Both? Good heavens!" exclaimed Wickenshire. "My mama and Lady Alice both?"

"Uh-huh. The rooster crowed for both of them. Right away. The very moment they knocked."

"You are not disappointed that he did not crow for you, eh, little one?"

"Uh-uh. I do not have one gentleman I wish to marry yet."

"But she will," warned Lady Vermont with a most unexpected warmth. "Such a dear child will keep you extremely busy when she makes her come-out. She will have gentlemen callers forever at the door."

"Most likely," agreed Wickenshire. "The coach awaits us, ladies," he added, bowing with considerable flourish. "Will you accompany us to the front door?"

Alice expected to take Spelling's arm for the trip down the corridor but he did not offer it. He smiled at her but took Delight's hand instead. The two of them hurried off ahead of the others and it was left to Ducane to accompany Alice in the parade to the foyer and to offer his other arm to Lady Vermont as well.

Why does Neil not escort me? Alice wondered as she progressed up the corridor. Is it because of Grandmama? I ought not have confided in him that, mad or not, I will likely always love Grandmama. Well, but it is true. Though my mind tells me I ought to abandon all concern for her, my heart will not allow it. I cannot help what my heart feels. If Neil despises me for it and will not have me because of it, then I must go on without him.

I cannot go on without him, she thought then, her lower lip beginning to quiver. I love Neil Spelling and I love Papa and I love Grandmama and I do not see how I can possibly sacrifice one of them for the other.

"By Jupiter, will you look at that!" Ducane exclaimed as they approached the already open front door. "An eight-horse hitch! And all decked out for Christmas! What a beautiful sight!"

"Oh, Grandmama," said Alice, "have you ever seen such an exquisite sight? Silk flowers and red bows, gold and silver bells. And only look at the green and gold ribands streaming from their manes and tails."

Lady Vermont did not answer. Her gaze, as they stepped out of the house, was fixed on the coachman.

Alice looked to the box and discovered her Papa resplendent in a many-caped greatcoat of sky blue with silver buttons and silver trim. Glowing black Hessians set off the silver gray of his breeches and a red winter rose bloomed on his lapel. The hat upon his head was tipped rakishly back from his brow, freeing black curls mixed with silver to scatter across his forehead as he smiled down at the dowager Lady Wickenshire with eyes as filled with promise as the first day of spring.

"Devil," hissed Lady Vermont quietly. "But I shall keep my promise to Diana. I shall pretend the blackguard is nothing but a coachman this entire day. Completely beneath my notice."

Once inside the coach, with warmed bricks and straw at their feet and fur throws to cuddle beneath, the ladies made a cozy party. The gentlemen, dressed to the nines, rode proudly along beside them. Alice peered out the window to discover Spelling peering in at her and smiling. He tipped his hat and winked. Alice could not help but smile back. "He is not upset with me," she whispered softly to herself.

"Good. You are smilin'. That means you are not angry with Cousin Neil for not 'scortin' you to the coach, does it not?" asked Delight quietly from the seat beside her.

"No, I am not upset with him," Alice responded. "I was confused though. Why did he not offer me his arm?"

"He could not 'cause he had to help me with my muff an' we had to hurry to get in the coach before anyone else."

"Hurry to get in the coach before anyone else? Help you with your muff?" Alice glanced down to see the most enormous muff balanced on Delight's knees. "Wherever did you find such a muff as that, Delight? It is large enough for you to crawl inside of it yourself."

"I founded it in a old trunk. And it is perfeck. But I could not climb inside the coach with it. Cousin Neil had to hold it for me."

"He did?"

"Uh-huh. Would you like to put your hand inside? There is a secret in it."

"A secret?" Alice looked about the coach to find that none of the other ladies were paying the least attention. The dowager countess had engaged Lady Vermont in what appeared to be a most serious conversation, and Sera was quite occupied in making faces through the opposite window at her husband, who was similarly occupied making faces in at her.

"Yes, I should like to share your secret," Alice replied, turning back to the child.

"Then just put your hand inside my muff."

Alice did as she was told and pulled it out again hastily, her eyes wide with surprise. "What?"

"It's Lord Nightingale," whispered Delight. "Cousin Neil fixed my muff up special inside, so Lord Nightingale would be toasty warm. It has got sable inside of it! And I am helping to keep him warm by plugging the ends with my hands."

"Oh, Delight!" Alice's eyes lit with laughter.

"Sera does not unnerstand," Delight continued quietly. "The Reverend Mr. Longfellow is *'specting* Lord Nightingale and Mrs. Siely is 'specting him, too. Everyone is 'specting him and now they willn't be at all disappointed."

"Is he wearing his Christmas going-to-church clothes in there?" asked Alice. "I cannot think there would be room."

"Cousin Neil has got Lord Nightingale's clothes in his coat pocket. We are going to run off to the convenience right as soon as we get to church and put them on him in there so that no one will see him until he is done up all right and proper."

Alice looked out the window at Mr. Spelling once again, and making a perfect *O* of her lips, she clasped one hand in front of them. Spelling laughed aloud to see it and with the greatest of caution, tugged Lord Nightingale's hightopped hat from his pocket for her to see, then hastily hid it away before anyone else should take note of it.

What a scoundrel he is, Alice thought joyfully. What a

larkster to so please Delight and have his own fun at one and the same time. And he is not upset with me because of Grandmama! No, he is not, or he would not be laughing with me now. Oh, I know that we will find a way, she thought, her hope rising as she glanced at Lady Vermont. I know we will find some way to help Grandmama. Neil is so very good at devious little plots—even Sera says that he is—surely between us we will be able to devise some means to keep Grandmama from the madhouse and from tormenting Papa as well.

The little church in Swiftinwhold was as full as it could hold that Christmas morning. The Reverend Mr. Longfellow, who had never in his lifetime understood the passion for brimstone, hellfire and severe dreariness expounded by many of his fellow parsons, rejoiced at the energy and cheeriness of his flock. "As we celebrate the birth of the Christ child," he observed at the start of the service. "As we celebrate the birth of hope and salvation upon the face of the earth, so let us also rejoice in our own personal hope, in our own private salvation, for we are the children of a strict but a loving God and we *shall* find true happiness and mercy beyond imagining."

He might have said a word or two more, but he noted at the rear of the church a bit of a disturbance. He cocked an eyebrow. His round little cheeks flushed. He stepped down from behind his pulpit and peered nearsightedly down the main aisle. All heads turned to see what the Reverend Mr. Longfellow could be peering at that would cause such a look of wonder to grow on his face.

"Oh, no," squeaked Sera. "Nicholas! Oh, no!"

"Oh, yes," Wickenshire whispered. "Do not be upset, Sera. She was most determined, you know. And he does not look at all cold or frightened. But how the devil did she get him here?"

"Nicholas, do not use that particular phrase at the moment."

"Oh. Sorry. But how did she? Neil had something to do with it. It was he went with her to the privy. And he looks guilty as sin. No wonder they were so long in returning."

"I cannot bear it," Sera replied hoarsely, covering her face with her hands.

"Sera? Darling? It is not such a very bad thing. You minx! You are not upset at all," Wickenshire accused then. "You are laughing behind your hands."

Sera nodded and peeked up at him over her fingertips. "I c-cannot h-help myself."

Lord Nightingale, in hat, tail coat and tiny, pristine neckcloth, perched proudly upon the muff that Delight carried carefully in both hands. "FatherChris misssss Ibe," he declared exultantly to the entire congregation as she carried him up the aisle, escorted with great decorum by Mr. Spelling. "FatherChris misssss Ibe. Come tashare yer piepie PIE with ye!"

To his credit, the Reverend Mr. Longfellow did not quite burst into guffaws, and he did return to the altar and proceed most dutifully with the service. But not a single soul in the church that day could fault him when his eyes wandered from time to time in the direction of Wickenshire's pew, or when his lips, without the least inhibition, curved unswervingly upward and a chuckle escaped him in the oddest places during the worship. And no one of the entire congregation could hold it against the good parson when he declined to present the sermon he had most diligently prepared and instead invited little Delight to bring Lord Nightingale forward to sing for them all.

As the congregation took its leave of the good parson at the church door, all had attained the joyful mood which Mr. Longfellow had hoped to instill in them that day. And even though Lord Nightingale had strayed in his singing from "God Rest Ye Merry Gentlemen" into "I Saw Hiram Kiss

Yer Sister"—or more likely because he had done so—the Reverend Mr. Longfellow was certain that this particular Christmas Day was going to prove jolly and memorable to each and every one of his congregation.

Tucked back into his muff with only his hat removed, because he did not wish to have the rest of his fine dress taken from him, Lord Nightingale muttered, mumbled and nestled down cozily on Delight's lap inside the coach. "You were the verimost splendidest part of the entire thing," Delight informed him cheerfully while they waited for the other ladies. "Everyone was thrilled with you."

"Nice touch, bringing the old pirate, Wickenshire," Squire Hadley observed as he greeted the earl at the foot of the church steps. "Most enthusiastic service we have had in Swiftinwhold since the Wednesday evening that Mrs. Catenwall decided to give birth to her Tommy in the nave. A Merry Christmas to you, lad, and to your lady as well."

"Merry Christmas to you, Squire. I dare say you have your hands full, eh? You have brought enough company with you to fill the church all by yourself."

"No, no, not quite so many as that, but— Well, by Jove!" exclaimed the squire, waving at the dowager Lady Wickenshire as she entered the coach and staring as Spelling handed Alice and Lady Vermont in after her.

"By Jove what?" asked Wickenshire.

"Said she could not remain. Had to meet her granddaughter for Christmas. Odd she did not mention Willowsweep."

"Who?"

"Lady Vermont, Wickenshire. Lady Vermont. That was she entering your coach?"

"Indeed."

"Appeared upon our doorstep two days ago. Took the last chamber we had free in the entire house. Thanked Mrs. Hadley graciously for inviting her, but made it clear she must be somewhere else on Christmas Eve."

"I had no idea you even knew Lady Vermont."

"Do not," Hadley replied with a bewildered shake of his head. "Not to speak of."

"Then why did Mrs. Hadley ask her for the holiday?"

"Did not," Hadley responded. "But what were we to do? Cannot turn an old lady out into the cold. She plainly did not realize that we did not invite her. Well, she is your guest now, I see."

"Yes," Wickenshire replied, "and we did not invite her, either."

Twenty

Sayers, having joined the party from Willowsweep as they departed church, sat down to a sumptuous Christmas luncheon with them perfectly unaware of the tension at the table. He did not think it at all odd that Sotherland should seek permission to carve the Christmas goose in Wickenshire's stead. Nor did he take note of the way in which the duke glared at Lady Vermont with each slow, prolonged thrusting and slicing of the knife into and through the tender meat of the fowl. Sayers accepted his portion of everything with great good cheer, ate enthusiastically and entertained his table partners with spirited conversation. Unnoticed went the uplifted nose of Lady Vermont as she bluntly and pointedly ignored Sotherland's presence. Unnoticed, too, went the dowager's commanding glares at both Lady Vermont and the duke. Sayers, who had thought to be alone this Christmas Day, and without the journals he longed for as well, reveled in the joy of his inclusion in the Willowsweep household. By the end of the meal his happy enthusiasm and conversation had driven away all but the tiniest anxieties in all of the party over what might become of the rest of the day.

"Not the time to be threatening old ladies, I expect. Not likely she will attempt anything dastardly today, do you think, Ducane?" Sotherland asked as the two strolled side by side toward the Gold Saloon. "Want my girl to have an enjoyable Christmas. Had a wonderful time at the church, she did, what with Lord Nightingale's performance and all. Do not want my disgust for that old harridan to ruin the remainder of the day for her."

"Aunt Fiona will not attempt anything at all today," Ducane assured him. "The dowager Lady Wickenshire made it clear that if she should, she would be locked away at once. I spoke to Aunt Fiona after services, returned her money to her. Entire scheme is pointless now, I told her. Spelling is on the verge of applying for Lady Alice's hand, and once they marry, neither you nor she will have Alice for your own any longer."

"On the verge," replied the duke quietly. "How long does he intend to totter on the verge, I wonder? Expected him to demand my presence in private first thing after he rescued Alice last night. Fine figure he would have made, standing before me, bruised and battered on my daughter's behalf. Amazed he did not see the advantage of it."

"I would not have done," offered Ducane.

"You would not? Why not?"

"No telling but you might have battered me even more."

"Rubbish!"

"No, sir, not rubbish. You are a formidable gentleman. I cannot fault Spelling for thinking twice. What is this?" Ducane added, as they turned into the saloon.

Spelling took a seat beside Alice upon the gold-striped settee and grinned mightily at her. "What do you think it is?"

"I have never seen anything quite like it," Alice replied.

"I have."

"You have? Where?"

"In London. You have never been to London, I think."

"Never."

"I live in Town. Always have. Should you like to live in

London, A-Alice?" he asked, cautiously resting one arm along the back of the settee.

"I will like to live anywhere that y—that my husband—chooses," Alice responded, her shoulders tingling from the very nearness of his arm. "Do not tease me, Mr. Spelling. What is it we are looking at?"

"A stage of sorts. For puppets."

"Puppets? Truly?"

"They are everywhere in Town at Christmastime. Alice?"

"Yes? What is it, N-Neil? You seem so— Is there something you particularly wish to say to me?"

"Yes."

"What?"

"I—I wish to say that—that—" Spelling stuttered to a halt as the Duke of Sotherland and Ducane seated themselves in chairs arranged directly behind the settee.

"I should discover another place to rest my arm, Spelling," the duke leaned forward and whispered in Spelling's ear, the one farthest from Alice, so she could not hear. "If you do not and it should slip the least bit, I will be obliged to chop it off."

Spelling removed his arm from the back of the settee at once. But then he took a deep breath and returned it to its former position.

Behind him, the Duke of Sotherland smiled.

When all the seats, arranged in a semi-circular fashion before the little stage, were filled and the small audience abuzz with speculation, Jenkins, in his finest clothes, entered the Gold Saloon and strolled up before them. He bowed with a considerable flourish. "Good day to you, ladies and gentlemen," he said. "We welcome you to the home of the Willowsweep Thespians as they present their extraordinary drama, Lord Nightingale's Christmas."

"Chris miss!" called Lord Nightingale from the chandelier as up popped the stocking covered in feathers.

"Once upon a time in the land of Egypt, which was merely a hop and a skip from Willowsweep . . ." Jenkins continued, the parrot puppet hopping and skipping back and forth across the stage as only a parrot puppet could, its feathers billowing about, ". . . the bedazzling Lord Nightingale traveled to the tiny village of Bethlehem to pay his taxes."

"Too many windows," squeaked the puppet Lord Nightingale as it hopped along. "Too many windows, too much taxes. Board some of them up, I will."

In the audience, Wickenshire smiled as the back of his neck grew warm. His mama gazed around Lady Vermont and winked at him.

"He was almost there when night came," Jenkins said. Abruptly the painted blue sky that hung behind the puppet was stripped away and the sheet that Delight had painted to look like the night sky appeared from beneath it.

"You done that excellent," commented a tiny unseen voice as the audience oohed and aahed appropriately.

Jenkins went on. "And night arriving, Lord Nightingale thought he would stop at the nearest inn."

Up from behind the stage rose a little desk cut from paper and behind it a stocking with dark green button eyes and a paper hat set rakishly atop dark yarn curls.

"I wish to have a room for the night, please," said the Nightingale puppet properly.

"Don't got none lef'," replied the other puppet. "I be the innkeeper an' I say we has run outta rooms. But I gots a stall in m'stable. Gimme money, an' I'll let ye sleep there."

"Villain!" squawked Nightingale from the chandelier. "Bite villain! Villain!"

"No, he was not a villain," Jenkins offered calmly. "Merely an innkeeper whose rooms were full. But just as Lord Nightingale was about to hand the innkeeper his money, a gentleman came in with a very pretty lady on his arm." Two more puppets popped into view. One of them was a weary-looking stocking with a floppy hat and a colored neckcloth, and the other, the very lovely lady puppet with yellow curls, faded blue dress, purple shawl, amazing bonnet and now, an obvious bulge where her stomach should be.

"We need ta 'ave a room, sir. We went all the way ta Beth'lem. Me awalkin' and Mary aridin' on are donkey. Went fer ta pay are taxes," said the tired gentleman puppet. "We is weary and 'ungry, an' needs a warm place ta stay 'cause we kinnot go no farther. Mary kinnot, 'cause m'heir is pendin'."

Sera stifled a whoop of glee, leaned against her husband and bestowed a quick kiss on his chin. "His heir is pendin'," she whispered.

"Too late," said the innkeeper puppet. "There bean't no rooms and this gen'leman be takin' the last stall in m'stable."

"But we is tired and 'ungry an' m'heir is pendin'," sighed the weary puppet.

"Ain't no other place," replied the innkeeper. "Ever'body's full. No room ta be 'ad in fifty miles o' Bethlehem."

"Well," inserted Jenkins, as the puppets huddled together, whispering to each other on the stage, "it turned out that the gentleman and his lady wife could not have paid the actual price of a room even if there had been one. They barely had enough money to pay what Lord Nightingale was to pay for the stall in the stable."

"Never mind," squeaked the Nightingale puppet. "You will need your money to buy food on the way home. I will pay for the stall, but you and your lady wife may sleep there because your heir is pendin'. I am a macaw, you know, so I will just go sleep in a tree."

"Ye kinnot sleep in a tree," the lady puppet protested. "I willn't allow it. Ye'll freeze ta death! Come an' sleep wif us in the stall. Joseph an' me willn't mind, will we?"

"Uh-uh," the weary gentleman stocking replied. "We willn't mind atall if you sleep wif us in the stall."

"And so Lord Nightingale did just that," Jenkins proclaimed as a curtain at the front of the stage was drawn closed and a good deal of scurrying, whispering and thumping could be heard going on behind it. "It was a very big stall, actually," Jenkins went on, placing one hand upon the stage to steady it as the whole thing began to rock a bit. "And there was straw enough for all of them, even the donkey."

"Hee-haw! Hee-haw!" brayed a long-eared stocking as the curtain opened to show a lantern, a little pile of straw, and all the puppets sound asleep and snoring loudly.

"And then it happened," said Jenkins decisively. "Oh, Joseph!" the lady stocking exclaimed, awakening from her sleep and standing straight up minus her bulge. "Oh, Joseph, yer heir bean't pendin' anymore! He is borned!"

"He is borned!" exclaimed Joseph. "Mary, he is borned! Best wrap 'im up in yer cloak afore he freezes." Whereupon Mary dropped beneath the stage.

The Nightingale puppet rose and yawned and looked downward. He yawned again and then addressed the weary Joseph. "Right handsome lad, he looks to be."

"More 'n that," responded Joseph. "He be Jesus, the Saviour of the World. He be borned ta bring hope ta us all."

"Is 'at so?" the Nightingale puppet said in surprise.

"And then an angel from on high appeared," Jenkins intoned, as up popped Ducane's clocked stocking with bright blue eyes, red lips, golden wings and a tipsy halo. It flew-hopped back and forth as Mary lifted a purple bundle to the stage by the most expedient means of clamping a bit of it in her mouth.

"The Son of God be borned!" cried the angel loudly. "Peace be on earth an' good wills ta all men."

"Is he really the Son of God and the Saviour of the whole world?" the Lord Nightingale puppet asked.

"Uh-huh," replied the angel, coming to a stop beside him. "An' the shepherds are comin' ta adore 'im pretty soon now. An' three wise men from the East will be acomin' ta bring 'im gifts."

"I ought to give him a gift as well, I expect."

"Indeed ye ought. What 'ave ye got?" asked the angel.

"Well, I have got some money, but that is to pay my taxes. I will lose my head if I do not pay my taxes."

"Don't want ye ta lose yer 'ead," the angel responded.

"I know what!" the Nightingale puppet exclaimed. "Straw is not the verimost softest thing to lay a baby in. And that old purple shawl willn't help much against the cold. I will give him some of my feathers to lie in. They will keep him warm and make him comfy. That will be the verimost best gift a macaw like me can give him."

"Hallelujah!" shouted the angel. "This blighter be willin' ta give the baby Saviour pieces of 'imself! That be a better gift than all the monies in the whole world!"

"And so Lord Nightingale stripped away as many feathers as he could spare," Jenkins recited soberly, though his lips kept curving upward and had to be forced down. "And until Mary and Joseph finally left the stable, the baby Jesus was warm and comfy and happy. And for the whole rest of his life, Lord Nightingale was warm and comfy and happy, too. It was the best Christmas Lord Nightingale ever had. The end."

The audience applauded and all the stockings on the stage bowed quite properly. "Chris miss!" shrieked Lord Nightingale, bobbing merrily up and down on the chandelier. "Yo-ho-ho Merry Chris miss!" And he soared enthusiastically into the air, circled the room three times and landed on Spelling's shoulder just as that gentleman and the entire party stood up from their seats and applauded more loudly than ever.

"He gave the baby pieces of himself," Alice said to Spelling, standing on her tiptoes to whisper into his ear.

"Kiss Howdedo m'pretty Kiss," said Nightingale in Spelling's other ear.

"I wish to give you *all* of myself," Spelling replied, taking her into his arms. "Every bit of me, Alice, body and soul. I love you, and it is my greatest hope that you will consent to be my wife. Will you?"

"Neil!"

"I have not got permission from your father," Spelling added hurriedly. "But I will. No matter what he demands of me, I will do it. No matter what he requires from me, I will provide it. If I must get myself made an earl, I will manage it somehow. Only please say that as soon as I have brought him 'round, you will marry me. Please say you will, Alice."

"Indeed, I will," assented Alice, her eyes shining. Spelling leaned down and kissed her mightily amidst all the company and the lingering applause. Then he felt Nightingale leave his shoulder and a firm hand replace the bird.

"That last exchange of words had best have consisted of a proposal of marriage, Spelling," Sotherland growled. "And an acceptance on your part, young lady, or ears will be chopped off and heads will roll!"

"Howdedo m'pretty!" Lord Nightingale declared. "Kiss! Hiram! Hiram kissyersister."

"Papa, Neil has just now asked me to be his bride!"

"Yes, your grace, I have," nodded Spelling. "And she has consented to have me. And though you may be opposed to it, I give you my word that—"

"Papa is not opposed to it, Neil," interrupted Alice excitedly. "He promised that I should have you if you asked."

"He did? Hallelujah and Merry Christmas!" Spelling exclaimed to the entire room and kissed Alice soundly once again just as the troupe of tiny thespians came wiggling and giggling out from behind the puppet stage and bowed. The applause soared to a rousing crescendo for the thespians and the lovers both.

And then Ducane ceased to applaud. He stood frozen for a moment, his mouth open, his fine, tawny eyes fixed upon the little performers. "What the devil," he gasped as the applause ceased. "It cannot possibly be." Long strides carried him to the front of the stage. He stared down at the children in disbelief. "Until two days ago, I could not even remember her name, and yet here she stands before me—twice," he murmured, going down upon one knee before Maryrose and Becky. "What are your names?" he asked, his voice thick with disbelief. "From where do you come?"

"This is Becky," Delight offered at once. "And this is Maryrose. They are orphans."

"Orphans? Are you?" asked Ducane of the two girls who were shrinking back from him in awe.

"Uh-huh," conceded Maryrose at last, placing protective arms around her sister.

"Maryrose," Ducane mumbled. Then, "Maryrose," he said, studying the elder of the two whose eyes were bright blue, and whose hair was a fine reddish brown. "What was your mother's name, Maryrose?"

The child pursed her lips in the most distinctive fashion. "Our mother were Mary Dalrymple Fisher," she said most decidedly. "Mary Dalrymple were 'er name afore Pa married 'er, but she did so like the Dalrymple part that she were a'ways asayin' of it."

" 'Cause it soun's like laughin', that be why," added Becky, staring at Ducane. "Do Dalrymple soun' like laughin' ta you?"

"Yes," Ducane responded, as the others of the party gathered more closely around the little tableau in order to discern what went forward. "To me it sounds very much like laughing and dancing and happiness. I knew your mother, my dears, when I was very young."

"Ye did?" asked Maryrose cautiously.

"I did. She made my life gay. She filled it with love. Oh, but I should like to return her the favor."

"Then you ought to take them both home with you," Delight suggested innocently. "An' make them part of your family, like I did Nicky an' Lady Wickenshire an' Cousin Neil an'—"

"Enough, minx," interrupted Wickenshire, who had come to stand beside her, one arm around Sera and the other around Delight. "Why do you not take them home with you, Ducane?" he asked. "I assure you, we can spare them."

"I don't have a home," whispered Ducane hoarsely. "I live in two rooms in London. I don't have money enough to raise two sweet young girls as they should be raised either, but—"

"There are any number of ways a thing can be done if a fellow wishes sincerely enough to do it," Wickenshire observed.

"Believe me," Ducane said, gazing from one to the other of the girls. "I sincerely wish to do it. I will find a position somewhere. Perhaps some lord's secretary. Yes, I can do that, I expect, though I do not know much about such things. I shall not mind to do it, if it will provide the means to stand guardian over these two for Mary's sake."

"Of course you can do it," nodded the dowager, crossing to put a supportive hand on Ducane's shoulder.

"And you may have these," Wickenshire said, tugging a leather pouch from his jacket pocket, untying it, and pouring brightly colored stones out onto his palm. "Neil was good enough to point them out to me. We were going to give them to Sayers for a Christmas gift, but I think they will be of more help to you. They are not worth very much money, but—"

"They are worth a little," finished the dowager for him. "I thought Mr. Sayers would like them, because they once belonged to Elaina Maria. Keepsakes. There are tales concerning them in her journals. Most are gemstones, merely, but they will provide you with a bit of security."

"Elaina Maria Chastain's? They were hers? And you have read her journals, your ladyship?" asked Sayers, his hands resting upon Jem's little shoulders as he stared at the gems in Wickenshire's hand and then at the dowager.

"I did read some of them, Mr. Sayers. And they were quite interesting. But I cannot think where they have gone. They were in a little room attached to the passageways at one time, but they have apparently been moved since last I saw them."

"What is journals, Nicky?" asked Delight.

"Books, m'dear."

"Big books with writing in them? Real writing?"

"Yes, real writing, not print."

"Well, we knows where they is," offered Jackie and Jem simultaneously. And without another word Delight and the boys scampered off behind the stage, each returning with an enormous leather-bound journal.

"I thought they might have some verimost ancient stories in them," Delight explained. "There is more of them up under my bed."

Sayers stared at the leather-bound volumes. His heart pounded so violently that his face began to turn red.

"Aunt Diana," Spelling said, standing toward the rear of the gathering, his arm firmly around Alice, "are those the ones?"

"Indeed, Neil. Nicholas?" she said then, her eyes bright with laughter. "Nicholas, I do believe the very best Christmas gift we can give Mr. Sayers is the loan of these journals for as long as he requires them. That will please him even more than the gems would have done."

"The loan of Aunt Elaina's journals? Well, I cannot think why not," shrugged Wickenshire. "I am not likely to have the time to read them any day soon. And Delight, you are too young yet, I think. Take them, Sayers, and a Merry Christmas to you."

"Nicholas," murmured Sera softly, beside him.

"Hmmm?"

"Nicholas, is Bobby Tripp anywhere about?"

"Tripp? Why?"

"Because I—I am not feeling just the thing, Nicholas. I think—I think—Bobby Tripp had better ride for Mrs. Parkins."

"Ride for— Sera, Bedazzler is not due until— Ohmigawd—" spluttered Wickenshire, sweeping his wife up into his arms and carrying her from the room. "Ohmigawd! Mama!"

"Jenkins heard and is already dashing for the stables, Nicky," advised his mother, hurrying after him. "Take her up to your room, darling. Fiona, we may require your help."

"I am going with them, Neil," Alice said, bestowing a supportive kiss upon his cheek. "Sera may need me. You will watch over Papa, the children and the guests, will you not?"

"Herewecomea was sailllling," Lord Nightingale sang, as he shuffled along the back of the sopha in the Gold Saloon.

The children had taken their puppets and packed them away; the gentlemen had manhandled the stage back up the old servants' staircase into the little room. They had returned all of the furniture in the saloon back to where it had been before the performance and then Jem and Jackie had run off to do their chores, though Ducane had stopped Maryrose and Becky from doing the same. "Because you are not going to work here anymore," he told them, as he settled down with them on the carpet before the fire. "You are going to live with me and be my almost-daughters."

"How long does it take for a baby to get borned?" asked Delight with a little sigh as she plopped down beside Spelling on the sopha. "We have been waiting forever."

"Oh, speaking of that," Sayers said, taking his attention from one of the journals like a man jolted suddenly back into reality. "Spelling, this is yours now." Whereupon Sayers got to his feet, fished about in his waistcoat pocket, and produced the loveliest ruby-and-diamond ring.

"Oooh!" gasped Delight. "How beautiful!"

"Yes. It is Aunt Diana's," Spelling replied.

"And you may as well take these," Sayers added, tugging a small packet of letters from his inside pocket. "I intended to give them directly to Lady Alice, but who knows if we will ever see her again? How long *does* it take for a baby to be born?"

"However long the baby decides it will take," replied Sotherland as he paced the length of the room. "Now, who the devil is that?" he muttered as Jenkins approached the threshold and was nearly trampled by a tall white-haired gentleman who pushed past him into the room.

"What is this, a wake?" cried the gentleman. "It is Christmas! There is a baby being born upstairs! Two lovely little gels have found a home! By Jove, look alive, lads! Find the brandy; fill the glasses!"

"Manthe mainsail!" crowed Nightingale excitedly. "Scuttle theblackguard! Pirates!" He took flight on the instant and landed on the gentleman's shoulder. "Yo-ho-ho! Ol'FatherChris missss Ibe! Cometashare yerpie pie PIE!" the macaw proclaimed proudly, tugging at the gentleman's hair with great enthusiasm.

"Oh, so Nightingale has inherited my position, eh, Neil? Not an excellent choice, but not bad, not bad."

"Uncle Ezra?" Spelling stared at the gentleman, midway between joy and fear. "Uncle Ezra? No one said you were coming."

"Got a note, before dawn this morning," Ezra Spelling replied. "Jenkins sent a note. Lady Vermont is here, it said, and all the cups in her cupboard are cracked."

"Damned true," Sotherland replied. "End her life in a madhouse if I cannot find something to do with her."

"You will be Sotherland," Ezra observed. "Fiona's Devil and the father of my nephew's beloved, Jenkins tells me.

Jenkins tells me everything. Told me most of it coming up the stairs. Good man, Jenkins. Dependable. I will take Fiona. Yes, and those three by the fire as well. Take the lot of 'em."

Ducane, who had gained his feet at Ezra Spelling's entrance took each of the girls by a hand. "What the deuce is he talking about, Spelling? Take those three by the fire?"

"Means I will have you," Ezra Spelling answered for himself. "Got a place large enough to live, have you? Able to support two gels? Cannot raise 'em in rooms in London, though that is what Jenkins tells me you mean to do. Well, I have got a house for you. More than a room or two. Empty as well. Tivally Grange it is called. I be in need of a man to run it."

"A man to *run* it?" asked Ducane, mystified.

"You do know something about farming, do you not? Well, no matter, you will learn. Learn a bit about smuggling as well, but that cannot be helped. You will live in the Grange, do the best you can with the land, and I will see you are paid handsomely for it. I, meanwhile, shall move to Wilderly Crossroads and keep a sharp eye on Fiona. Enjoy that, she will."

"You are proposing to move in with Lady Vermont?" asked Sotherland, thoroughly mystified. "Without the benefit of marriage? At her estate?"

"She will revel in it," Ezra Spelling assured him. "Two good friends together again. Hearty companionship. A bit of adventure to keep her young. Too old to bother with marriage, unless she wishes it. Eighty," he added. "Fiona is eighty if she's a day. And I am older still. Nightingale, what is that I hear? Listen. By gawd, but it is the loveliest song in all the world. Our Nicky is in heaven now, Neil, m'lad. This Christmas he will never forget, eh?"

"It's a baby cryin'," said Delight, her eyes wide with wonder. "Cousin Neil, it's a baby cryin'!"

"Just so," smiled Spelling. "Old Father Christmas has brought Sera and Nicky a baby."

"A girl!" cried Alice, rushing so fast that she barely missed a collision with Jenkins as she turned into the saloon. "Neil, Sera and Nicholas have a baby girl and she is the most precious thing. And her name is to be Joy Noelle," she said, laughing as she ran into Spelling's arms and he lifted her and spun her around and around. "Oh, oh, look!" she exclaimed as her feet touched the carpet at last. "Neil, Papa, Delight, everyone, only look out the window. It's snowing!"

"Just so! About time there was snow for Christmas in Devon. Merry Christmas to us all!" cried Ezra Spelling, laughing merrily as he went from one to the other of those present, shaking one hand after another.

"Harry mustmess!" Lord Nightingale crowed proudly on his shoulder. "Tarry migglemiss! Yohohoho Merry Christmissss!"

Dear Reader,

And so, a Happy Christmas to you all from Lord Nightingale and the gang. May your holiday be a joyous one and may God bless.

Now, I'm going fishing. I will, however, be pleased to hear what you think of the Lord Nightingale series. You may e-mail me at regency@localaccess.net or write to me at 578 Camp Ney-A-Ti Road, Guntersville, Alabama, 35976-8301. My thanks to those of you who hung in there for the entire ride.

Judith